PRAISE FOR
THE BRIGHT FREIGHT OF MEMORY

"Greg Fields' third novel, *The Bright Freight of Memory*, follows the lives of two boys from a poor neighborhood through adulthood and old age as they seek, in different ways, to come to grips with life. A cast of minor characters interwoven into the captivating plot place the story in a context revealing both tenderness and unfeeling cruelty and the inevitability of misunderstandings in human relations. As always, Fields's prose is elegant, with a musical lyricism reminiscent of Pat Conroy, and the way he ends the tale is heartrending. With this novel, Greg Fields has once again firmly established himself in the ranks of America's finest fiction writers."

—RAY CARSON RUSSELL, author of *Philurius College Blues*

"A story of childhood trauma somersaulting through adulthood and grappling to define one's lot. Through elegant descriptions and his signature lyrical prose, Greg Fields illuminates the grit and gruel of boys turned to men while straddling the unforgiving wedge between what they were born into and who they might have become."

—RACHEL STONE, author of *The Blue Iris*

"Fields's novel masterfully delves into the lives of flawed protagonists, revealing their lifelong struggles and isolation. The prose is both profound and moving, poignantly capturing their journey from hopeful youth to troubled adults. A compelling read that resonates with tragic realism and literary excellence."

—GLENN R. MILLER, author of *Doorman Wanted*

"Greg Fields has joined the pantheon of Irish and Irish American writers so gloriously paying homage to the *ould sod* and the luminous literary legacy it has inspired. His new novel, *The Bright Freight of Memory*, captures powerfully the generational angst that haunts the Gaelic-born and their progeny long after their ancestors are gone to the grave. In elegant and elegiac prose, Fields illustrates the inner workings of inherited trauma from Irish plights of famine, diaspora, alcoholism, and loss of identity and family. Poignant and profound."

—DEBORAH HUFFORD, author of *Blood to Rubies*, winner of the American Writing Award for Book of the Year, Gold Medal winner of the Ben Franklin Award for Literary Fiction, and an Amazon top ten best seller

"In *The Bright Freight Of Memory*, Greg Fields paints a multifaceted portrait of the American Dream that grabs from page one and doesn't let go. Three teenage boys find themselves on the shores of a new country, contending with their own demons and the demons faced by any outsider. This is a searing ode to the flawed. Not everything goes to plan, and sometimes there may be no plan beyond that of survival, a shot of Scotch, and enjoying a stray ray of afternoon sunshine. Fields's elegant prose shows us there is beauty and nobility to be found in unlikely places. He shares his characters' inner and outer lives with us and ultimately, by celebrating both their flaws and strengths, leaves us a feeling of hope made all the more precious for having been forged in the cauldron of life's vicissitudes. Bravo."

—ALFREDO BOTELLO, author of *180 Days*, winner of the National Indie Excellence Award for Best Contemporary Novel

"Author Greg Fields reveals a sobering and thought-provoking glimpse of an aspect of life in Washington, DC, far removed from politics, headlines, sound bites, and the nightly news: the colorless, austere world of the streets, its inhabitants and inheritors. It's a downtrodden world where dreams and aspirations are not so much crushed or broken as they are stillborn. Survival, not success, becomes the motivating goal in life, and a person's resilience is determined by his ability to make the most of what little life may offer."

—STEVE JAM, author of *A Seventh Sense*, winner of the 2023 Independent Press Award for General Fiction

"Praise for *The Bright Freight of Memory* as Greg Fields deftly carves out characters, pushing past the shards of a broken heart to the soul of existence. In true Irish terms, Fields delves into the questions found at the bottom of a glass of scotch, of finding grace within a broken life and fighting to be more than a past set into motion before our existence. The promise of love fleshes out the hollow existence of a rejected heart's purpose as the reader finds themselves on a journey to accept the destinies of two men bound by violence and poverty."

—SHARON KRASNY, award-winning author of *Iceman Awakens*

"A stirring and lyrical meditation on Irish roots, a portrait of Irish immigrants and Irish spirit transplanted in the new world. Character and destiny are joined at the hip—and what characters they are—as Greg Fields unfolds their inner urges and deeper desires, their stories of love and loss, of hope and despair, of temptation and thwarted desire, of emptiness and the search for meaning and belonging. And always the roots of childhood camaraderie, of long-held loyalties and their meaning and value in the changing vicissitudes of life, connection, and dissolution. A wonderful writer. Highly recommended."

—MICHAEL SHANDLER, award-winning author of *Karma and Kismet: A Spiritual Quest Across Continents, Cultures, and Consciousness*

"How can a narrator be both relentlessly critical and understanding toward his characters? In *The Bright Freight of Memory*, Greg Fields's vibrant, lucid, sonorous prose makes space to include the loser, the homeless, the trickster, the children of the cursed, outcast families, heirs of '*detritus of dreams as shattered as the glasses from the final bottle*,' each one of them holding indelibly bruised souls.

"Never patronizing, Fields's compelling narrative holds the power of opening one's eyes to see how adventurous and free the life on the road can seem, and by sharing his characters' mirages, it enlarges one's perceptions and empathy through a compassionate and riveting reading experience. Storytelling is the strange alchemy that can provide for a unique moment of secret inner metamorphosis."

—HELOISA PRIETO, Brazilian best-selling, award-winning author of *The Musician*

"Compelling characters highlight a life on the streets that most of us are fortunate enough not to experience ourselves. Greg gives us a deep insight into the thoughts, feelings, and emotions of Donal, Matthew, and Gina to the point where we know them as acquaintances. An excellent read."

—ANGELINA KELLY, author of *The Priest and the Prostitute* and *The Waterproof People*

"Did you perhaps grow up with a group of friends from your neighborhood that, despite the years passing, had a core that transcended life's changes as you went beyond your first home and school? Matt Cooney tells his friends, '*The world is ours, if we just take it.*' This phrase sent my thoughts right back to my own old neighborhood, and to my first 'street gang.' We began to play outdoors together on the street at four years old, and we are still in touch a lifetime late. *The Bright Freight of Memory* is simple and deep, something to reflect upon, like looking into a still forest pool and noticing how much life it holds. Fields writes, '*We are all of us the outcome of accident, and change, and folly, and every life the compendium of intertwined threads.*' As you read this story, you'll find yourself considering your own life's threads and paths."

—ELAINE REARDON, author of
The Heart Is a Nursery for Hope

"A haunting and poignant exploration of the cycles of poverty, alcoholism, and despair that can persist across generations, 'all of us born to it, with no angels of redemption watching over us.' An easy and deeply affecting read, forcing the reader to confront the harsh realities faced by many Irish American families and the ways in which historical trauma and social marginalization can perpetuate suffering, whilst celebrating the tenacity of the human spirit and the bonds of community."

—ANNMARIE FEWER LACY, author of *Yankeeland*

"Greg Fields once again takes us on a journey into the depths of the human soul, compelling us to feel the raw pain of our existence: '*The elongation and eventual negation of an entire life*, he thought, gazing across to the square. *What I might have been. And what am I now? But I belong here, I think. I belong to this place. Nothing to wish for. I had my chance.*' His vivid and exquisite elucidation of suffering and acceptance in *The Bright Freight of Memory* further solidifies Fields's position as a key figure in America's literary landscape."

—DAVID WELCH, author of *Kelsey's Crossing*

"Greg Fields's latest novel offers yet another deep dive into the soul of Everyman. As I read *The Bright Freight of Memory*, I felt I was being slowly, inexorably weighted down by the experiences, sorrows, and dashed hopes of generations of Irish immigrants. Fields has a remarkable way of turning a curt phrase that embodies years of wisdom and as with the best literature sends the reader off into their own internal exploration. Remarkable writing, painfully identifiable and compelling characters."

—DEAN CYCON, author of *Finding Home: Hungary 1945*

"As both an author and lover of books, one comes across many styles, genres, and writing tempos. Rarely, however, do we encounter one such as that employed by Greg Fields in his latest magnificent work, *The Bright Freight of Memory*. Reading this tale, I was powerless, abducted, and mesmerized not only by Greg's natural literary flow and strong command of dialogue but by his exceptional character development. Anyone reading this epic piece will be relegated to being a very curious fly on the wall of Greg's fascinating tale and richly developed characters. I found myself red-eyed, staying up till the early-morning hours, and unable to put it down. Kudos to Greg on constructing such an elaborate, instant American classic."

—MIGUAL RIVERA, author of *Pivotal Universe*

THE BRIGHT FREIGHT
OF MEMORY

The Bright Freight of Memory

by Greg Fields

© Copyright 2024 Greg Fields

ISBN 979-8-88824-453-1

All rights reserved. No part of this publication may be reproduced, stored in a retrieval system, or transmitted in any form or by any means—electronic, mechanical, photocopy, recording, or any other—except for brief quotations in printed reviews, without the prior written permission of the author.

This is a work of fiction. All the characters in this book are fictitious, and any resemblance to actual persons, living or dead, is purely coincidental. The names, incidents, dialogue, and opinions expressed are products of the author's imagination and are not to be construed as real.

Published by

3705 Shore Drive
Virginia Beach, VA 23455
800-435-4811
www.koehlerbooks.com

THE BRIGHT FREIGHT OF MEMORY

GREG FIELDS

VIRGINIA BEACH
CAPE CHARLES

DEDICATION

To Harry Browne
Writer, Raconteur, Gentleman
A Lifelong Son of Dublin
And without whom this book would not exist

The world breaks everyone and afterward many are strong at the broken places. But those that will not break it kills. It kills the very good and the very gentle and the very brave impartially. If you are none of these you can be sure it will kill you too but there will be no special hurry.

—Ernest Hemingway, *A Farewell to Arms*

There are no verdicts to childhood, only consequences, and the bright freight of memory.

—Pat Conroy, *The Prince of Tides*

PROLOGUE

Our fathers sinned, and are no more;
It is we who have borne their iniquities.

—Lamentations 5:7

Are the sins of the father to be visited upon the sons? Or can a child born begin with a clear passage and no wisps of those who went before?

Jock Cooney had no stomach for such questions. He was neither a thinking man, nor even remotely spiritual. Life for him was subsistence, a restlessness for taking what he needed both to survive and then to find whatever pleasures he could grab within the surviving. The work, the women, the fire of the fight. And always there was the drink.

He learned these traits from his own father, and he from previous generations. Jock Cooney's great-grandfather Michael Cooney had spent his formative years in a workhouse, a blotted and shoddy building at the western end of County Cork. The Cooney family, such as it was, had been consigned there in the years following the Famine. Where others had found the means to emigrate during those hard years, and even more had died, the Cooneys lingered in poverty, trying and ultimately failing at farming, shopkeeping, and thievery. In time the authorities grew weary of responding to the tugging hands and pestering of the Cooneys and sent them to the workhouse in Midleton. Michael Cooney spent his days being beaten by teachers who did not care whether he learned a whit of anything, and spent his nights in darkness while vermin raced beneath the wooden plank that was his bunk.

On one of those nights in 1891, shortly after the lad had turned thirteen, Michael snuck away from his bunk out the door and into the early springtime cold. He took nothing with him but his soul. After a night of walking in the direction of the salt air, he found the docks in the Cobh of Cork. Exhausted and tattered, he snuck his way into the belly of a freighter, unnoticed by a callous crew who showed no concern for a young boy who might have been a messenger from one of the ship's providers, an apprentice cooper, or the latest nighttime playmate for their old captain. And if a stowaway, so what? Every man had his story, and so did every child. The crew would leave the lad to whatever he was about. He had no idea where the ship might be headed, nor did he much care. It was headed out, and that was enough.

In the hold, Michael curled into a corner behind several large crates of indeterminable content, one perched on top of the other somewhat perilously. Michael thought that if the ship were to pitch a certain way, they might topple and he would be crushed. But no matter. He had already felt himself crushed by weights more subtle but more sinister. He closed his eyes and slept for hours.

He kept that pace throughout the passage, slumbering during the day as best he could, then skulking about at night for food. He had become one of the vermin. The crew paid him no mind.

Once, as he slunk his way to the galley, a crewman on the night watch spotted him coming around a corner. Michael startled then turned to run, but the crewman clapped him on the shoulder before he could do so. "It's all right, boyo. I know you're here, and it's all right. Take what you need, but be quiet about it." Michael said nothing, nodded in gratitude, then turned back to the galley. "You're not the first, you know."

Protective anonymity followed, allowing him to forage at night as long as he remained invisible when there was work to be done. The crew continued to ignore him, and one night near the end he found a mug of porter on a galley table with a note, *For the lad.*

When the ship docked after a crossing calmer than most, Michael emerged from his corner before the cargo could be unloaded. He wore the same clothes from the workhouse, had not washed in weeks. But he had eaten, slept, and emerged disease free. During the commotion of the docking and the preparations for unloading, he worked his way to the deck for his first breath of sea air in days. When the ship at last moored, Michael walked down the docks and approached one of the longshoremen.

"Where are we?"

"What do you mean, 'Where are we.' Are you daft, boy? Don't know where you are. Get the hell out of here."

Michael walked the port and noted the markings of the place. *Alexandria, Virginia.* Unnoticed as before, he passed the entry point and found his way into this new space.

What followed for Michael mirrored much of what he had left. He stole food from a small market that first day, slept in a green park with no one around. The next morning as he walked the city he saw a fountain with clear, cool water spraying in all directions. As onlookers gawked his way, he jumped in to cleanse himself, a line of filth drawing away from his shirt and the thin pants he had worn for weeks, a dark line in the clear water, the grit of Ireland. When he at last emerged he went back to the park to dry himself in the sun of a new springtime.

Arrested for the thieving he needed to do to survive, Michael was remanded to a thirty-day term in the Alexandria jail. "Another Irish rat," remarked the judge as he passed the sentence, paying no mind to either the boy's age or that he had nothing in this country to give him ballast.

But there were others like him in the Alexandria facility, and he heard what they told him. "Across the river is where you need to be."

"There's a corner of Washington for the Irish. Swampoodle, it's called. Find it, then ask for Thaddeus McCarthy. He's a contractor. Builds things, and he's busy as hell. He'll take you on and give you an honest pay."

So it came to be. Michael Cooney embarked on a life of hard work, just enough pay to meet his needs, and a desire to find any pleasure he could claim. Days of sweat, nights of strong drink, loose women, and the occasional brawl. He never saw his family again and took no knowledge to his own grave of how they lived the rest of their lives. Nor did he care. Michael Cooney was here, he was alive, and he would go on, one way or another.

His son, Eamonn, followed the tradition of sharp living, as did the grandson, Brendan, both working the building trades and patronizing the local pubs. No one ever made enough to do anything else, nor did they aspire to anything different. This was what they knew, and who they were meant to be.

When the grandson married Lucy Halloran, who gave birth to a squalling boy to be named Jock, the course of all the Cooneys had been charted. One could seek to alter the flowing path of the Mississippi more easily than the energies of those young men born to carry the Cooney name.

The sins of the fathers.

CHAPTER 1

When the door to his room kicked open, Matthew Cooney curled into a protective ball on his bed, tucked his knees into his chest, and sought to make himself as small as he could. His father tore the belt from around his waist, turned the buckle outward and swung at the prone boy lying fetal in front of him. The buckle struck arms and legs and ribs. Even in his rage, Jock Cooney knew enough not to aim for the head. It was not for fear of hurting the boy. But head shots left marks, and such marks begged questions that he preferred not be asked.

The first blow hit a shoulder and burned the flesh. The second blow found his stomach and burned the soul. Matthew closed his eyes against it, this inarticulate assault. He braced his muscles against the impacts, closed his eyes and whispered a Hail Mary. This would pass. It always did.

Tonight his father raged, swinging his belt with the vigor of a man seeking retribution against an unfathomable wrong. What that wrong was, eight-year-old Matthew Cooney had no way of knowing. A bad day at work, a cutting remark from a stranger on the street, perhaps his mother's scowl when his father finally walked through their door, well past a dinner that sat cold on their table. His father did not bother to explain his grievances as he pummeled his young son. He swung his belt and choked out animal-like sounds that a young boy could not decipher.

Matthew, the avatar of his father's frustration and madness, his impotence and inconsequence, absorbed the beating. He did not cry; Matthew would never cry. His father would not draw the tears out of him, no matter the force of his fury.

At the end of it, six or seven strikes, his rage spent and his own shoulder aching from the throwing of the blows, Jock Cooney hitched his belt back into his place. "Goddamn you," he muttered. "I wish you'd never drawn breath. Look what you've done to me," then stumbled out the door. "Look what you've done to me," he mumbled into a narrow, empty hallway. Matthew heard thumps as his father lurched against the walls, heading back then out the door to find his next drink.

The young boy lay still to calm the fire of his father's wrath. He did not try to reason its genesis. He had done nothing wrong, at least nothing that he could recall. Instinct told him that his sins were mere interpretations, that his father saw things his son did not, and that the violence of rage needed no provocation beyond the simple fact that he existed.

After some time Diana Cooney gently entered the room to check on her son. "Oh, Matty," she whispered. Matthew continued to stare at the ceiling.

"I'm so sorry, Matty," she mumbled through a sniffle. "I couldn't stop him. I couldn't. Are you okay? Of course you're not."

Matthew turned to her. "It just hurts a little."

His mother sat on the edge of the bed and gently stroked his shoulder. "Why does he do that, Mom? Why does he beat me for no reason?"

Sniffles gave way to tears, and Diana reached to hold her son tightly. Matthew did not move to her embrace, but neither did he retreat. In his mother's embrace, Matthew smelled the tinny whiff of cheap whiskey. He had become accustomed to it, the same odor that wafted off his father every night.

"Your father is an angry man, Matty. It's not his fault. Really, it's not. And it's not yours, either. It's just the way things are, just the way he is. I expect someday you'll understand it all better. When you're older."

"And when I get angry, too?"

"Pray God that the rage passes you by, son. The rage that landed squarely in your father's heart."

"Does he beat you, too, Ma? The way he beats me?"

"Don't concern yourself with that, Matty. I'm fine. He's still my husband, and still your father."

"Sometimes I hear things that sound like he does, but I just hide my head. I crawl under the covers until it all goes away."

"We look out for each other, don't we, Matty?" Diana Cooney sat back and reached into a side pocket to draw out a flask. "I know what your father did hurts, and probably hurts a lot more than you show me. Here—" And she offered the flask to her young son. "This helps take away the pain."

Matthew looked at the flask, then back at his mother. "What is it?"

"Never mind what it is. I think it'll help you. It'll help you sleep. It'll help you forget this very bad night."

"That's the stuff that makes Dad crazy. Why are you trying to get me to drink it."

"Because it calms the heart and soothes the soul. Try just a sip. To take away the pain."

Curious, Matthew tentatively grabbed the flask. He held it to his nose and sniffed the bitterness. His mother had always tried to protect him, to do what's best for him. He trusted her. There was no one else to trust.

He lifted the flask and let a few drops fall onto his tongue. And with them, they echoed the burn from outside his body and caused his tongue to flame. But he did not spit it out. Very gingerly he drew the liquid back to his throat, then swallowed. Fire raced down the length of him, and his stomach roiling.

"Jesus, Mom. That was awful."

"Don't think about the taste. Just let it sit there inside you and calm you down," she said, and for the first time all night she smiled. "It'll do that." She rose then, kissed her son on his forehead, turned toward the door.

"Good night, son. You're strong, Matty. Don't ever forget that."

Diana turned off the light as she left, but her son did not sleep. In the small room that was his, he listened to the night sounds—the passing of cars on their dingy street, the clatter of metal doors that closed, the voices of those who still wandered this part of the city. His father was out there, one of the wanderers.

Matthew wondered where that wandering led him, what he would find when he got to wherever he bounded. A space without a son, it would be, and without a wife. Without a home to drag down his besotted, lost dreams. A space where his father, Jock, could extinguish his anger at least for a time before it rose again and consumed all those unfortunate enough to have to share this life with him.

The young boy at last turned toward the wall and pulled his covers tight. His head felt lighter. Perhaps it was the drink his mother had given him. Perhaps there really was something to it that calmed the heart and softened the soul. His shoulders ached, as did his ribs, in all the places where his father's buckle had met its mark. Sleep would come, fitful and unfulfilling, but on this night, the best he could do.

Matthew took his bruises to school, and while he sat bored at his desk listening to the droning of wiser minds, they festered and chafed. He took his bruises to the corner store when he ran errands for his mother. He took them to the streets, where his friends hid their own wounds, yet still shared laughter, a bit of mischief and good times.

No one could see them, but he knew they were there, that they would continue to dive beneath his skin and leave whorls of blue and green and purple on the tenderest parts of who he was, of who he wanted to be. Such were the bruises that his father gave him that night. Such were the bruises that would not heal.

Matthew grew through the wounds. His father became a vaporous figure, wafting in and out of his life, the occasional phantom. The beatings continued, but they lessened, whatever point that Jock Cooney needed to make having been well established. Mostly they avoided each other, until, on a day shortly after Matthew turned twelve, there was nothing left to avoid. An empty whiskey bottle thrown against the living room wall, a slap across the face of Matthew's mother, who was drunk as well, a final slamming door, and Jock Cooney disappeared into whatever contours his life had formed, leaving behind the detritus of dreams as shattered as the glass from that final bottle.

Jock's departure was not mourned. Nature did not take notice, and so the next morning dawned in full, bright sunlight, traffic rolled through Washington in its usual way. Winds did not howl, banshees did not keen.

Matthew rose with his usual reluctance and prepared himself for school, his mother still insensate on the living room couch. He finished the piece of bread that was his breakfast, slurped from a bottle of soda, and made his way out the door to head for school, pausing to pluck stray pieces of glass out of his mother's hair.

Despite it all, Matthew grew well. He carried a genetic predisposition to good health, it seemed, so that flimsy meals, or meals missed altogether, did not slow his growth, nor did the restless nights of too little sleep. His features would turn rugged – a strong chin, high cheekbones that seemed almost defiant, and a shock of light brown hair that fell across a broad forehead. His eyes, dark and somber, seemed to burn with every glance.

He brushed aside the common worries and uncertainties of boys entering puberty. He had seen much worse and survived in one piece, physically and mentally. Matthew knew that his path to manhood was well set, and he would honor it as it came to him.

A bit taller than his mates, and now certainly bolder, he became something of a leader. He did not aspire to this. But when Matthew Cooney met them on the sidewalks of their neighborhood, his friends looked at him with more respect than they gave each other. They would most likely have been unable to explain this deference. Perhaps the young Cooney emanated things they could sense but not understand, an aura of unspoken violence, a subtle threat that Cooney's depths might be deeper than their own. That, despite the commonality of their place and time, Matthew was not exactly like the rest of them.

He had a smile, broad and uninhibited, that too rarely spread across his face, but when it did it brought a light that his friends enjoyed. On the good days, Matthew implied a sense of mischief, a curiosity about what they might be able to pull off together, or, if they were reluctant for an adventure, what he might be able to pull off himself.

Matthew dismissed the very processes of life that had shown themselves to be facades masking the realities of loss and heartbreak. The institutions of family and community, the aspirational rigidity of school, the artifices of social standards, good behavior, and compassion for one another became illusions. Not to be taken seriously, any of it. A game, it was, the ultimate scam that sought to fool onlookers into notions of security, promise, and reward. It was early on that Matthew Cooney came to believe that the only rewards this life might offer would not be those that came to him for doing the right things, but only be those he claimed for himself.

— ◆ —

A summer's day from the before years, that time when boys could spend their days seeking sun and amusement. Boys they were then—

Matthew Cooney, Donal Mannion and Johnny Duncan, on the cusp of the demands and disappointments that come with age, but now thirteen years old and in full command of the small spaces that constituted their world. Inseparable that summer, the three of them. Each day a pass through the streets, through their friends, limited only by the constraints of time and the boundaries of their imaginations.

City boys, a breed apart from those who grow up in wider spaces and cleaner air, different from the boys whose lives swirled around the nodes of family, responsibilities, expectations, and safety. Not for them, these things. The three would head out their respective doors in the morning, breakfast no more than a piece of toast or stale cereal, charged to find their friends and the adventures that they might create together. Into the streets. Aimless and spontaneous, but never lost.

They knew these streets. They knew the stores that might give them a special boys discount on gum or candy, the buses that went to the places downtown where the museums and Mall might create a new canvas. They knew which dogs wandered around which corners, who might smile at them as they passed on the sidewalk, and who might cross the street to avoid them altogether. These were their streets, the domain of thirteen-year-old princes desperate for a realm of their own.

Their families existed in name only, each one disjointed and broken in its own way. The three clans lived on the same block, a tatty strip in the city's poor northeastern end. But there was a fabric there, and the boys knew it. Stores and shops and sidewalk stands that created what passed for a neighborhood. There were the bars, too, a lot of them. Those would come later.

"Are you guys hungry?" Matthew Cooney's question was rhetorical. They were always hungry. Too little food in their home kitchens, and usually no one to cook it.

"What do you have in mind?" asked Johnny Duncan.

"Something to do," Matthew muttered. "Something I want to try," and with that he sauntered ahead of his friends to the end of the street where Dominick Salvaterra sold fruits and vegetables from a small stand near the corner. Dominick's fruits were well regarded, and this morning, as most mornings, a crowd of women shuffled around his bins eying the produce.

Matthew ambled into the group of shoppers. "What's he doing?" Donal asked Johnny as they watched him inspect fruits he could not buy. Who had money for such things?

His eyes alive and darting, Matthew slipped between two women looking at the bananas. As did the ladies, he picked up a bunch. Unlike the ladies, who tested the firmness of the fruit then put the bunches back into the bin, Matthew slipped his under his jacket. He did not run away. Instead, he shifted over to the apples, and likewise surreptitiously grabbed three Macintoshes. He showed neither impatience nor hesitation. *Look like you belong here,* he told himself. With a firm step, he turned back down the sidewalk and returned to his friends.

"I did it," he whispered to them. "Always wanted to try that. No one suspected a thing, and here we are. Come on, let's find a place where we can eat these things." Donal and Johnny looked at each other with wide eyes, jaws slightly open. "Jesus, Matt, that's stealing."

"So it is," he replied, "and it feels great. The world is ours, boys, if we just take it."

The first step in what would be a long journey. Matthew's world, there for the taking. Years later, he would sit back on a bench not far from where he had stolen his first fruits. A taste of banana flicked through his memory, and he smiled at the new morning sun.

Another morning, the trio, feeling the sparkle of youth that a dulling summer could not entirely extinguish, snuck off to find a way to the shore. No buses ran there, at least none that they could afford. They would have to beg a ride.

It took a while, and along the way they had to endure a lecture from a middle-aged man who picked them up outside the city to take them on their way and to tell them the right way to live their lives. "Work at it, boys. A day's lark is fine here and there but find a purpose and stick to it. And thank God every day that you're drawing the air you breathe . . ." and so on. The boys feigned interest, the price to be paid for free transit. Matthew rolled his eyes then closed them as he slouched down in the back seat.

At the shore gulls flapped and squawked near the planking of the boardwalk and sun dripped like honey onto the backs and faces of bodies stretching themselves in the sand or splashing through waves strong enough to ride but gentle enough to pose no threat. Matthew had not seen the likes of it, had not known such a day might be.

In his part of the city there were pigeons, dull winged and dirty, and the sun sent down spasms of heat and sweat rather than honey. Water flushed from hydrants shot upward in violent sprays then flowed to sewers, capturing the dreck of the gutters as it washed away. Mid-August, the baking days of the dull throb of summer, to be survived until the tawdry, wet days of fall squelched these flames and pointed its bony finger to death of the year, to the death of time itself.

In late afternoon, after all three lay long enough in the sand to feel the heat rise off their thin and pasty bodies after several splashes in the water, after gossip and the usual adolescent regard for the girls in swimwear that accented curves and valleys and flamed burgeoning hormones. Donal turned to his mates.

"We need to find something to eat before we head back."

Matthew rolled to an elbow and smiled a wicked grin. "Should be no problem, boys. Leave it to me." And he rose, brushed the sand off his arms and legs, then headed toward the food shacks along the boardwalk.

"What do you suppose he's got in mind," asked Johnny.

"It's Cooney," said Donal. "God knows what he'll come back with." And the two rolled onto their backs once more to await whatever came next.

They did not wait long. Matthew reappeared within a few minutes. He stood above them, then dropped a plastic bag with several sandwiches on Donal's chest.

"Damn, Matty. Where'd you get all this?"

"No need asking, boys. I have my ways. Let's just keep the bag out of sight, though. Its owner might recognize some identifiable markings."

"Jesus, Matty." But still they ate . . . all of it. Sandwiches, chips and fruits. Donal pulled out several small round foil-wrapped pieces from the bottom of the bag. "What are these?"

"Chocolate, I'd wager," said Matthew. "Chocolate money. Something the rich folks like to play with. Makes 'em feel proud to nibble on coins."

Duncan laughed. "You've always had a nose for the coins, Matty."

"It's a nose I'll keep, Johnny. We need the coins to get by, chocolate or otherwise. Don't ever forget that."

"We'd best head back," said Donal through a quiet burp. "It might take a while to find a ride."

"No lecture from the drivers, though," said Matthew Cooney. "Won't stomach that, boys. We need the coins to get by. And we'll find them, one way or another."

"Even if they're stolen?" asked Donal.

"Especially if they're stolen," replied Matthew. "Everyone steals, Donal. We're just part of the herd." With that, Matthew Cooney turned to the roadway, extended his hand, and feigned his most innocent look to beg a ride.

— ◆ —

Father Lemmon's Saturday morning catechism class demanded little attention. Matthew leaned back in his chair and gazed at the ceiling as the padre droned on about obligation. Diana aspired that her son follow the family tradition, that he come into the church as had every Cooney progenitor since St. Patrick collectively raised them from their heathenish druidic tendencies. When Matthew balked at the notion of spending an hour each Saturday morning in the presence of God and the sour priest who was his neighborhood representative, she cried and begged and pleaded piteously. Matthew had finally acquiesced if only to quiet her tears. Now he sat in this airless room while the sun shone brightly outside.

With him were the boys he knew, Donal, Johnny, Eddie Moore, and two or three others from the street. None had been regular at Mass, but here they were, appeasements to their parents' expectations.

Father Lemmon was explaining the mechanics of the fast days, those occasions when true believers punished their bodies to elevate their souls. None of it made sense to Matthew, or, really, to any of the other boys who sat quietly while Lemmon explained that every Catholic, even after his sins have been forgiven through the brutal honesty of the sacrament of penance, must satisfy a merciful God's judgment for temporal punishment. And there were plenty of occasions for the need to do so—the weekdays of Lent, the Assumption, the Immaculate Conception, the Ember Days, and on and on.

Christ, Matthew thought. *Maybe we should fast on the days when Jesus took a dump.* And then Lemmon made a tragic mistake. "Any questions?" he asked. There were never any questions. But today, Matthew raised his hand.

"Father, I've got a question."

Warily, Lemmon turned his way. "Yes, boy."

"What if the night before a fast day a piece of food gets caught in my cheek at dinner?" With that, Donal bowed his head to look down to avoid laughing, and Johnny looked out the window to avoid any eye contact.

Matthew continued. "And then it doesn't come free until the next morning, and I swallow it. Is that a mortal sin, Father?"

Lemmon turned his eyes to the ceiling and shook his head. Before he could answer, Matthew went on. "I know you'll probably say it's the intention that matters, but what if I knew that that piece of meat was tucked there the night before, but I didn't pick it out in time. What if I saved it for the next day just because I was too lazy to swallow it when I first found it?"

The old priest opened his mouth to reply, but the boy continued to plunge ahead. "And let me add another consideration. Say all this happened when I was on an overnight flight to Japan, flying to Tokyo, and in the middle of the night we passed the International Dateline. Would that make a difference?"

With that, Donal burst a snorting laugh, Johnny put his head down on his desk and roared, and the rest of the room let go with hoots, except for a couple of the more proper boys who sat stunned by the Cooney boy's insolence.

Lemmon's face grew red, then a light shade of purple. He would not tolerate a mockery of doctrine. "Silence, boy," he roared. "I expect you to say nothing for the remainder of this class. And know that your arrogance and sass is itself a serious offense to God."

Matthew smirked, "I expect God has seen far worse." He was rewarded with a slap across his cheek.

Matthew turned his head to absorb the blow, then looked back up at the priest. "And I've seen far worse, too, Father." He rose and walked out of the small basement room, never to return.

— ◆ —

At the end of the block was a convenience store, part of a chain that had dropped similar shops in various corners of the city, corners that sat away from the downtown mall, away from the government offices and administrative complexes, away from the swank shops on Connecticut or Wisconsin Avenues, and all throughout Georgetown. Those were the parts of the city where people came and went, days spent making a mark or buying a deal. There was no need for such stores in those places. But in the neighborhoods that lined the edges, these shops were anchors, small stores that sold almost anything one might need—food, motor oil, tobacco, ice, and the cheap liquor that was kept behind the counters.

For the boys on Matthew Cooney's block, the store was a gathering place, an institution of sorts, a constancy as they grew older. Each day the boys would wander in, usually after school but sometimes in the mornings. No need to browse the aisles. They knew what was there. A candy bar, maybe a bag of chips, and then out to the curb to see who else would come by. There would always be someone, always be the chance for a challenge, or an adventure, or a dare. A chance for something new.

The store anchored Matthew's days. He went there for space, often for some illusion of peace, and no one would ever chase him out or tell him to move along. The clerks knew that the boys had nowhere else to go. For the most part they were harmless, just lads on the edge of manhood looking to be boys just a while longer. They bought things and kept to themselves.

On a Thursday afternoon, Matthew sat on the curb that lined the very small parking area and nibbled slowly on a stale bar of chocolate that had no doubt been sitting on the shelves far too long. He paid no mind to its chalky, grainy texture. Chocolate was still chocolate, no matter how cheap.

It was Johnny Duncan who was the first to show. He nodded at Matthew, then went into the store. "Be out in a minute." He emerged with a day-old pastry and a bottle of water then took a place next to Matthew on the curb.

"Anything happening today?"

"Not a damn thing." Matthew took a small bite of the very bad chocolate. "Wish I could tell you different."

"So what can we do about it? Wanna go over to the park? Might be a game going on there."

"Nah, I don't feel like playing ball. You go ahead if you want. I think I'll just hang here and see if something comes up."

The two boys sat in silence pecking at their food until a red Corvette shot its way down the street, roaring in its sleek power, carving down a street it owned by right. At the next corner it spun a quick right turn and sped off. The boys heard its muffled power fade off in a new direction.

They looked at each other and Johnny smiled. "Jesus, I'd love to have a car like that. Go as fast as you want, go wherever you want to go."

Matthew looked down and smiled for the first time all day. "You think you'll ever own something like that, Johnny?"

"Why not? If I want it, I'll find a way to get it. Make a lot of money, then go buy it."

"As easy as that." Matthew chuckled, mostly to himself. "If it were that easy, everybody'd have one and it wouldn't be special. Your dad would be driving you to school in a Corvette with the top down, and no one would even notice."

"What the hell is wrong with you today, Matt?"

"Nothing . . . nothing that wasn't wrong with me yesterday, or the day before. I just don't feel like chasing dreams today. A waste of time. Corvettes, or fancy houses, or a soft bed to sleep in. Just dreams."

"Jesus, Matty." Johnny took two bites of his pastry to finish it off, then stood up from the curb. "I'm going to go play some ball at the park. You comin'?"

"You go ahead. I'll see you later." Johnny threw the pastry wrapper on the ground, grabbed his bottle of water, and headed off to the park a few short blocks away. Matthew sat where he was.

No place else to go, and the day drawing down. Alone there on his curb. None of the others had shown up or wandered by. At the park, most likely, on a bright afternoon like this, with gloves and mitts and bats. Matthew stood and stretched to loosen a back.

The end of the day, and an empty night ahead, resentment bubbled up from some space deep inside. It traveled up his throat and perched on the edge of his tongue, although he could not speak it. It flamed his blood and made his muscles taut. Matthew Cooney became a rope pulled tight and straight, a stone rounded by the pulsations of the water that flowed against it.

He headed home, slowly, head down and hands in pockets. A single block, but he would take his time. No hurry to go where nothing waited for him. His father was long gone, and his mother would be nowhere he could reach, sitting in a friend's living room nursing a drink, or lost in her own bottle at the kitchen table. This he knew, and there was nothing he could do about any of it.

With his thoughts away in the ether and his head down, Matthew did not see the boys coming toward him, talking and joking among themselves. They were a bit younger, perhaps nine or maybe ten, and they showed no care for anything other than their friendships. As they passed three abreast, one bumped Matthew's shoulder. He turned to them and pushed the back of the one closest to him.

"Hey. Watch it." The younger boy reeled from the push, and his two friends spun around. "Jesus, lay off, would you? It's just a bump. Or are you some kind of tough guy?"

Matthew wasted no time. The taut wire snapped at once. His fist shot forward and caught the boy on the chin. The younger one fell to the sidewalk, and Matthew stood over him.

"Yeah. I guess I'm a tough guy."

The two others huddled around their fallen friend, who did not rise. Instead, he crumpled into the arms of his friends, sobbing. One of the others sneered up to Cooney, "A real tough guy, beating up on a little kid," he said, then wiped his friend's tears with a napkin he pulled from his pocket. "Real tough guy," and he, too, sniffled through wet eyes.

Matthew turned back to his walk. His heart numbed, insensate, as his legs pulled him homeward. Over his shoulder he heard the boys tend to their friend. "Come on, Tommy. You'll be okay. That guy was nothing."

When he got home he entered an empty house. Just another day, hooked onto the end of all the others.

CHAPTER 2

In late October, shortly after Scorpio's emergence, Emma Mannion pushed out her first child into an indifferent world devoid of warmth or welcome. She had stumbled to her car in labor, no moon to light the way, and only the pockmark of distant stars for guidance. And in the stumbling, she felt an earth beneath her feet that would be forever changed.

In the hospital's birthing room, Donal Mannion had drawn his first squalling breath under a dark moon. He had no choice in the matter. His small frame, coated in his mother's blood and the uterine fluids that slid him forward, squirmed in the new and short-lived freedom of a foreign realm, one that, for the moment, did not suffocate. His papery lungs had filled for the first time. Eyes that did not see blinked insensately, and his lips tremored in anticipation of nourishment. Donal Mannion had arrived.

His mother gave him her breast, and then she gave him his name. *Donal*, it would be, a name both resonant and evocative, calling again to her still young mind the romanticism of the land that her family had left generations ago. There would be no *d* at the end of it, no Americanization of a name that originated on Irish soil. Emma Mannion intended that her son knew who he was, and where he came from.

No moon to light his way. Only the pockmarks of the stars in a dark and lowering night sky. Donal Mannion, Son of Man.

Emma's husband's father had carried that name as well, the original Donal Mannion, a grand and legendary figure whom her man adored. Donal had left Ireland at an early age, no more than twenty, intoxicated by the lure of Amerikay and its riches. The Great Depression hit Ireland no less than it did the United States. With no job, no education to speak of, and no prospects, Donal Mannion the Elder sold his small stake in the family farm to his brother, giving him just enough to book passage to New York and what he expected to carry him through two or three months once he got there.

The new country fascinated him, and he tried his best to drink in every sight, every sound, every sensation of this grand place. Donal, charmingly glib, had a knack for making friends. He found that a quick wit, a kind word, and a good story caused men to seek his company and women to seek his charms. For a clever man willing to put himself forward, work was easy to find.

He spent three years in and around the New York loading and unloading trucks, sorting produce and tending a seedy bar in Breezy Point, where sour, sullen Irishmen congregated to drink and to fight. After a time the luster faded, and he knew it to be time to move on once again. "Too damn many people here," he muttered into the shoulder of his new lover, a girl he had met earlier that night and whose name he could only vaguely recall.

"What do you mean, man? It's only you and me."

"And a couple million of our closest friends. God, woman, how can a man breathe when he's surrounded on all sides?"

Before moving south, he went to sea.

In the broken days, those days when purpose eluded him and the daily struggle for meaning and pleasure seemed most tawdry, Donal Mannion the Elder would wander the streets near the rooming house in the nub of Queens where the poor people lived, looking for something, some satisfaction for an unarticulated hunger, some spark that might light a roar of passion, an explosion, something so vivid and vibrant that it could be neither denied nor destroyed. Perhaps the streets of Breezy Point offered a hidden secret that might lend itself to wisdom.

On a spring day during the wanderings, Donal Mannion found himself at water's edge, the same sea had crossed not long ago from a native land. By then, the glitter of the new land had faded. *What really is the point of it all? There must be something better,* he thought.

A schooner—a schooner of all things—moored at a dingy pier that was usually reserved for the smaller boats. Maybe in Gloucester or Boston, where they played around with such things, but this was Queens. The days of the sailing ships had well passed. Lines and rigging had been replaced by iron and steel. *Odd enough,* Mannion thought. *There may be a story here,* and he approached it.

"Hallo," he called to a man tying down one of the jibs, and when the man looked up, "I haven't seen a boat like this in too many years."

Only too happy to be distracted from his tasks, the crewman walked to the railing to respond. "Not too common, is it? But it's great fun."

"Why the hell am I looking up at a schooner in Queens? What does a boat like this bring to the table?"

"Not a damn thing. We're not a working boat. Pleasure cruises only, for those with enough money and time to be nostalgic. We sail up from New Jersey, tie up for a few hours to give the guests a chance to walk the piers, eat bad food and feel like nineteenth century aristocrats, then we sail back. Beach Haven, about two hours down the coast."

Donal shook his head and turned away. No story here, it turns out, unless it be the wastes and indulgences of memory, those things that make the past something it never truly was. He thought of the schooners of Kinsale, the tall ships that sifted in and out of the Cobh of Cork. Gone now, all of them, made old and obsolete by the press of time. And replaced now by pleasure boats out of New Jersey that played upon time's ghosts.

No point to it. None of it. Donal Mannion went back to his rooming house, gathered his things, went to the cabinet downstairs where he knew his landlady kept a small cache of money, took what he could, and headed out the door. There was a train south, he knew. Always there would be a train south. He would take it, and try something else, something new, something farther away. To Washington, perhaps, where the Irish gathered in a neighborhood called Swampoodle, or maybe even deeper down the line, somewhere away from the sea, and the faulty, tarnished memories of the lost times.

The restlessness, then, would come to young Donal's blood through that of his grandfather, his namesake. He could not know this as he lay in newborn innocence, staring into the wondrous and wondering eyes of his young mother and swathed in the warmth of blankets that made him appear even smaller than he was.

— ◆ —

Emma Mannion brought her new son home to the small apartment she rented in northeast Washington. Space was scarce, so Donal spent his first nights sleeping in a second-hand crib in the corner of the single bedroom, his mother close by to keep watch.

It was just the two of them then. Donal's father had disappeared shortly after Emma informed him of his seed growing in her womb. One night here, the next day gone. She had not heard from him, had no idea where he might be.

Just as well, she thought, recalling that David Mannion had no job, no way to contribute to keeping things together, and a too-violent temper that had driven away whatever warmth they had shared. Emma relied on her own small income as a secretary, and regular support from her own family, still perplexed that she would cast her lot with a feckless Irishman when the world was filled with fine Scottish Protestant boys.

Her well-heeled mother and father had been thrilled when she told them that she was pregnant, and thrilled all the more when she came to them shortly thereafter to tell them that her man was nowhere to be found. This child might have a chance, especially if they could help him along.

Emma, stripped now of the cumbersome burden of a derelict husband, felt at first the rush of a heady freedom. There would be no more arguments, no threat of the back of a hand or a voice raised so loudly that it reverberated off walls too thin to muffle such abuse. She would spend her days working quietly and tending to the wonder of her son.

But the nights were another matter, and Emma sank too soon into loneliness and loss. She was still young, still attractive enough to draw the attention of men. What chance to do so, though, and really, what was the point? To her mind men brought pleasure in small measures and pain in huge doses. So at night she would feed young Donal, play with him or watch him play with his toys, then put him to bed. Quiet, then, into these nights that contrasted so starkly with her husband's boisterous and often violent enthusiasms, that filled with the empty blathering of evening television or the ticking of clocks. And as baby Donal grew, the quiet grew more intense, pressed into her tender core like a wound, and the loneliness turned to acid.

She did not know when the drinking began. At some point, when the despair crept under her doorway like a fog, she turned to a bottle, just to take the edge off, she told herself, and to help her sleep. Emma had no predisposition to alcohol. As a young woman she drank socially, and never alone. But aloneness had a different meaning now. No comfort in it, no healing, no reflection or regeneration. A permanent condition it was, nothing soothing about it, and no end in sight. So the easing of it became a nightly ritual. Emma felt the despair of being locked in place, and the place she was locked into was dank and still.

As Donal grew and became more self-sufficient, she had more time to herself, more of what she did not want. No point to any of it, she told herself. She grew slovenly, the house untended and neighbors ignored, a spiral drawing toward the destitution of her soul and the collapse of dreams. Mother and son moved to a smaller place in a corner of the city that no one cared about. The bottles moved with them, and Emma faded it seemed by the day.

Emma considered the whimsical playfulness of the Fates, the whispers of Chance, the guiding hand of unseen Providence, unseen and unknowable until the manifestations of their games become apparent. What confluence of accidents had led a brash young man to abandon his native land to come to a new country and spawn a generation of sons, one of whom would claim a naïve girl to mother a son whose soul was plucked from the ether to carry forward that very name?

Would there be a Donal Mannion born in Washington if Caesar had not crossed into Gaul, if Charles Martel had fathered a daughter rather than a son, if Strongbow had not seized Dublin in 1170, or if the French fleet had successfully landed in 1798? Does a farmer's flirtation with a country lass in County Clare in 1825 lead to a newborn's cry in 1964? We are, all of us, the outcome of accident, and chance, and folly, and every life is the compendium of innumerable intertwined threads that span the centuries that came before us.

And if young Donal's father had decided to stay, had found within himself the commitment to wife and son that he so clearly lacked. What then? Would Donal Mannion have grown up in a shoddy and shabby neighborhood, scrambling to find food enough to fill his stomach and motivation enough to drive his days? Would his mother have spent her days fretting over a son tending wild? Or would the boy have known temperance and balance, or slept in a comfortable bed in a warm and wide house with room enough for friends and dreams? Would the magic genie of youth grant his wishes for security and strength and purpose?

Donal Mannion became what he was to be, the complex product of forces centuries old from across the seas, and the immediacy of impulses in the next room. Unknowable, and as immutable as time itself.

— ◆ —

With a simplicity that extinguished aspiration, Donal Mannion grew up with all the necessities and none of the luxuries that pampered the lives of other children. A small apartment, regular meals that provided a minimum of both taste and nourishment, and what passed for a mother's devotion brought him through the first part of it all. Years later, in retrospect, Donal would look back to this part of his boyhood and remember almost none of it. He recalled swatches of peeling wallpaper, the cold of the bathtub before warm water gushed out, and once, when he was four or so, the path of a mouse that made its way from a kitchen cabinet to its refuge behind the old refrigerator.

School was nothing more than an obligation, sparking neither an inordinate curiosity nor the satisfaction of uncovering the wonders to which such curiosities pointed. In the early years of it his teachers sought to amuse while they taught, creating games and contests that demanded some attention to adding, subtracting, spelling, and good behavior with tawdry rewards such as an extra carton of milk or an orange. In short order Donal saw through the gimmickry. During the afternoons he let his mind fly through the classroom window to the streets, to the sky, to all the places a boy's imagination could craft. His teachers droned on, and he did not particularly notice.

Donal anticipated his Saturdays with a fervor that blocked every frustration, insult, and stretch of boredom that permeated his weeks. School was out, but, really, what else was there in these languid, hot, often humid days that stretched one into another?

To be sure, he tried his best to ward off the languor. He and his friends would haunt his city's dense streets, looking around each corner for something new, something that would spark curiosity or response, or, best of all, a bit of mischief. There might be a fruit stand where the boys could nip an apple or an orange, just for the sport of it. Donal had little taste for fruit of any kind, so what he stole he would throw away, or, if in a favorable mood, give it to his best friend, Johnny Duncan.

Their mischief sometimes expanded beyond a simple pilfered banana. If the keeper of a corner market looked preoccupied, lazy, or too distracted to pay enough attention, they might snatch a pen, or a pair of nail clippers, or, once upon a dare from Matthew Cooney, a submarine sandwich. But Donal and Johnny measured their risks, and in the main stayed away from anything overly foolish. They ate the sandwich, but they never went back for another.

While others floated into and out of their circle, it was these two, Donal and Johnny, that formed the core of the boys roaming the neighborhood looking for engagement.

There was a precipice for young boys like this, a divide which presented the chance to turn left or right. The direction of the turn would set their futures, and, with the turn, determine who they really were, and wanted to be. Donal and Johnny had one parent each—Donal's overwrought mother, and Johnny a father who provided just enough to keep him fed, clothed, and housed, but offered little more of himself, a man more in love with his bottles than with his son. Home itself for each boy was confining, neither physically nor emotionally expansive, as stark and minimalist as a monk's cell, or so it seemed. They were not bad boys. Not yet. Perhaps never.

But during the hot and indolent summer, they looked to each other, their floating passel of friends, and the thick streets of Washington to fill their time and to stimulate a young boy's sense of being alive. They gave little thought to the future. It was enough to surmount each day as it came, and to do so with a hint of adventure if they could find it.

It was the weekend that drew them, that focused the ennui of their days to a single aspirational point. No matter that in the summer each day could bleed into the next, all the same. On the weekends people were out, they were animated, and, because there were more of them, things always seemed more alive.

There were street fairs and art festivals, places where people gathered. The noise and aromas drew them, even if they had no interest at all in the event at hand. Donal and Johnny went for the smell of cheap foods frying in sidewalk stands, for the different voices and accents, for the shouts and the cries that reverberated through the streets. It didn't matter where. A half hour or so on a bus or a hop over the Metro turnstile to dash for a train, and there it was. Playgrounds of tawdry things overwhelmed by a press of bodies from the human smorgasbord that walked the pathways there. Donal and Johnny set out each Saturday. They pressed the streets, ate mealy hot dogs and drank warm sodas.

And in the process, they were boys again, on the proper side of the precipice.

Once, when they were younger, the two stole away on a Saturday dawn with money taken from the jars on their kitchen counters that captured random coins and pocket change, supplemented by the twenty-dollar bill Johnny had found two weeks prior at the Georgetown Art Fair, a prize of inestimable value. Johnny had seen it fall after being too carelessly tucked into the back pocket of a man walking away as he munched on a taco. Johnny pounced at once, catching it almost as soon as it hit the pavement. He had not a thought of returning it to the taco-muncher.

"Geezus, Donal, look at this!" he said as he turned back to his friend, unaware of what it was that provoked Johnny's lightning strike. "We're rich, man."

"Ah, Johnny, shouldn't we give it back to the fella who dropped it?"

"Are you an idiot, man? If he doesn't care enough to take better care of things, then that's his loss." Johnny fingered the bill, held it toward the sun, viewed its lines and hues, things too rarely seen in his young life, then firmly plunged it into a front pocket of his jeans. "We'll keep it."

"What are we gonna do with? Where should we spend it?"

"We'll save it for something special. No need to spend it just to spend it. Someday we'll do something really great with it, something we've always wanted to do."

And it would be on a Saturday that their fortune would find its purpose, a day to remember. They met at the bus stop to take the series of buses that would bring them twenty-five miles into Virginia, to the Prince William County Fair, the state's largest and one which promised new experiences. It took more than two hours to get there, and too much of their stolen funds to get in, but by noon there they were, wandering through agricultural barns, smelling the pungency of prized livestock—the earthiness of horses, the thick stink of cattle, the meaty blight of the hogs, the clucky nervousness of the poultry. They eyed the racetrack where later that day there would be a tractor pull and watched the workmen build the mounds that would later be soaked to create a deep muck. Wondrous, it was, all of it, and as foreign to the eyes of two young city boys as the Pyramids at Giza or the Eiffel Tower.

The Midway seemed a land of fantasy, replete with games, rides and bizarre displays of two-headed dogs and vegetables with human faces. The afternoon would be for the Midway, a confirmation of why they had come here. After a lunch of lemonade and French fries, the two counted their remaining money, set aside what they would need for the return to the city, then calculated how many rides, how many games, and how many snacks could fit within their very limited budget.

Among the Midway rides was a roller coaster, modest and rickety, pretentiously named the Cyclone. Neither had ever ridden a coaster. Neither had a frame of reference for comparison to the mighty, looping, soaring coasters at the great parks. Donal and Johnny looked up at tracks splitting the sky, heard the roar of the wheels and the screams of the riders, and got in line.

It was the Cyclone in particular that brought them back to where they belonged. The rush of wind combined with the press of gravity, the sweep of outward momentum around sharp corners, and the hint of fear, the whisper of uncertainty.

In a life weighed down by the press of boredom, of cynicism, and of loneliness, how priceless, how timeless, were those moments of uncertainty to the boys, when fear might push out the best and deepest aspects of one's character and open a window to vistas obscured during the hot and deadening week?

"Hey, Don,"

"Yeah, Johnny?"

"Let's do the Cyclone again."

"Yeah, let's do it again. Let's do it all again."

Boys once again. Nothing more than boys on the right side of the precipice.

That night, after the long trek home and with stomachs gurgling from greasy, grainy food, the boys went back to their homes. Johnny Duncan found an empty house, his father gone for some indeterminate time.

"Hey, Ma," Donal said as he passed through his own front door. Emma Mannion sat at the kitchen table nursing a beer. She looked up without expression.

"I didn't realize you were out," she said, then took a long draught from her bottle.

— ◆ —

An indolent autumn afternoon, school done and nothing at hand but the boring end of a lifeless day. Donal and Johnny kicked stones across the schoolyard, now empty except for some late-staying teachers making a play at diligence. Like the students, most of the teachers sought just to get through their days without undue burdens or annoyances.

A school in the city, reached either by a short bus ride or a long walk, fenced and gated, its old stones wearing into dirty browns and grays, and now Donal and Johnny sat on one of its outer walls and kicked their stones. Each may have had some homework for the night—math problems or some reading, things of that sort, nothing overly challenging that might lead to failure or provide any excuse for not pushing them ahead year to year to what passed for a finish line, complete with a properly stamped and sealed diploma. Neither boy cared very much. Donal liked to read, and so the English classes weren't so bad, but the rest of it was worthless. Assignments were just something to be done as quickly as possible, handed in, then on to the next one.

"Hey Johnny. Have you ever noticed Janie Donovan? "

"What about her?"

"Do you think she's cute? She's got that nice smile and that long hair."

"Hadn't noticed, Donal. Seems that you have, though."

Janie Donovan wore long blond hair, a sweet smile, a soft body accentuating burgeoning breasts, and a reputation for wickedness, insofar as one could develop such a persona by the age of fourteen. And she wore that reputation as overtly as any skirt, blouse, or pair of jeans. She had spent her earlier years stealing paper and pencils from her classroom, tripping other girls in the lunchroom so that trays and the tacky, starchy foods they carried splayed over linoleum floors, and sneaking away the completed homework of the smartest students to copy and then destroy. As the hormonal tempests of adolescence came to crash upon Janie's well-formed shores, her wickedness took on new dimensions.

Donal had indeed noticed her, but he hadn't the first clue about what it all meant or what he might do with these nascent stirrings. Girls occupied spaces he could not enter—mysterious, possibly enchanting, but to this point in his young life, as foreign as the Amazonian jungles or the valleys of the moon.

"Yeah. I think she's pretty cute. Don't know what to do about it, though."

"Christ, Donal, just do something. Anything. Go talk to her sometime and tell her that you want to get to know her better. The worst she could do would be to tell you to fuck off. Then you go find someone else."

"So you're an expert on this, Johnny? I haven't seen too many girls flocking around you."

"Nah, I'm no expert. But I know what you've got to do if you want to get to know a girl. You can't just sit around and hope she'll come to you. Go get her if you want her."

Janie had noticed Donal as well, just as she had noticed most of the young boys in her environment. Aware of her unique attributes, Janie kept a running inventory of those who might be drawn to what she had to offer. Naturally curious, she was, and the mischief of her younger years testified to that innate curiosity. Most of her life revolved around a central question but unspoken question of, *What would happen if I . . .* The asking triggered a food fight, the theft of a book she might want to read from the local bookstore, agitate the family next door by playing her music too loud, and so on. The world levered on action and response, and Janie had always been fascinated by the responses to her actions. How much could she get away with, and how would it feel to read the lifted book, to eat the stolen candy? She had rarely been disappointed.

Boys held her interest. She marveled at the form of their strange bodies, the curve of their muscles, their mysterious hills and valleys. The way they joked and laughed and teased and flirted to win her attention. Such a marvelous playground they created, and Janie's curiosity led her to explore every inch of it. It was only natural.

She noted the boys, cataloged them in her mind according to type—the jocks, the quiet ones, the thinkers, the bad boys; according to appearance—height, hair color, their flaws and assets; and according to willingness—those who wouldn't, those who might, and those who most definitely would.

She dismissed those who wouldn't right away. Their obvious reticence, based on fear or ignorance or that vilest of roadblocks, a sense of morality. They barely existed, floating around the periphery of her days with neither recognition nor thought.

It was the boys in the middle who drew her, those young men confused and uncertain about their emerging sexuality but unwilling to ignore it. With some encouragement, they could be brought forth to explore it, and Janie, obsessed with her own explorations, might be a suitably exciting guide. These boys presented challenge, and opportunity. Their presence excited her beyond measure, and certainly well beyond the predictable satisfactions of those boys, advanced within their tribe, who actively pursued her for the pleasures she might bring.

On a humid Thursday afternoon in mid-November, a day remarkable for both its heat and its promise, Janie Donovan sidled next to Donal Mannion in the yard behind their school. Donal had grabbed lunch from his backpack and was walking toward a cluster of his friends when he felt Janie's shoulder nudge his own.

Startled, he turned to her. "Oh, hi Janie," who said nothing, but merely smiled, leaned into Donal's shoulder and brought her lips to his ear where she blew softly a breath of scented, warm, whispery air into the young man's center, then turned to walk away. She did not look back.

Donal said nothing as he joined his friends, none of whom had seen anything. The remainder of the day his already thin concentration wafted away completely, his classes a complete waste of time against the demands of fantasies, his puzzlement, and a continual adolescent tumescence that would not ebb. When the final bell sounded, Donal rushed to the yard to search for Janie, but she was nowhere to be found. A vapor, or a dream

On the walk home he said almost nothing as Johnny and the others went on about football, the classes they hated, and their older friend Matthew Cooney's disappearance from the neighborhood. "Hey, Mannion," Johnny said at one point. "Where the hell are you?"

"What do you mean? I'm right here."

"I don't know where you are, Donal, but you sure as hell aren't here. What's wrong with you today?"

"Leave him alone, Johnny," said one of the others. "Maybe he's in love." The rest of them laughed. Donal shrugged and walked on wordlessly.

The next day Donal spent the morning canvassing the school for Janie, trying to anticipate where her classes were. But he didn't know her, really. He didn't know what classes she took, what she might be interested in, or who her friends were. Janie stood alone now in his psyche, Aphrodite fully formed and singular.

He found her at lunch. Or perhaps she let herself be found. She seemed to coalesce right before him, yesterday's smile returning as she watched him walk toward her in a schoolyard that may or may not have been crowded. Donal lasered his sight on Janie alone.

"Hiya, Janie."

Janie said nothing behind her smile. Her eyes, dancing with mischief, locked onto Donal's.

"So what was that about yesterday? Jesus, you knocked me halfway to the moon."

Janie leaned in closer and put her hand on Donal's forearm. She responded in a whisper, "You're cute, Donal Mannion. I think I want to get to know you better. I thought I might get your attention."

"You've always had my attention, Janie. How could I ignore someone as gorgeous as you?" He smiled as he said this in a fourteen-year-old's attempt at suavity. Meanwhile in his deep caverns, Donal's heart beat a quick tattoo and his breathing deepened. He hoped Janie would not notice the first drops of perspiration appearing on his brow.

She touched his forearm. "That's sweet," she whispered, then rose on her toes to deliver Donal Mannion's first kiss, a light peck to his cheek. "Very sweet," she whispered again.

"So how should we get to know each other better?" Donal asked in false confidence, trying consciously to control his tone to keep it from cracking.

"Meet me here in a few hours. Eight or so. I'll wait for you if you're late. We can go get something to eat, then we can see what happens." Janie leaned in again and found Donal's ear once more. A soft breath, then a flick of her tongue along its edges. "We'll see what happens," she whispered again before turning to go. "I'll wear something nice," she called over her shoulder to Donal, too stunned to move. He watched her walk to the sidewalk then turn down the street, regarding her almost playful steps and the firm, well-shaped line of the legs that made them.

What was Donal to do with those hours in the late afternoon, where his anticipation mixed with uncertainty, sapping whatever confidence he might have? He walked home, drank a glass of milk, then set about his neighborhood, trancelike from street to street, seeing no one and not sure what he would tell them if he met them. He knew he was not himself, as some inner ganglion of nerves subtly transformed his perspective, the way he walked, the curves and lines of his face.

After a time he returned home to wash away the day's dirt, to change his shirt, to comb his hair and to spray himself with a cheap scent he had never used before. Half an hour before the appointed time, he headed back to the schoolyard, his pulse, like his emotions, charged.

When Janie came into view, Donal's throat parched. She wore a white tank top that ended just above her very tight waist, accenting her very full breasts, and her jeans clung tightly to her curvy hips. She had loosened and brushed down her long blond hair so that it hung down to the small of her back. As she neared, Donal caught the floral perfume, rich, aromatic, and exotic, that Janie had dabbed on wrist, cheek, and a swanlike neck.

She smiled as she walked to him, said nothing, grabbed his wrist as she raised on her toes to kiss his cheek. "I was afraid you might not show."

Donal swallowed hard, his composure shredded. He breathed her scent, looked into blue eyes that held his own, and felt his knees tremble.

"And where else would I rather be tonight."

So began the arc of the evening, one that Donal's fantasies had constructed. Years later, he would not be able to recall just what they had done during the early part of it—where they had gone to eat, or what they had had at whatever cheap neighborhood place they found. But he would remember clearly the flirtations and encouragements. He would feel again Janie's foot running the length of his leg under the table, and the way she leaned forward from time to time to push her breasts forward. He would see again the flip of her hair and hear the sultry tenor of her voice as she told him that she had always been curious about the "real" Donal Mannion. He would smell once more the exotic, erotic scent that seemed to flow from her every pore.

As they left the café, Janie took Donal's hand and pulled him to her. There, on a gritty and grimy sidewalk on a tatty northeast street, she gave him his first real kiss, lips and tongue dancing over his own, instructing him instinctively to reciprocate and escalating his already uncontrollable tumescence. "There's a park two blocks over," she whispered. "You know it, I'm sure. And you know how quiet it is over there once the sun goes down. No one's ever around." She kissed him again. Donal said nothing and let her lead him there, her hand around his waist.

It did not last long, this first coupling. Donal's uncontained excitement rushed him through the act, despite Janie's guidance. At the end of it, she giggled. "That was sweet, Donal. But so quick. That was your first time, wasn't it?"

Donal felt himself blush, looking away into a copse of trees across the empty green.

Janie reached her hand beneath his legs once more. "There's nothing to be ashamed of," she whispered. "Everybody needs a first time. And then there's the next time," she cooed as she rubbed him there. "And the time after that."

They did not count the hours. Sometime after midnight, they rose from where they lay, rearranged their clothes and headed back to the streets that would take each of them their own way.

Later that night, as Donal tried to coax himself to sleep, he considered the wonder of it all—the intensity of passion, the press of young, firm flesh, the quick breaths, yips and moans, the indelible sensations of strength, and connection, and eventual release. The hint of danger and the threat of discovery. The ecstasy that a woman's body might provide. A new world opened to him, and Donal Mannion, ever the explorer, committed himself to investigating every corner of it.

Donal and Janie never shared another meal, never went on anything that could be remotely described as a date. For the rest of that year they barely spoke, although there were occasional nights when they might find themselves overcome by the same urges and with no one else to exorcise them. Partners, but never lovers. Never friends.

Janie had been an experience, nothing more than that. What more could a woman be?

CHAPTER 3

Since he was a boy, Donal had been enchanted by stories and poems and rhymes and the swirl of a good word. He had come to love the way the language could soar and dance and eddy in ways that stirred the heart and inflamed the mind. Part of it, he thought, was being Irish. He shared blood with the great voices of a tradition rooted in storytelling and rhapsodic lyricism. Yeats and Joyce, Behan, Swift, Synge, and Kavanaugh, and so many others, writers he'd never know but who spliced the roots of their culture to grow new shoots that spiraled brilliantly to the sky, to the light. Donal never felt more Irish than when he picked up a book.

But, as Irish as he was, Donal was no scholar, and classroom walls made him claustrophobic. With just enough effort to get the job done, Donal completed his high school classes and made ready to receive the sheet of parchment that gave him a validation that the first phase of his life was done.

So it was that the world beckoned in all its illusory splendor. He had nothing to keep him at home other than a hard-drinking mother, increasingly oblivious to her surroundings and those who moved within them. And if his love of the written word could be his admission ticket to this beckoning world, so much the better.

Donal scoured the job listings. While he was qualified for nothing, he felt capable of everything, a young man's hubris. He made the calls to the proper places that might have need of someone fresh and eager, someone able to work the language and charm the words on the page in front of him. He sought out the newspapers, marketing firms, and firms providing technical writing.

In reasonably short order, he was invited to speak with the head of a small advertising agency 16th Street near Farragut Square. The job was providing draft copy for local print ads, copy which more senior admen would edit. Davis, the manager, went through the preliminaries, then got to the heart of the matter.

"You have no qualifications," he said. "Fresh out of school. You've done nothing in this field."

Donal leaned forward in the chair opposite Davis's desk and smiled through his reply. "Ah, but I have the best qualifications anyone could bring to this job. I have an agile mind and an articulate tongue. You'd do no better than to bring me on board."

"You also have the arrogance of youth," Davis said, grinning.

"Isn't it grand?" Donal answered, then threw his head back and laughed. "I won't deny it. But I'll do you well, Mr. Davis. Give me the chance."

Davis did, and two weeks later Donal Mannion joined the firm as its youngest and rawest associate. Most of his coworkers were years older, none going out of their way to welcome him or coach him on whatever intricacies there might be in this work. No matter to any of it. Donal had his first job, and with it, the intoxication that comes with self-reliance. He wore it as a new skin.

Once he had the offer in writing, he secured a place of his own. His meager starting salary wouldn't support much luxury, and he didn't bother to look at the high-rise apartments in the city's northwest quadrant. Maybe later, after he made his mark. For now, his needs were simple, and so he took a small furnished flat not far from his neighborhood. A single bedroom, a kitchen and something that passed for a bathroom in an old building without an elevator. His flat was on the third floor with a window that overlooked the back of the even older building facing the next street over.

Donal packed up his small belongings, his clothes and a few of his books, kissed his mother goodbye as she sat at the kitchen table with a glass of whiskey and tears running down each cheek, then bused over to his new place. He had the weekend to settle himself, to adjust to his new surroundings and to wander these less-familiar streets.

And so Donal Mannion, his schooling finished but his education just begun, left his home and, fresh and eager, joined the world. He would write ad copy for a small firm struggling to find enough clients to meet a weekly payroll. Donal would write, and network, and charm those around him. And he believed that, in due time, there would be a partnership, and that that partnership would open new doors, would give a platform for his brashness, his intellect, and his creativity. His work would change the way society looked at the products and services it consumed, and, in so doing, change the way it looked at itself. He would be an engine of introspection, a prophet of change, a herald of social adjustment. He imagined it all, and set himself to the tasks that lay at hand, the work that would elevate the inherent character and goodness of Donal Mannion, Son of Man.

— ◆ —

Carole, her name was. Or maybe it was Caroline. Donal wasn't exactly sure.

The night had been a fog, beginning early on in the basement apartment Johnny Duncan had let back in the old neighborhood. He moved in shortly after Donal had found his own place and he needed to celebrate. Not only did he have a place of his own, he had a new job to pay for it. Johnny's father knew a guy who needed someone to drive one of his panel trucks. Johnny was well underage for that type of driving, but the man was desperate. Payment would be in cash, and it would be generous. A few trips down the coast to the Carolinas and Georgia, hauling God knows what in the back and unloading it, packed in tight crates, at selected addresses. His eyes dazzled by the prospect of earning money more quickly than he had dared dream; Johnny had not an ounce of curiosity about the cargo.

Johnny's new boss had supplied the refreshments for his party. Two kegs of beer sat in opposite corners of the small living space, and bottles of vodka, gin, scotch, and rum sat on the floor along one wall. Next to the bottles was a bowl containing some sort of fruit-like mixture, fed with occasional pours from whatever bottle someone put back nearest the bowl.

The party opened to the neighborhood, no invitations needed, and the neighborhood responded. Donal descended the steps to faces he had grown up with, and to many he had never seen before. The room jammed elbow to elbow, music blasting through it all, the press of young bodies creating a haze of heat and smoke.

Johnny edged his way through the mass to greet his friend. "You made it," he yelled above the noise, handing Donal a beer.

"Wouldn't miss it, Johnny."

"I had my doubts, now that you've gone uptown."

"Northeast isn't uptown. And I've yet to be invited to anything remotely resembling a party with this crew." Donal took a deep draught of the beer, then said, "Tell me something I want to know."

"Like what?"

"Like which girls here are the easiest. I've missed you, buddy," and they were off.

It was three beers along, complemented by a glass from the mystery bowl, when Donal sidled next to a girl he had never seen before. She looked to be even further along than he was at the moment, slouching a bit against the wall and looking aimlessly around the room, smiling as much to herself as the rest of the world. "Hey." She looked at him, said nothing, took the half-empty beer from his hand and drained it, then deepened her smile. "Hi," she replied. "Who are you?"

"Donal Mannion, at your pleasure, sweet girl."

She giggled. "Right now my pleasure is another beer. Go get me one," and Donal did, with one for himself. They found an unoccupied corner.

"I haven't seen you around here, Donal Mannion. Where do you come from?"

"About two blocks over. I grew up here, with Johnny and Eddie and a bunch of these other degenerates. I suppose we're celebrating tonight."

"What are we supposed to be celebrating?"

"Johnny's new place. Getting out on our own. A new job. The fact that we're still alive. All of it. Maybe the better question is what is there *not* to celebrate?

"You make it sound so easy."

"And why should it be anything else? Look around, right here. Music, and good drink. Old friends, and new people to meet, and dancing, and laughter. Who would want to be anyplace else?"

She smiled up at him coyly. "I take it you're a Romantic, Donal Mannion. A bit of a poet."

"Not at all. Just a guy starting out, and drunk enough to speak what he feels. God, it's all so much fun, isn't it?"

She said nothing. Instead she leaned into the young man and kissed him fully. Her lips parted, and Donal felt the silkiness of her tongue flick across his own. "So much fun," she whispered.

Later, after more beer, after grinding against each other as loud music played through them, after breaking into uncontrollable laughter for no reason other than the fantastic, phantasmagorical realization of pleasure, and youth, and freedom, and the limitless frolicking of drunken hearts, the two stumbled up the stairs.

"Let me take you home," slurred Donal as they reached the street.

"No," she said. "Take me to your place. I want to see it." She kissed him again and rubbed her hand on the outside of his growing tumescence. "I want to see everything you've got."

Carole? Or Caroline? No matter. She was what he wanted that night, and she reciprocated his desire. And in the morning he rolled over in sudden recollection of who she was and how she had come to share his thin, very narrow bed. He looked at her now for the first time, watching her sleep. She was not unattractive, although, he knew, it would not have mattered in the moment. Donal had not seen her clearly in the dim light of Johnny's basement flat, the darkness of midnight streets or the backseat of the cab that had taken them across town. Now he looked at her as the morning crept in under the blinds. *A brunette. I thought she was a dirty blond.* Her face seemed harsh in the morning light, her coyness stripped bare as she lay beside him, mouth slightly open and her makeup smeared on the pillow.

Donal left the bed and made his way to the bathroom, after which he stepped to the small kitchen to launch a pot of coffee. As he did so, his companion awoke, and he turned to her. "Coffee?"

"No," she shook her head. "I never drink it." She rose from the bed and wrapped the sheet around her. "I've gotta go," she said as she gathered her clothes. "Got things to do." She dressed quickly and walked briskly to Donal in the kitchen. She reached up and kissed his cheek.

"You're a sweet kid," she said, then turned to the door. Before she got there, she looked back over her shoulder. "What was your name again?"

"Donal. Donal Mannion."

"Strange name," she mumbled, opening the door. Donal was pleased. He would not have to face the awkward and uncomfortable urge to evolve a friendship, or, even worse, a role as lover. Nothing more than a pleasurable and transitory experience.

Donal Mannion stood at his window, coffee in hand, and watched Carol, or Caroline, run to the corner to flag a cab. He picked up the sheet she had used to wrap herself and threw it back onto the bed. His head hurt, a hangover that would lay him low for most of the day.

Donal sat on the edge of the bed and sipped his coffee. When he had finished, he stood again, threw back his head and laughed, then thrust a fist toward the ceiling, punctuating the air with the strength of a young man's joy, the lightness of a young man's heart that has just stepped into new light.

— ◆ —

Donal settled into patterns that were not unpleasant. He spent his days at his desk, creating copy for advertisements promising cheap tires, amazingly efficient cleaning products, lawn services, and quick relief of constipation. At day's end he would return to his simple flat, pour himself a glass of scotch, watch television or read a bit before going to bed at a reasonable hour. He took his work as seriously as circumstances demanded and sought to be good at it.

Some nights he would write, or at least try to, the first disjointed attempts at creating something. In his fantasies, he envisioned himself a novelist, someone insightful enough to regard the human condition, and gifted enough to write about it with lucidity and purpose. The copy writing deepened his incipient respect for language and ways it could be used.

He did not know the elements of writing—how to craft a narrative or develop characters that were three-dimensional. And his understanding of the mechanics of the language never went beyond high school English. But he knew stories from the way he listened. Passing conversations stayed with him, and in his fancy he interpreted the people who held those conversations. He guessed their backgrounds, their motivations, and their aspirations, creating whole personas on the basis of a casual sentence, a facial expression or a type of posture. Donal had no real idea of what to do with all this imagining, but he continued to gather it as raw material, ore to be smelted into some lasting form as he found the time, energy, and insight to do so.

On the weekends he cast aside all pretense of respectability. Carol-Caroline was not the last woman he would bed through the drink and music of a Friday or Saturday night. He loved the hunt for, and the young women of Washington seemed equally eager to share the quest. Nothing meant anything, and Donal passed from week to week, from woman to woman, without whim of conscience, regret, or introspection. Occasionally one of his partners might call him the week afterward and suggest they do it again. Sometimes he would do so out of mutual attraction and sympathetic lusting. Other times he would ignore the contact, uninspired by what had come before and convinced that there would be better connections to be made randomly in the days ahead. Use once, then discard. All of it was great fun, and all of it fed his growing notion of who he was, and what he wanted to be.

In point of fact, during the week Donal Mannion consciously tried to invent himself as a responsible, young, and budding professional, someone with ambitions, accountability, and respect for all the right things. He told himself that he would manage his own life, and do it well—answer the obligations thrust upon him, fix what needed fixing, show compassion where it was due, and pay his bills on time. He would continue to evolve as he sampled things new and different that came to him over time, digesting the impressions into new conclusions that led to new forms.

Even as the city defined him as he grew up on its neglected streets, he would in turn become part of the city. He would seek to know it from the inside, contribute to its pulses and rhythms, assess both its worst and its best, and always seek to gravitate toward the culture and art and aesthetics that made it what it was. He would visit the museums on the Mall. He would try new restaurants when he could and ride the buses across town just to see what was there. He would wander the streets of Georgetown and stick his head into the bookstores there to rummage through the discount bins and feed his own authorial dreams. He would pay attention to public events and read about the issues of the day. He would subscribe to the *Washington Post* and watch the local news while he sipped his scotch.

All this he would do as a young man eager to grow roots, to develop a sense of place and purpose, and with it, a sense of self.

Donal at twenty set himself upon these things. And when twenty became twenty-one, and then twenty-two, and on to twenty-three, his days remained the same, his dreams stayed fixed and focused. He would work as hard as required, he would toy with being a writer, he would seduce whom he could when he could, and he would go on being Donal Mannion.

— ◆ —

On a formless day, a springtime Saturday when the city shook off its gray winter coat through blossoms and blooms, Donal wandered the streets near his apartment. He had slept late and eaten well. What lay ahead was a lazy afternoon, followed by whatever mischief his night might conjure.

Near Mount Vernon Square he passed a bookstore. The window displayed best sellers, but it also held a corner for the classics, the books which most attracted him. The store itself stood recessed from the sidewalk, small and quaint, and from it wafted the odor of strong coffee.

Once inside he sought the sections for literature and poetry, then sniffed along the shelves. Unlike in most stores, the holdings were arranged chronologically rather than alphabetically. He made his way past the eighteenth and nineteenth century authors to find the twentieth century Americans. While he was leafing through an edition of *The Great Gatsby* he caught his first glimpse of Annie.

She was sitting at a corner table with a cup of espresso, thumbing through the pages of a book. Donal noticed first the piercing green of her eyes. He had never seen eyes quite that color, and quite so sharp, boring through the pages in front of her effortlessly, laser-like and insightful. Brown hair hung loosely past her shoulders, and even though she was seated, Donal could tell the curve of a firm, lithesome body.

He took the Fitzgerald to the coffee bar. As he passed her table, he noted that the book in her hands was Edith Wharton's *Ethan*

Frome. He saw an opening, and he had no intention of letting the whispers of Chance go unheeded.

Donal stopped at her table. "*Ethan Frome*," he said. "I remember reading that in high school."

She looked up at him, expressionless, and he went on. "A good read. Forbidden love, won and lost. Ethan is left quite sad in the end. Sophomore English, it was, one of the few things I remember." He flashed his best smile. "What do you think so far?"

"About the book? Or about you?"

"Either."

"The book is melodramatic and overwritten, fine for its time, but too dull for my tastes. And you seem to be someone anxious to catch my attention by using one of the cheapest and tackiest openings I've ever heard. So I've not made up my mind about you."

Donal shook his head and laughed quietly. "You've seen through me. Do you mind if I share this table? Not a whole lot of space in here."

"I can tell you've got a touch of persistence. Sit, then."

"Donal Mannion," he said as he pulled in his chair.

"Annie Maxwell. And it's an interesting name you have. I've never met a Donal."

"Named after my grandfather. Came over from Ireland, honoring the family trait of running away. A trait he passed on to my father."

"So are you running away, too, Donal Mannion?"

"No. Not yet. There's nothing to run away from now, is there? Nothing that I can see." He looked calmly into her magnetic eyes and smiled again.

"A bit of a flirt, you are. You know nothing about me."

"Ah, but it's the discovery that can be magical, don't you think? Look around. We're surrounded by people in this huge city, and most of the time we go out of our way to ignore each other. We pass someone on the sidewalk and we avoid even looking at them, as if the very act of acknowledging them is an intrusion. It's awfully cold out there. We owe it to ourselves to open up to one another as best we can, to not be strangers. So tell me about yourself."

"I'm as common as my name. A girl of the city, and nothing special in any of it. I work, I eat, I sleep. And I like to read."

They spent the next hour sharing resumes, dancing along the edges of a visceral attraction. They spoke of where they grew up, where they worked, the patter of two curious people uncertain of one another. Donal learned that Annie Maxwell provided administrative support for a downtown law firm, that she lived alone and had done so since she took her associates degree two years before, and that she did not believe in God and had little faith in mankind. She knew herself to be attractive but did not cherish that attribute because it tended to draw the wrong type of man, the superficial ones looking for the next thrill.

"Are you one of those, Donal Mannion?" she chided. "Another in a string of cheap yet exciting experiences?"

"Perhaps, Annie Maxwell. But perhaps not. Perhaps I'm as distinctive as my name."

Intrigued by this young man sitting next to her, intrigued by his delicate mixture of gentility and boldness, intrigued by the soft tenor of his voice and the quiet confidence behind it, Annie Maxwell dared herself to step beyond her usual reserve. Nothing to be lost. She would not abandon her defenses. But she was intrigued.

"There's a place I know in Georgetown," Donal said. "I go there every other weekend or so. They play the blues, and sometimes I just sit in a dark corner and let the music go through me. You can do that with the blues, and when you leave you feel cleansed, as if all the bad things in your life were just thrummed away. If you've got the inclination, I'd love for you to join me tonight."

"Do you think I need cleansing?" she teased.

"We're all soiled by what we do, girl. We all need to be cleansed. Come with me tonight."

They were off, then, the young Donal and Annie, an amalgam

of fortune and unspoken vulnerabilities, to be leavened by time and temper and thought into new forms previously unattainable in their young lives. Nothing unique in that, as the gods continue to amuse themselves through the pliable humors of mortals. Annie and Donal, the product of whim and fancy. As are we all.

Later that night, after the last set, after last call and the dim lights raised to full brightness, Donal walked Annie into the cool spring night air. She did not resist when he held her hand. Nor did she resist when he turned her toward him and gave her his first kiss. Years later he would still be able to note the exact spot on the sidewalk where that kiss occurred. Annie's spot, it would forever be.

When the kiss broke, Annie nestled into him, then leaned her lips to ear. "Find me a cab," she whispered.

Empowered by the fusion of the blues, the scotch, Annie's gentle scent, the pressure of her firm body and his usual design, he whispered back, "Shall we share it to my apartment?"

Annie stood back. She continued to hold his hand as she said, "No," then watched the slight sag in Donal's shoulders and a passing glower of disappointment touch his brow. In an instant, both disappeared.

"I'm not one of your conquests, Donal. I'm not going to sleep with you tonight. And perhaps never. But I like you, Donal Mannion. You intrigue me, and I want to get to know you better. Can you stand having me as just a friend, at least for the moment?"

"I don't know," he said, then looked away from her, down the street, his eyes searching for anything that might keep him from looking into her eyes. "I've never had a woman who was just a friend," he said in little more than a whisper. Then he turned back to her, "But then I've never known Annie Maxwell until today, haven't I?" He smiled and kissed her forehead.

"We can share a cab back to your place," he told her. "Then you'll get out and I'll ride on to my own apartment, alone and abandoned at the end of this perfect night. All my evil designs cast aside in respect for your honor." His smile told her it was all right.

They flagged down one of the cabs that cruised that part of Georgetown at the end of a Saturday night. In the rear seat they held onto each other, and before Annie got out she cupped his face in her two hands and gave him a deep and lingering kiss. "Call me, Donal. Be my friend and call me."

As he rode the few blocks to his own flat, Donal's head spun in new directions. He had never experienced such a woman. She was intrigued, she had told him. And now, he found that his burgeoning interest matched her own. Annie Maxwell would compel a pursuit, and Donal Mannion never saw himself as one to turn away from a challenge.

CHAPTER 4

Annie Maxwell's curiosity about this new man clashed with her customary reserve. Something about him that carried a different feel to it. Donal Mannion was pleasing to her eye—tall, a thatch of dark hair with just a touch of blond, a strong and narrow face, and an angular body that moved artfully, at times sinuously. But she had known attractive men before. He had his rough edges, to be sure. And despite his best efforts, Donal was no gentleman. That he had been raised through the streets came clear in a sometimes-brusque manner, a blurted, unintended profanity, a tinge to his voice that rasped the harsh tatters of street life.

Under it all hid a boyishness that his halting attempts at sophistication could never hide. He dreamed, did this new man. To be a writer, to have a voice that others heard. To live away and apart from these streets. To know which fork to use in the best restaurants. To engage the respect and admiration of his friends, and to know the pleasures of his woman. The rough edges could not hide this, nor could the hints of a youth spent with too weak a rudder. Donal never spoke of his family, and rarely mentioned his friends. He had come from very little, yet here he was.

Annie was no Romantic. She did not anticipate flowers or music or magic. She had had enough experience with the falsified, superficial manifestations of young men's pursuits. She had no use for such things. Annie did not know precisely what she expected, but whatever it was, however her time with Donal Mannion might unfold, she wanted it to be genuine, infused with honesty, respect, and integrity, an appreciation of each other as individuals with spirit and form. Only then, if she were convinced that such was their basis, would she celebrate with her body, and with her heart.

For his part, Donal entered the chase with enthusiasm and excitement. He found outlets for his own frustrations to counter Annie's reserve. Donal still had the occasional physical encounter, haunting the same bars as he had done at the beginning and finding the same pleasures. But those were short-lived. If in fact Annie Maxwell inspired him, he would need to focus. And so he put aside the shallow and tawdry to concentrate on this new and beautiful wonder.

As Annie perceived the subtle nuances that constituted Donal Mannion, so Donal evaluated the ways in which Annie was set apart. For one, she was not easy. Not just physically, although that was Donal's standard point of reference when meeting someone new. It became apparent from their first night together that Annie would not immediately yield to Donal's avarice. She would require a bit of work before Donal exacted his pleasures.

As the days went on, Donal came to realize that nothing about Annie was easy. She revealed herself piecemeal, guarding who she was, what she thought, what she felt through a steady reserve that only provided glimpses rather than panoramas. Donal gently probed, never pushed, and let Annie show herself as she became comfortable to do so.

As he regarded the well protected vault of her heart, he had no clue how she felt. Annie betrayed little through expression, motion, or word. On one of their early days together, at a table in a coffee shop, after Annie had told him about her day at work, Donal reached across to grab her hand. She did not pull it back, but neither did she return the playful squeeze he gave as he twined his fingers into hers. She looked at him quizzically. "Why'd you do that?" she asked.

"Do what?"

"Grab my hand."

"Jesus, Annie, do I need a reason? I wanted to touch you, that was all. A bit of support after your day. A bit of affection, I suppose. Maybe just to let you know that I'm here, and that you should see me."

She smiled. "I see you, Donal. You need have no doubt of that."

"But do I see you, Annie Maxwell? Or are you merely an illusion?"

"You'll just have to wait on that, man, to see if your illusion vanishes into mist," she teased.

Donal shook his head. This all would take more effort than he had ever had to make before. He expected she would be worth it. Something this hard to land had to be worth it.

He dismissed his usual methods of pursuit, which customarily consisted of making sure his partner drank enough to blur her judgment. In fact, Donal had no fixed plan. He did not court, he did not date, he seldom gave a thought to any woman past the first conquest. Nor did he have anyone who he could ask for advice. His friends from the old neighborhood had scattered, and those that hadn't, whose experiences were no different than his own, would be no help. He dared not open himself to his colleagues at the agency, exposing what they would see as naivete and immaturity—which, of course, it was.

And so Donal got creative. He made sure that they spoke often, every other evening just to keep the pulse beating. On the weekends he would head to Annie's place in late morning so that they could spend the day quietly together. Donal would lead her on walks around the neighborhood or share time with her sitting in the bookstore where they met, sipping coffee and saying nothing. On a nothing Wednesday he showed up at her office unannounced, a single rose in hand, and took her to lunch. He treated her to dinners he could not afford at places serving food he did not know. He spent a huge sum for two tickets to a Boardway play that made its way to the Warner Theater downtown, just to impress.

Annie, though, was not impressionable. She had experienced such gestures before, from young men more seasoned than Donal, smoother and more polished. Still, her innate defensiveness began to thaw. What Donal did for her and with her in itself had little impact. She had seen better. But she had never seen a better effort, or more commitment from any man trying to win her. It didn't matter what he did, how flawed or uneven or awkward those efforts might be. He stepped outside himself to come closer to her. What mattered was that he took the risk to do so. Her resolve melted away in stages, and Donal Mannion began to assume a new light.

— ◆ —

"ManΩnion," a bark more than a word. "Do you have the final draft on the Anderson project?"

"Workin' on it, David. A couple of things don't seem to fit right. Should be clear by the afternoon."

"Damn it man, it's been a week. Close the damn thing out and move on to the next one. You're like a barge stuck in a canal, backin' up the traffic. Damn it man," and David Davis, the owner of this small and somewhat disreputable agency which buffed the public image and drafted shiny advertisements its clients, turned back down the hallway to his small office in the corner.

Donal eyed the text he had drafted, but all he saw were crooked lines. He saw neither the neat and orderly arguments for a product's unique qualities, nor did he see the point in arranging them. All he saw was Annie, dangling seductively, just beyond his grasp.

Out the window a jay clattered in the oak tree near the parking lot. "And your complaint is what, small bird?" Donal muttered to the window. "A lost mate? Too little to eat? A morning too cold by half?" He chuckled at the similarities. "Perhaps I should find a tree of my own."

His work occupied no space within him on this blurry and blurred morning, and a quiet agitation stirred energy, and purpose, and life itself. In his mind he saw Annie. Only Annie. Relaxed over coffee in their bookstore or walking next to him through Mount Vernon Square. Teasing him, touching him, laughing and alive. He could not shake her. Not this morning, and perhaps not for mornings to come.

Against it, his work rang hollow, his workdays meaningless with sensations that were transient and shallow. All of it there for him to regard, to fit into neat and tidy text, to sanitize into a pitch into neat patterns that pointed its readers to what they did not need and might not even want, a process that within these office walls defined Donal Mannion.

The Anderson account can wait, he told himself. This day called for something else. A long walk, perhaps, or maybe a drink. Maybe several.

Donal stacked the Anderson drafts into a neat pile, then pulled them into his tatty briefcase. He would work on them later. Rising, he looked once more out the window to the old oak. The jay had stopped his chatter and was nowhere to be seen. Flown off, then. And so would he.

On the way out he stopped at the front desk to let the receptionist know he'd be leaving. "So soon, Donal. Mr. Davis won't be pleased."

"Mr. Davis is seldom pleased, Carol, and certainly rarely with me. Tell him I'll have the account in question on his desk first thing tomorrow morning."

"I'll tell him, Donal. Can I offer him a reason?"

"Just tell him that he has no idea what it means to be me. I'll deal with it all tomorrow."

Out the door then, and into a bright late morning. For no apparent reason, Donal thought of the boys from his neighborhood, Johnny Duncan and Eddie Moore and even Matthew Cooney, probably somewhere behind bars. All of them rogues in their own way, all walking along the same barren tracks. *Born to it,* he thought. *All of us born to it, with no angels of redemption watching over us.*

— ◆ —

Annie represented the unknown side of things that had always seemed illusory to Donal. Composure, a measure of grace, a sense of self, none of which Donal saw in himself. Annie had come of age in another place, just across the river but as foreign to Donal's world as the snows of Kilimanjaro. What she wanted, what she sought for herself, she pursued in steady, measured, and choreographed steps. No rushing, not with her job, with where and how she lived, with her man. All would come about in time, the result of purpose and process.

On a springtime Saturday night, the cusp between May's gentility and June's portent of the sweltering summer ahead, Donal and Annie had a quiet dinner at a bistro on 16th Street near Annie's apartment, then walked to Thomas Circle where they found an open bench. There they sat, breathing in the fresh billow of the evening, and said little. They kissed, confidently and open.

"You fascinate me, Donal Mannion. Do you know that?"

"And how do I do that? Tell me how fascinating I am."

"You make your way so easily. Nothing disturbs you, and you accept the things that come your way. You accept me, even though I know I frustrate the hell out of you sometimes. You're not driven, yet you have everything you seem to want. How is that? How can you live your life so effortlessly and still be so content?"

"There are a lot of things I want that I don't have. But what I do have is all that I currently need. And how contentious can a life be when I'm sitting next to you on a soft spring night?" He leaned into her to kiss her once more.

"Then do you expect everything you want to come to you on its own?"

Donal smiled, looked into her eyes. "The best things come to us when we're not looking. And it's wisdom that lets us claim them." He held her hand. "I did not plan for you, Annie. Yet here you are."

When they reached Annie's apartment, she pulled him inside, plunged into him with her full body, her fullest soul. "Tonight," she whispered. "Stay with me."

Their lovemaking unfolded at last, as measured as Annie would have it and the culmination of Donal's pursuit. In contrast to Donal's past experiences, there was no rush, no devouring, no wanton abandonment to the most basic and primitive impulses. The two shared themselves gently, almost mechanically, with a rare tenderness and a ready attention to the other, an exploration of what might be. Donal found it unspectacular. When the act softly ended with neither loud cries nor moans of passion, he rolled to his side to look at his newest lover. He had rarely been so satisfied.

— ◆ —

It had been a glorious morning. The drive to the hills had begun under the bluest of skies, sharp and crystalline, carrying the whispers of a soft cool breeze that promised to keep the sun in balance. They had found their trail and walked two miles or so into the Blue Ridge, Annie skirting occasionally off track to step into the surrounding brush or to wander a few yards beyond into the deeper parts of the woods. The Shenandoah was trees and sky, streams and flying things, and always the possibility of something unforeseen and unexpected. A chevron of geese flying low enough to touch. A deer or a bear. A kiss from a nervous lover stolen under a canopy of chirping birds.

In a clearing several yards off the trail they had spread their lunch. Now, food consumed, wine in hand and the warmth of the sun lulling conversation and the thoughts that fired it, Donal Mannion regarded the lady who lay across from him. A wondrous journey it had been, the two of them. She had become his quest. Rocky, broken, and bumbling, but a quest nonetheless. In the end he knew that Annie Maxwell had come to take him for who and what he was—a young man of boundless intentions and finite abilities, temperamental, shallow, and eternally lost in a world that swirled around him too quickly and too coldly, yet someone whose battered heart persisted in beating and indulged the constant impulse to welcome into it the lovely souls his meandering journey encountered.

— ◆ —

"Tell us about yourself, Donal. We're all ears."

The dinner had been Annie's idea. She had little occasion to mention Donal to her parents, but she saw a need to bring them together. Transparency, it was, in addition to checking a box on a list of things that had to be done. They had been seeing each other for longer than most of Annie's past endeavors, so it seemed the thing to do.

On a Sunday Annie drove them to her parents' house across the river in Alexandria. Donal took the drive with a measure of calm. He knew he could be charming enough. One of his colleagues had told him that his personality was adaptive, that he could laugh when others were laughing, stay serious when need be, engage in deep conversations if that the agenda called for it, speak of the things he knew and had sense enough to stay silent on those he didn't. So a meal with James and Theresa Maxwell should present little challenge. Besides, what really was at stake?

"I'm a dull story, I'm afraid, Mrs. Maxwell."

"Oh please. It's Theresa. And James."

Donal smiled, "Not Terry, or Jim? I admire people who use their full names. I think there's a bit of integrity in that.

"And you've never been Don or Donny, I assume," she responded with an equal smile. "We are who we are, is that right?"

"Exactly. No need to build illusions around ourselves, or take shortcuts to our identity."

"So what's your identity, Donal?"

"Very humble, to be sure. I grew up in the city. I write advertising copy for a cranky boss in a downtown office that's too brightly lit and work with other people who are finishing their degrees and writing novels and saving for summers in Europe. By comparison, I'm rather dull, as I said. I expect some day I'll try my hand at writing a novel, but I don't expect to finish any degree or scamper around Europe. It's enough to take each day as it comes."

"Do you still have family here?"

"My mother's still in the city, living in the house I grew up in. It's in the northeast, near New York Avenue."

"Isn't that a pretty rough area?" said James, silent to this point. "I can't think of much that's up there."

"There really isn't much," replied Donal. "Nothing but corner businesses, pawn shops and liquor stores. But any part of the city is rough now, don't you think? It's become that way. For what it's worth, I'm pleased with where I grew up. I made good friends, I slept well at night, and I learned some very practical lessons, I think. All I could ask of a boyhood."

James Maxwell, across the room on the sofa next to his wife, shifted his head and grunted, then took a long sip of his pre-dinner bourbon. The Maxwells lived in a well-spaced housing development, with wide yards and a small park at the corner. Annie grew up here. It was what she knew. Donal learned that night that when she set out to make her own way, her parents did everything they could to keep her on this side of the river. They begged her to go to college locally. "George Mason is really so close. You could study whatever you wanted and still live here and sleep in your room. Or if you really wanted to live away, there's UVA or James Madison. You're certainly smart enough."

If college were not her preference, then perhaps she could find a job close by so that she could temper the demands of a real job with the securities of home. Then, after a time, she could go on to something else, her confidence and self-assurance buffed with minimal stresses.

But the city drew her, that web of streets and people and buildings that whispered the seductions of exoticism, romance, and the mysterious aura of the new. She had been to the museums and to the restaurants, all within the safe embrace of her parents or well supervised field trips. Now it was the streets that lured her, not the finery. She would find out who she really was, and she would live her life freely while doing so. Behind their silence, her parents carried deeply bruised hearts.

Through dinner, Theresa had designed to show Annie the depth of flavors her gentle rebellion had cost her—cranberry glazed pork tenderloin, summer squash with honey and cinnamon, broiled brussels sprouts with garlic and olive oil, a homemade key lime pie. Donal held forth on the meaning of his work, his notion that he might actually have a voice in shaping the way society might view the goods and services that came to his accounts. He told what he knew of his grandfather, "the first Donal Mannion, the one with all the nerve," and how that nerve placed his descendants on these shores instead of slumping farms and homesteads in Ireland. He spoke of the pride he took in living in a flat that others might think as dark and small, but he knew to be truly his own, and Annie rewarded him with a soft smile.

Pie consumed and after-dinner coffee grown cold, Annie pulled them to the doorway for the drive back across the river. "Such a pleasure to spend time with you," said Donal as he shook James's hand and nodded at Theresa. Both had been content to let the young man carry the conversation throughout the evening. James had said no more than a handful of words all night. Who, really, was this young man who pursed his lovely, spirited daughter? Could he be trusted? But then, Annie made her own decision these days.

On the drive back, Donal turned to Annie. "What was that all about, Annie? Did I make the impression you wanted me to make?"

"I didn't expect anything of it, Donal. I just thought you all should finally meet. You did fine. I think they really liked you."

"Your dad may not share that conclusion. He seemed pretty apart all night."

"He's always that way. Usually the less he says, the better for all concerned."

"So that's out of the way, then. The meeting of the parents. What comes next?"

They had arrived at Donal's street, and Annie pulled the car to the curb before his building, then turned to him. "Whatever you think is right, Donal Mannion. The journey continues, no? Take us somewhere."

— ◆ —

It had been several months since the two had seen each other, but Donal Mannion sat now at a bar with Johnny Duncan. Friends since boyhood, but now too rarely together, Donal obligated downtown, and Johnny still wedded to the old neighborhood. It was Donal who made the call, inviting Johnny for an end-of-day drink at The Black Hand, a dark, tatty institution of a pub a handful of blocks from where they had grown up. A place familiar to them both, with drinkers cradling their glasses in relative silence, as dour as the walls, and bartenders willing to let them be.

"Uptown Donal Mannion," Johnny called out when Donal walked through the door. As Donal's eyes adjusted to the dim and woody interior, Johnny hopped off his barstool and came to his friend to shake his hand. "You've got the first round. And maybe the second."

"Still hustling your drinks after all this time, eh, Johnny?"

"The price you pay for success, Donal. Most of us have never come near it."

The two spent the first two rounds reviewing the neighborhood, the girls they knew, their best times and their worst fights, and their friend's whereabouts and disappearances. "Christ, I haven't seen Cooney in almost two years," Johnny said. "No idea where he is or what he's doing. And Eddie just got his girl pregnant. I assume you'll be invited to the wedding."

Over the third round, a warm scotch that eased the blood and loosened the tongue, Johnny leaned across the small table and looked his friend in the eye. "So tell me, Donal. Where do you find your women now that you've gone uptown? I'll wager there are a thousand places where the drinks are expensive and the women are hot. Not like these neighborhood bars. Am I right?"

"Wouldn't know, Johnny. Haven't done much of that since I moved. And I'm hardly uptown. I live in a one-room flat, and my nearest neighbors are the winos and junkies in Mount Vernon Square. Nothing uptown about it. Just another place to live. Christ, Johnny, I'm just a copy writer."

"Yeah, but you've got a downtown office."

"A downtown cubicle."

"Okay, then, but it's a downtown address. So you go to a bar, mention to the ladies that you're working for Hendershot and Blubberbutt, or whoever they are. You don't need to mention what you do. That's got to catch some attention."

"Like I said, Johnny, I haven't really put it to the test."

Johnny paused as he considered, then his eyes grew wide, and his mouth opened just enough to let a quiet gasp escape. "Oh my God. You've got a woman." Donal looked up and smiled shyly. "My God, that's it! Jesus, Donal, give me details."

"I'm not one to share details, Johnny, you know that. Let's just say she has my attention.

"Where'd she come from, then? How'd you meet her?"

"Just by chance. A bookstore, if you can believe it. She caught my eye."

"Many have caught your eye, Donal, but no one's been able to hold it. Gorgeous, I assume." Donal nodded. "Uptown girl? Lots of money?"

"She grew up across the river. Suburban girl who wanted to try the city. I've met her parents. Nice enough, although I got the sense that Dad didn't really approve of the city boy. She's stubborn, though. I like that about her. She stands her ground, and she holds her own. Never really met any women quite like her."

"Jesus, Donal. This sounds serious. I greatly fear, my brother." He sipped his scotch, then asked quietly, "So what comes next?"

"Why does anything have to come next? We're just enjoying ourselves in the moment. Nothing wrong with that."

"If that was the case, then we wouldn't be having this conversation, now, would we?"

Later, after the fourth round followed by a tequila shot for the road, the two staggered out of The Black Hand and onto a sidewalk that spun beneath their feet. There they hugged the familiar graces of friendship, and Johnny turned to stumble the few blocks back to his flat. After a few steps, Johnny turned back to Donal.

"Hey, Mannion," he called. "You got yourself a job and a woman. You're the best of us, man. Don't screw it up."

— ◆ —

And so continued the slow assimilation into what would be, what would have to be. Donal Mannion, buoyed by the sense that he might in fact surmount the peculiar challenge of Annie Maxwell, pursued her with diligence, care and as much empathy as a poor boy from the city's tawdry streets could summon.

There remained much about Annie that he did not know. She had not abandoned her self-protective instincts, and she gave pieces of herself only gradually. Donal had not met her friends, nor had they returned to her parents' home. She showed him no pictures of herself, and she did not speak of places she'd been or, inevitably, the other men she had known. Annie remained squarely in the moment, silently asserting that Donal accept her as she was, that any additional layers would be peeled back reluctantly, and only over time.

But the two had drifted together, of that there could be no doubt. They reserved each weekend for each other—day trips to the Virginia countryside, nights at the movies, drinks at the bars and pubs where they felt most comfortable, quick lunches and leisurely dinners,

Annie cooking in her small kitchen new recipes that experimented her innate creativity. At the end of most of these nights they would find themselves in bed, holding close to one another the marvelous revelation of another soul residing in another body that came to be more than merely a physical emanation. Their nights held more peace than passion, but both came to anticipate the wash of harmony as their disparate spirits claimed a common warmth.

On a night in late May, after the ebullience of a new springtime in which the two had flourished, caressing their attraction for each other as if it were a rare jewel or a holy relic, unexpected yet precious, Donal Mannion sat at the narrow window in his flat that looked onto the broken pavements of the parking lot behind his building. In his hand he held a glass half-filled with red wine, the remnants of a bottle that Annie had given him two days ago.

"You need to diversify your alcohol intake, Mannion," she had told him. "All you drink is the hard stuff. But there's a sophisticated world out there, and you need to be able to walk through it knowing at least a little bit about where you're going."

Donal eyed the bottle as she handed it to him. "But I don't really like wine, Annie."

"That's because you've never had anything more complex than Boone's Farm. Your palate's undeveloped. As is most of you. But I'm here to help, so drink this when you get to the point of expanding your worldview."

To his surprise, he came to enjoy the way the red lined his wineglass—another of Annie's gifts—then filled his nose with a strong floral scent that prefaced the velvet of the wine itself. A good wine, it was, and he drank from it now, fully cognizant of the power of this singular and bizarre Eucharist, Annie herself inside the wine.

It's been time enough, he thought. *My Annie, the ultimate accident. I've chased her all this time, and she's not yet turned me over.* He sipped his wine, his forehead furrowed. *She could do better, I know, but still she's here. Always here.*

As the evening drew on through a lowered sun, the room grew cooler. Donal finished his wine, then moved to his kitchen to pour another glass, ending of the bottle. He turned on the small lamp on the table near the chair, and the sudden light flashed out the window so that a cat in the parking lot below stopped in its tracks and looked up at its source before scampering behind a dumpster.

A partner. A lover. Stability. A constant now. That's what I wanted, wasn't it? That's what all this was about, as I recall. The pursuit of Annie Maxwell, just to see where it might go. So here it is. He sat back and closed his eyes.

Let us be lovers
We'll marry our fortunes together . . .

Donal opened his eyes and smiled. Perhaps this quest, the mysterious challenge of Annie Maxwell, might at last be coming to fruition.

— ◆ —

Donal Mannion married Annie Maxwell on a sweltering Saturday afternoon in early September. When he had asked her to be his bride, she hesitated, genuinely surprised.

"It's so clear to me, Annie. We're better together than apart, and we need each other. At least I need you. Be there for me. Be my wife."

Donal bought a modest ring, all he could afford, and they reserved Annie's girlhood parish of St. Lawrence in Alexandria. Theresa Maxwell gushed when the two shared their news at a Sunday dinner that Annie had asked her mother to prepare on short notice. "We have news, Mom. Let's have dinner, a nice dinner, all together this weekend." James Maxwell's mouth stretched as best it could into a thin smile. He shook Donal's hand and said nothing.

They insisted on a small wedding, no more than immediate family and a few close friends. At last Donal would meet those who shared part of Annie's childhood. He did not tell his friends. There were only a handful of them, really, and he knew them to be too rough for this. Most wouldn't cross the river, and all of them would be uncomfortable in a suburban parish. Donal could not imagine Johnny Duncan in a coat and tie, squirming to be polite. He imagined Eddie Moore looking to see if he might lift a plate or some cutlery from the reception. The others would make for the bar, no doubt grow raucous, maybe even start a fight, or finish one begun nights ago at the neighborhood pub.

He would tell them later. Perhaps they might even hold a separate party down the road. But this day would be for Annie, in Annie's world.

When Donal told his mother she looked at him as if he had sprouted wings and flown a lap around the kitchen. "You can't be serious," she said. "Annie, is it? The smart one with the dark hair? The one we went to dinner with a few weeks ago?"

"Yes, Ma. You liked her, or at least you told me so at the time."

"I've met her only the once."

"You'll meet her again, I would expect. We'll be moving into Annie's apartment downtown. You can help us fix it up."

"Her place? What'll you do with yours?"

"I'll be rid of it, Ma. Her place is much nicer."

Emma Mannion stared into space, sipping at her drink saying nothing more about it. When the day came, she sent her apologies to the Maxwells, citing a migraine rather than a severe hangover, and did not attend the wedding.

So it was a simple affair. A wedding mass, then an intimate dinner in the Maxwell orbit, attended by Maxwells and their friends, Annie glowing at the center of it. Donal held her hand, kissed her attentively when the glasses were clinked, and aunts and cousins took their pictures.

Afterward they drove in Annie's old car across the bridge where they had booked a luxury suite at the Jefferson Hotel, a place neither had ever dreamed of entering. This would be their wedding weekend. Both had work again on Monday, so this was the best they could do. Her parents had offered to send them on a honeymoon of their choice, but they deferred. "Maybe later, Mom. Donal and I just want to be together. The wedding's the thing, not the honeymoon."

The wedding indeed was the thing. Donal Mannion made love to his new wife that night, vigorously and with purpose. He matched Annie's uncharacteristic moans with sighs of his own. He felt a completeness to it, the entirety of Annie and Donal.

Tomorrow they would wander the city. They would go to their favorite museums and sit on the Mall to watch young people throw baseballs and play soccer. They would eat what they wanted when they wanted. And at the end of the day they would return to their suite and make love again, seeking to hold fast the wispy elations of newness, of promise, or each other. They would clutch each other, and in so doing, strive to drink the nectar reserved for the gods themselves.

It was the middle of that night, their first night as man and wife, that Donal rose while Annie slept peacefully, unclothed beneath the thick coverlet. He stepped carefully through the dark to the minibar and withdrew a small bottle of scotch, which he took to the window that opened onto 16th Street. There he stood, naked and vulnerable, looking at the city's lights which still twinkled gently. Not everyone in Washington was asleep, despite the hour, nor was Donal Mannion.

He stood and sipped his scotch, stretched his back and yawned. A large dark bird, perhaps a hawk on a night hunt, swooped outside the high window. Donal looked back over his shoulder at Annie's sleeping form, lovely in the half-light.

And in the peace of this night, in the aftermath of a day filled with the indelible etchings of time and place and memory, he thought, *Now what do we do?*

CHAPTER 5

SEVEN YEARS ON

A cold night, one of the coldest he could recall, and cursed by a wind that whipped and snapped off the Potomac to rob all feeling from fingers, toes, and heart.

Matthew Cooney crumpled up the newspaper that served as his pillow and nestled as best he could under the overcoat that doubled now as his blanket. Enough of an overhang from the tacky tobacco store, closed now behind an iron grid, kept him from absorbing most of the snowflakes stinging like tiny darts. He had seen nights like this, far more than he cared either to count or remember. He would face this dark night as he had faced every night for the past two years, resolute simply to see the next morning.

Almost no one was on the streets, the combined effect of winter bluster and Christmas Eve, which, if nothing else, promised the rarity of a white Christmas. Christmas Eve meant little to Matthew Cooney. Christmas was just a day, the same this year as any other Friday. He would spend it as he spent most days, shuffling among strangers who chose not to see him, wending his way to the mission where, at the end of the priest's blessing, he would find at least a cup of hot coffee and a muffin, then setting himself up in the park with a paper cup in front of him and a look of quiet pleading in eyes that scoured each passerby for sympathy and spare change. If he were fortunate, he might collect enough for a meal at McDonald's, filling his stomach with grease and gristle and quieting his mind enough to allow him to get an early start in his quest for the perfect door front. It would have to be recessed from the sidewalk, dark enough to afford him some bit of privacy, and close to a heating grate. Those were hard to come by.

Cooney's Christmases had always been a blur. Even as a child, one blended into another, and none held enchantment or wonder. The yelling, the slaps, the cold were indistinguishable one year to the next. He had grown too old too soon, the excitement of holiday meals and Christmas carols and cards sent or received obliterated by poverty and the resentments it engendered. The best Christmas gift he ever received was a carton of smokes from his father. His mother rarely left her bottle long enough to give him anything.

When Matthew turned eleven his father despaired of family life altogether and left for parts unknown. Matthew never saw him again. His mother, now with more reason than ever to climb into her cups, did so with a deeper commitment, and ceased to exist at all in present and responsible realms. Matthew turned to the streets. As tatty and dangerous as they might appear, it all seemed more stable to his young eyes, and even younger heart.

Incapable of sustaining himself he turned to the usual crimes—theft, some petty and some not so petty, a few drugs bought at wholesale and sold at retail, and, in a grand gesture of hubris, an attempt at armed robbery. He was an amateur, though, and no match for a liquor store that was a regular target for those on the edges. The owner stepped on a hidden alarm and feigned confusion and fear long enough for the squad cars to roll up to the door. The police drew their arms, Matthew Cooney threw his down, and he found himself a temporary home through a two-year sentence.

When paroled, it was back to the streets. *No one hires an ex-con,* he thought, *especially one with no schooling, no skills and no hope.*

Matthew knew his lot, and he accepted its heartbreak. There was, he believed, no longer a heart to break.

And now, on this bitter Christmas Eve, Cooney settled into his doorway. No miracles. No bright star to light his way. Nothing but pelting snow. In the early evening of it all, he drifted into what passed for slumber.

"Cooney. Matty Cooney. Is that you?"

Matthew roused at once as a man's hand gently tapped his shoulder. Instinctively, he reached for the knife he kept in a side pocket of the coat. "What the hell? Get off me," he barked, squinting against the darkness to see who this was.

The man drew off at once. "Jesus, Matt, it *is* you. What the hell are you doing out here on a night like this? I knew you once, don't you see. Johnny Duncan . . . I'm Johnny Duncan."

Matthew peered upward, scowling as he racked his memory. Maybe, once, a few years back. When he was another man in another time. When he was a boy, there might have been a Johnny Duncan.

"My family and I lived three doors down from yours. We ran together a bit before, well, before you left. A bit of mischief, a game or two, all that. D'ya remember at all?"

Matthew grunted as the vapors of recollection put a face to the name, and he saw the grown version of that face kneeling before him now. "Johnny Duncan," he whispered. "Yeah."

"What the hell are you doing out here, Matty? You've no place to go? No place to be? Christ, man, it's Christmas Eve."

"Just the way it is, Johnny, and nothin' to be done about it. Go on your way now. There's nothing for you here."

Johnny reached down and placed his hand under Matthew's arm, then pulled him upward. Matthew resisted, stumbled as he tried to pull his arm away, but found himself too weak. Johnny got him to his feet.

"And there's nothing for you here either, Matty. I don't have the first clue what happened to you, but I'll tell you man, I don't give a damn. I see a man I knew sleeping in a doorway on Christmas Eve and I know he shouldn't be there, no matter who he is or what he's been. You're coming with me."

Matthew stepped away as best he could, but Johnny held tight to his arm. "I'm goin' nowhere, Johnny. Leave me be."

Johnny let go his grip and turned to face his long-lost friend fully. He sighed and shook his head. "Do you recall that we were in the same catechism, Matty? Do you remember what we learned? More than just a few chosen words, the rubbing of the beads and Sunday Mass. That teaching gets into your blood and you can't ignore it. *Christmas*, Matty. It's part of who we were as boys. Part of who we are. Even if it's only for one night. You're comin' with me, Matty. You're not sleeping in this cold. Not tonight."

Matthew said nothing.

"I have a flat not far from here, with a spare bedroom. It's yours for the night, along with a hot meal. Tomorrow you can sort things out. Stay or go, as you choose. But every Christmas Eve demands a stable for those in exile."

"Those in exile. I'm hardly the Christ child, Johnny."

"You're as close as any of us from what I can tell. Come along, now. For old times, and for who we used to be. There's no star, and no wise men, and you won't have to sleep with the goats. But there's a manger for you tonight, Matty, if you'll have it."

Matthew Cooney hesitated, then gathered his overcoat and a small bag of belongings. With an unsteady step he came to Johnny Duncan's side. Together, then, into the night, through the wind and the cold and the snow, to hear the angels singing hosannas in soft and gentle voices.

— ◆ —

"It always starts small. You take something little, then next time something a bit bigger. And it gets in your blood, then, and you begin to think that you can take whatever it is you want, and whenever you want it. Leads to trouble, all that. But it always starts small."

Matthew leaned back against the cinderblock wall that separated his cell from all the others. His mate, a scared and trembling young man of nineteen, hovered on the edge of his cot, fidgeting with uncertainty and the latent terror that comes from the first time inside.

"I started with an apple," Cooney continued. "It looked so damn good—round and red and full of life, and I was hungry. Always hungry back then. So I waited for the storekeeper to turn his head and slipped one into my pocket. Then I walked away and down the street, as easy as you please. I even smiled at the keeper and told him to have a good day. That was it. I stole an apple and loved the eating of it. I was on my way."

"So what came next," his mate asked. Derek was his name, and he carried a voice made high with tension and fear.

"It's a dangerous thing when a poor man learns that thievery might fill both his stomach and his pockets, things that had always been empty. The usual things. A bit here, a bit there. When I had the chance, I might try to rifle a shed and sell what I carried off." Cooney paused with a chuckle." I learned in short order that selling car parts was nowhere near as profitable as peddling pharmaceuticals that were in high demand. I knew some people who did so, and folks like that can always use an expanded labor force, as it were. I got into the trade, and I did fairly well. Always wanted more, though. Always looked for another score. Big or small, it didn't matter."

"And that's why you're in here?"

"My own stupidity. Or maybe it was ego. I tried to graduate to the next level of crime. A convenience store holdup that went south. The judge had seen me before on the small stuff. This time he thought I needed a vacation, told me that I had been working too hard. I have the next several months to consider my career choice."

Matthew turned to look past his mate to the hallway, where a guard was leading a new resident to his own cell. He turned then to

Derek. "And what about you? What brings you the honor of being my new roommate?"

Derek shifted, tension melting into a scowl. "A friend of mine shows up on a Friday night in a new car, a Jaguar 'Hop in', he calls. 'This thing roars like a jungle cat.' I knew it wasn't his. Couldn't be, not on a mechanic's wages. But in I go, and off we go, and it was great fun until we got stopped for obvious reasons. We ran into some woods next to the stretch we were racing. It didn't take long to find us. All of it was his idea. I was just along for the ride."

"But it wasn't the first time, was it?" Matthew asked. "They wouldn't put you in here if it were the first time you played some mischief."

Derek looked away. "Couple of small thefts. Nothing big. The judge knew me, too."

Matthew looked back to the hallway, empty now, and chuckled. "Small thefts. It always starts small, don't you know? Then it gets in your blood. And here we are, Derek. Here we are."

When Matthew Cooney's sentence ended, he had no place to go. The clerk had asked for a permanent address upon his discharge, and Cooney listed the house where he had been a child. But that house did not exist in its previous form. Father gone all these years, mother vanished into a bottle, no job waiting for him. The state had taken its compensation for his crime, then spat him onto the streets, its obligation finished.

So it was the streets that had absorbed Matthew Cooney. He did not object, and in fact had looked forward to what he saw as the freedom and license of being his own master. There would be things to steal and women to buy. There would be liquor to drink. He envisioned a community of those like him, those cast aside by a society in which they could not fit for whatever reason. He would not be lonely. And to it, he had really been on his own all these years anyway. He had stolen, he had fought. He had survived. This would be no different, except for the fact that he was a bit older, a bit stronger, and immeasurably wiser.

Matthew had left the jail with a backpack of essentials and headed downtown. There were squares and parks and green spaces where he could find a place to sit and reflect on how all this would work. He knew it would. There he would introduce himself, quietly, confidently and with force if necessary, beginning this new phase, which really was no more than an extension of his previous phases. He knew he'd survive, and likely do so with a bit of flair and adventure. He was Matthew Cooney.

So he had come to the streets, and there he stayed until Johnny Duncan plucked him from the sidewalk on a blustery and bitter Christmas Eve.

— ◆ —

Matthew paused at the window of Johnny's three-room flat, a cluttered, disjointed space of failing plasterboard and exposed wires. He looked onto the street two floors below him. A cold day, and no one about. Papers blew through the soggy gutters, and he could sense again the carpet of cigarette butts and candy wrappers coating the sidewalks. Dingy, it was, all of it, both inside and out. Dingy, too, the man who regarded it.

Matthew turned back to what passed for a kitchen, took a final sip of his morning coffee, and headed out. Nowhere to go, but it was the thing to do. He would add to the clutter of the streets and leave the flat to its rightful owner.

Johnny made a hot breakfast for his stray friend Christmas day. What he did not make was any suggestion Matthew go back to the streets, or stay just long enough to fit himself back together and find a place of his own, or even to help him look for space in a local shelter. Johnny said nothing of the sort, that day or any of the days that ensued, so the two of them fell into a routine of comings and goings.

Johnny Duncan drove a city bus, sometimes at odd hours, and so Cooney often had the run of the place. He did not abuse this special situation. He took nothing, other than the comfort of a predictably warm bed at the end of cold days. When he rose he would go back to his streets, back to the park where he would put out his paper cup and try to engender pity. Most days it worked, and he would come home with enough coins to feel as if he were contributing to this very nontraditional household.

This day, cold and lonely, he took his place on the usual bench near a statue of some Civil War general seated on a horse. He was not a reflective man, but today, warm enough under his thick coat, well enough fed and well enough rested, away from the immediate dangers of loss and abandonment and irrelevance, Matthew Cooney regarded this very small sliver of time, this accidental comfort against the series of failures that had deconstructed the fibers of his life.

It wouldn't last, this he knew. There would come a day, very soon no doubt, when he would take his smattering of belongings, give Johnny Duncan a firm handshake, and set again on his damaged journey. This was who he was—Matthew Cooney, architect of grand failures. He would fail again, and fail better, and he knew it to be his lot.

But on this morning the sun shone through air so brittle and cold it might break, and ducks quacked plaintively on the nearby pond, and a church bell tolled Matins. A young mother scurried by in a bundle of gloves and scarves pushing a pram with an equally bundled baby. The city breathed alive again in short and small sips.

Matthew looked upward, shuffled on the bench, and looked up to the sky's piercing blue. Failure perhaps, but Lord, wasn't some of it grand and beautiful?

But there were other days, some so damned cold, and each morning colder than the last it seemed. Wind and the occasional flake of snow, the perpetual graying of the sky. And the worst of it when the piercing slanted rains of winter that saturated whatever clothing he wore, burrowing into the very marrow of an already frigid soul. Winter, damn it all.

Matthew shuffled his way to a tree at the far corner of the green, placed his pack next to him and settled onto the wet ground. No one would be about today, and so no need to claim a bench where the most used walkways met near the center of the square. No need to don his practiced expression of pathos and sincerity. No need to spread his quiet, unspoken plea before the best intentions of passersby who most often tried very hard not to see Matthew Cooney at all, save the occasional good soul who might drop a coin or two into his cup, and the very rare soul who might even pause to speak with him.

"How are ya, friend? Ya going to be okay?"

Such false concerns offered more to soothe guilty consciences than to break the dreariness of a homeless man's mindless and endless days. The flimsy offers of advice. "There's a shelter half a mile from here, down U Street. Have ya tried it? It'd be good to get out of this cold."

Matthew knew all the shelters, knew all the hostels. He knew the priests that offered morning blessings with warm muffins, and Cooney knew that it was the muffins and coffee that sustained him far better than a mountain of blessings ever could. What was a man then but what he ate, and where he slept?

He belonged here, Cooney did. He would live on the streets and scuffle his way from day to day, until there were no more days. No sense in fighting it; it was all he deserved.

His days with Johnny Duncan were over and had been for a while. Johnny's saintly act couldn't sustain itself, an act that made Matthew as constantly uncomfortable as a stone in a hard shoe. A warm bed and a few hot meals had not been enough to convince the homeless man that anything could ever be any different than what it was.

On a February day, another entry in the flaccid parade of days that held neither adventure nor meaning, Matthew Cooney found refuge under the branches of a great English oak, still dripping with the vestiges of last night's rainfall. It would rain again today, and the raindrops would find him once more. There was little he could do about it. Little Matthew could do against the rain, against the hunger, against the boredom. Cooney shifted again on the wet ground, pulled closer his tatty coat, and closed his eyes.

Where shall I go now? What shall I do?

Nothing, he told himself. *Nothing at all but draw breath on this cold winter's day, until I can draw breath no more.*

A man could live for years in this swarming mass of streets and time and never be seen, Cooney thought. He despised the clutter of obligation—the blinders that we wear, the obsessive focus on what's directly in front of us and what must be done, those to whom we owe allegiance or money or time. The streets of Washington teemed with it all, a jumbled mass of interchangeable bodies with interchangeable parts and interchangeable worries. No room for anyone else, and no call to notice what has no immediate value.

Matthew thrived on invisibility. *Nothing to it, really,* he would tell himself. *Just go about your day as if you knew every move to be made. As if you owned the city and everyone in it. No one pays any mind.* Mistakes came when one tried not to be seen or thought himself too bold. Lurking in doorways or clambering down dark alleys—any unnatural action—drew suspicion. Cooney detested attention, unless he were the one to be paying it to complete whatever task was at hand.

His one great mistake had been an attempt at daylight robbery, right in the open.

He had been invisible for years as Matthew Cooney the hustler, Cooney the petty thief, Cooney the entrepreneur, Cooney the Invisible Man.

On a sunlit late winter morning Matthew walked through the square where he usually spent his days. He surveyed this day—sunshine and enough warmth to keep away discomfort, the chatter of birds, the ever-present white noise of car traffic and the shuffling of the swarms coming and going to their places, heads down, absorbed and unsmiling. He had become familiar with the neighborhood and knew the surrounding houses well enough to identify those that might be worth a clandestine visit. The best thieves were patient, and really, there was no need to rush things. He had enough for the day, and for the next several days. The last house he had visited had proven generous. Again, he had taken just enough, but not so much that the losses would be noticed right away.

Cooney set off down the street adjacent to the square, the one where the fattest houses stood in sentry-like rows. A reconnaissance mission, nothing more. *No need to press things today.* Whatever he might see he would catalog for future reference, for those days when things might not be so flush. For now he was a happy man.

On the way he stopped into a bakery and picked three doughnuts and two bagels from the display case. Cooney reached into his back pocket and drew forth the bills to pay for it all. This day he had money. It had been a good week.

Back to the street, then, and into his walk. No rush. No hurry. He had the day to himself, and he might fill it with anything that caught his fancy. And, best of all, no one would notice him, this lone figure walking the dense streets, owning the city. This blurred human cipher., Cooney the Invisible Man.

— ◆ —

Strays, they were. Two dogs rummaging through the discards and throwaways that littered the streets in this part of the city. Northeast streets were seldom elegant and often dangerous, especially if one weren't familiar with the neighborhoods, such as they were. A fitting playground for these dogs, who, like many of the residents in this district, had no permanent sense of place or being.

Matthew Cooney joined his fellow strays on a summery midday, looking for God knows what. A familiar face, a loose woman, maybe an unattended store front, although these were few now that shopkeepers had grown more cautious, some even carrying handguns. The risks had become greater while the rewards had diminished.

In a green clearing between untended blocks he stopped his walking and sat down on the cool grass. The dogs had followed him there and they came to him as he sat, sniffing hopefully in his direction, perhaps smelling the remnants of the day-old roll that had been his breakfast.

"Sorry, fellas," Cooney said to them. "Nothing for you today. Maybe we'll both go on the hunt. Neither dog nor man should go through his days on an empty belly."

The dogs sniffed once more, snorted through the grass, which provided nothing but cigarette butts and the remnants of an old newspaper, then turned back to the sidewalk. A few steps on, one turned back to look again at the man with tired eyes. Matthew raised his hand to him, "Carry on, brother," he whispered, as the dog turned back to his companion and trotted across the street.

Matthew had always loved dogs. As a boy he had adopted just such a stray, a brindled mutt with huge eyes and too much fur, as ragged and as tatty as he was himself. When the dog followed him home, he took him inside to give him some food, a gesture of kindness that did not play well with Mrs. Cooney. She threw a glass at the poor beast while screaming a profanity at her son. From that day forward, Mattew took to sneaking the dog a portion of his own food, each night wrapping some meat or a section of a sandwich or a slice of cheese in a napkin and taking it to the sidewalk where his new companion waited, tail wagging and eyes alive.

Matthew named him Jake, a solid name for a tough dog, he thought. They carried on their surreptitious relationship for weeks. Sometimes during the day Cooney would seek out Jake and together they would wander the streets, finding whatever they could. On those days both of them ate well and basked in one another's company. In the autumn, when Father Lemmon preached a sermon at Mass about

Saint Francis, Matthew felt himself stir. *A saint who loved dogs,* he thought, *and all the animals. Loved them as much as he loved his fellow man. My kind of saint.*

Matthew went forth one cool December evening with his usual store of stolen food, but Jake was not in his usual place. He called for him, once, then twice, then set off to search the streets. He did not find him, not that night, nor the next, nor ever again. Had Jake been taken in by someone better able to love him, or, most likely, had he found a place to die alone? Cooney could not know. The young boy knew only that his dog was gone. He would never have another.

Now, in the cool grass, the hardened adult watched the dogs shuffle through the other side of the street. He leaned back into the coolness and closed his eyes to nap, another stray in a city of abandoned dogs, and a young man's abandoned dreams.

Matthew opened his eyes, stretched his legs, and like a cat arched his back in a dirty rainbow to revive the feeling along his spine. The bench, hard and unyielding, had dented his flesh. It always did this, and so no surprises. The cost of a quick nap in the afternoon sun, something rare enough on days neither too cold to chill the flesh nor too warm to open its pores too widely. Cooney loved his naps.

The small black dog he had noticed that morning lazed in the grass near Matthew's bench. It had been a good morning, a fine one, and Matthew felt the lift of a promising day within his tattered soul. He had come to the park at the usual time, full enough of the coffee and mealy muffin that was Father O'Hanlon's gift at the mission down F Street. Breakfast within him and the morning sun without, he had claimed his bench, set out a paper cup and watched the city go by, everyone with somewhere to go and someplace to be. The dog had come his way, and Cooney had beckoned him over to the bench. The two of them, then, strays sitting in a transitory comfort, until Cooney deemed it time for his nap. He lay back down along the bench, reached down to give the dog a soft chuck under his warm muzzle, then closed his eyes. A fine morning it was, and preface to a finer afternoon.

Cooney rose to the mid-afternoon sun. It had indeed been a fine day, and the night ahead promised warmth and clarity—a good night for sleeping, and the dreams that would come with it. He stretched one last time then headed across the way. In his mind the dice had been tossed and were bouncing now to however they might land. A young man, with swagger, brash and bold.

On the park's far side was a convenience store, the same one he had sought to rob those years ago.

"Good afternoon, Joe," he said to the man behind the counter, the same man at whom he had pointed his small gun. They had become friends of a type, bonded by shared experience and the chastening of things gone wrong.

"Back at ya, Matt," came the reply from one of the few people who knew his name, who recognized that Matthew Cooney walked this world. "The usual smokes?"

"Indeed. And I'll take a pint of the Four Roses, too. Something to warm me."

"A good day for ya?"

"Not really, Joey. We're a stingy city, it seems, and too few of us take pity on the homeless." He turned to the aisles to see what might be somewhat edible. The sandwiches looked like cardboard, and there was no call to even tempt the fruit—mushy bananas and apples that sank to the touch. Matthew picked two of the sandwiches and shoved them into his pockets, then went back to the counter.

Mid-afternoon, and he was the only one in the store. Joey Collins had laid out the whiskey and the cigarettes. "What else ya got, Matt? I'll ring ya up."

"Not this time, Joey. I'll call on your credit, if you'd be so kind."

"Ah, this again. Jesus, Matt, when are ya gonna pull yourself into something worthwhile?"

"I'm as worthy as I'll ever be, Joey Collins. Cooney the Beggar. It's my place in this world, and I'd be a fool not to honor it."

Collins reached for the whiskey to pull it back behind the counter. "You're a harmless man, Matt Cooney, despite your airs. I'm happy to give you what I can, and to keep you alive after the fashion it is. Now take the sandwiches and the smokes and get the hell out of here."

Matthew smiled, grabbed the goods from the counter and raised his hand in a gentle salute. "You're a good man, Joey Collins. A very good man." Back then to the street, to the bench, to the small black dog with whom he would share a bite or two of the second sandwich.

A good day indeed for Cooney the Beggar. For Cooney the Entrepreneur. For Cooney the Common Man.

A young man, with swagger, brash and bold.

CHAPTER 6

The special times spent together, the breaks from the obligations and responsibilities of daily living, were short-lived for the newlyweds. There would be no country drives when the apartment needed a new dresser to accommodate Donal's clothes, or the kitchen sink developed an annoying drip. Not magic enough to sustain tired weekday nights when neither wanted to fix even a simple dinner. Donal's tendency to toss his clothes in a corner clashed with Annie's propensity to keep a tidy house.

"Don't you ever make the bed, man? And why can't you put your dishes in the sink?" The fight for space on the tiny bathroom counter fueled fierce encounters testing the limits of their compatibility. And at the heart of it, did Annie and Donal feel enough for one another to overcome the inevitable logistical and emotional adjustments that allowed such lives to come together? Were there sufficient stores of patience and resiliency and love itself? After an observation became a comment leading to a spat that devolved into an argument, would either feel the need to soothe the other's hurt? Or would the small slits and slices of daily life fester into gaping wounds, deepening by the day and beyond the reach of simple emotional bandaging?

Their first Christmas, a scant three months after their exchange of vows, would be spent with Annie's family. She insisted, and Donal raised no protest. The holiday had never presented much for him before. He and his mother rarely did so much as put up a tree, and gifts were simple and cheap. Since he had wed, Donal had had almost no contact with his mother, so it would be Christmas Eve with the Maxwells, staying the night together in Annie's old bedroom, then finishing the next day with a traditionally overdone dinner. He would find a way to get through it.

Before they left their flat for the drive across the river, Annie flitted about in preparation, preening herself through her best casual outfit and a meticulous application of all those creams and liners that made her look her best. Donal sat in the corner and regarded her girlish excitement.

"Will we be doing this every year, Annie? Spending the great holidays with your family?"

"Just until we make our own traditions," and she came out of the bedroom to sit on the arm of Donal's chair. She leaned over and kissed his forehead. "When we have a family of our own. We'll do everything for our kids, especially when they're just so young, and each year we'll keep all that wonder alive." Annie gestured with arm, sweeping it in an arc. "Think of it, Donal. Gifts, and lights, and music, just the way we want it. And it'll all be our own."

Donal looked up at her gently. "Just Donal and Annie and the dozens of young ones we create, is that it? God, you're a dreamer sometimes, Annie. D'ya know that?"

"What else is there but dreams, man?"

Donal fought his discomfort, an outsider to this new family and their friends, many of whom stopped by unannounced on Christmas day as they had always done. He had met some of them at the wedding, but he remembered neither names nor faces. Donal and Annie together were a curiosity, but Donal alone seemed merely an anomaly, something out of place and perhaps slightly broken.

When they returned home late that Christmas night, overfed with an expensive and well roasted goose, a rich dressing and several types of pies, Donal undressed slowly while Annie unfastened herself in the bathroom. He looked out their bedroom window into a night sky through which a single snowflake wafted to the gray concrete below.

And as he watched that snowflake, he knew it to be no different than the day just passed—a fleck of whiteness and purity making its way to a gritty landfall.

— ◆ —

A lone fly buzzed around the surface of Donal Mannion's work desk, no doubt drawn by the crumbs of lunches past or the drop of sweetness from an overly juicy orange. Donal swatted at him once, then twice, then decided to let it be. He swiveled his chair back to the screen that showed more empty white than it should have.

Inspiration had been hard to come by. And really, how inspiring could the special services of a common dentist truly be? The account for Doctor Fontana, who wanted a flexible half-page spread that could be used for both a promotional brochure and placement in local press advertisements, had landed in his inbox. Now, the following Wednesday, Donal punched in more words that he knew he would eventually delete. He couldn't summon the spirit for this. He hated dentists.

This was no life for a newly married man, toiling with mind-numbing simplistic and meaningless commercial prose in a dusty corner cubicle with faceless colleagues who barely acknowledged his comings and goings. Six months following his wedding, he and Annie were in the same place.

Or maybe not. Maybe there had been some backsliding, a slight ebbing of that initial wonderment that comes with shifting into new forms. They argued sometimes, and on more than one night they had fallen asleep with their backs to each other. Their flat had begun to feel as cramped and as dirty as this dreary office space.

Donal turned his chair away from his desk and his too-empty computer screen. He stood then and made his way to the office at the end of the hallway. David Davis managed the firm. Gruff, he was, and disheveled. Everyone referred to him as "Davis." No mister, and certainly no use of a first name. Davis's office was not much more glamorous than Donal's own cubicle, but at least it had a door, which Donal closed behind him as he entered.

"Got a minute?"

"What's on your mind, Donal?" Davis looked up reluctantly from a messy spreadsheet. He managed this crew, but he gave little indication that he liked them. It was a relationship built on mutual suspicion and minimal tolerance.

"My position, Davis."

"What about it?"

"I've been here nearly seven years now and nothing's changed. The same tasks, the same expectations." He hesitated. "The same pay."

Davis leaned back in his chair. "Are you asking for a raise, Donal?"

"I suppose I am. And maybe a bit more responsibility. Some of the senior accounts, or maybe even sales. But I'd definitely like more money."

"You've been a married man for, what now, about a year?"

"Less than that. Six months."

Davis shook his head and sighed. "I should have seen this coming." He looked up at the younger man. "There's nothing I can do, Donal."

Donal said nothing as his own expression hardened.

"Look," Davis continued, "you're steady at what you do, but what you do is pretty basic. Ad copy. That's what you were hired to do."

"But I can do more."

"And I can't let you. Donal. You only have a high school degree. No college. That puts a lid on what you can do for this firm."

Donal sagged as he turned toward the door. He could argue, but what was the point? He could get angry, too. He would save that for later, for when he got home and told Annie about all this with a glass of scotch in hand and a burn in his heart.

"So I'm just a functionary, then. A weaver at a loom. Nothing more." Donal bit off as he reached for the doorknob.

"For the moment, yes. What did you expect?" Davis stopped. "It's nothing personal," he began again more softly. "Let me see if I can get you a cost-of-living adjustment. Won't be much, maybe two percent or so, but I'll see what I can do."

"Don't bother, Davis. It doesn't matter." As he opened the door he said, "It's good to know my place."

Back to his desk, then, and to the dentist that wanted Donal Mannion to cast him in glory. He would do the best he could, but what matter? No one was there to gild the image of Donal Mannion, or to make him appear grander than he was.

The fly returned, buzzed twice more around the desk, then flew off down the hallway, another parasite looking for something better.

— ◆ —

On a rainy night Donal fingered his glass of scotch while the television dribbled mindless sounds and shapes to which he paid no attention. White noise, that's all it was. Donal's mind was elsewhere.

Annie told him she would be home late and to take care of his own dinner. She would be heading out for drinks with some of her colleagues to celebrate one of their birthdays. Annie's office fit together more closely than Donal's, and they did such things, somewhat frequently it seemed. Usually once a week Annie would be late for this or that occasion, ambling through their door well after dark with a quiet smile and carrying a whiff of wine and smoke mingling with her cologne.

This night Donal's dinner sat in his hand. His day had been particularly rough, another mindless blot of words and images punctuated by Davis's discontented barking about deadlines and quality and God knows what else. After a time Donal came to regard it no differently than he did the television in front of him. White noise.

On TV an advertisement for a breath mint featured a beautiful and completely inaccessible woman blowing a waft of ice into a winter sky. At the time Donal began his work, eager and young, he would regard such ads critically to see how their arguments fit together, what impressions they wished to create, the scope of the fantasies that wove around mundane products, tying them to fame and fortune and sex. He could learn from these blips, draw lessons on imagery and touchpoints and emotionally evocative phrasing. Back then, he did all that. When he took it seriously. Now all he noted was the ice crystals blown from a sensuous mouth, wafting into the impossible.

He sipped his scotch and thought of a winter's day when he was eleven years old.

— ◆ —

It had snowed the night before, a rare event that dumped several inches into the city streets. Washington handled any snowfall poorly, and when the amounts grew to ankle-depth, all life froze to a halt. Buses did not run, businesses shut their doors, and plows pushed small drifts onto curbsides.

Best of all, the schools closed, and on that day Donal bounded out the door, mittened and hooded, to find his friends. They all were there that afternoon—Eddie Moore and Johnny Duncan and David Moynahan and even Matthew Cooney for a while before he grumbled his way down the street away from them.

They had never seen so much snow. The boys put it all to good use, beginning with a snowball fight with no allegiances, each boy looking for the closest and most vulnerable target. Donal learned quickly how to pack a snowball with just a touch of ice to create something firmer and harder than what the other boys did. When he plocked Eddie on the neck with a particularly well-formed unit, his friend went sprawling into a drift pushed up by a passing plow. That was enough for the rest of them to target Donal, all against him, and Donal ducked under the bombardment, retreating behind a mailbox as snow-and-ice covered arms, head, and shoulders. He had succeeded in bringing his friends together for a common purpose steeped in a pursuit of justice. He waved his arms in surrender, which did not prevent Johnny Duncan from rubbing a mittful of snow into Donal's face and down his neck.

And with the battle brought to a truce, the boys joined forces now to build snowmen. It was Johnny and Donal who sought to sculpt something spectacular, something the street had never before seen and would long remember through all future snows. It would be large, taller than either of them, and it would be well dressed. Johnny brought an old scarf for his neck, and Donal ran back inside to steal an old fedora—possibly his estranged father's—that had sat in their closet for as long as he could remember. Johnny found an old jacket that had been abandoned in the doorway of the liquor store on the corner. The jacket was thin and torn, and to his surprise, had a few coins tucked into a folded pocket.

There, then, in the late afternoon of this rarest of days, a snowman stood on the corner of their street, dressed perhaps slightly better than many of the sadder men who haunted these streets, standing as proudly as a pope surveying the hordes in Saint Peter's Square, a horde this day comprised of young boys consigned to these streets in search of something to believe in.

This lonely night, Donal thought back to that day, and to the proud, beautiful creation they had crafted out of water and cold. He thought then of the next day, when the sun returned. The snowman still stood on the corner. It had lasted that cold night, no one disturbing it out of either malice or carelessness. Untouched until the sun found it. Then, drop by drop, their snowman diminished and sagged. Neither the hat nor the jacket protected it. By day's end it had contracted to a lump slightly smaller than the boys, its head leaning forward now and the jacket slumping almost to the ground. The next day, when the schools reopened, the snowman had become nothing more than a pile of slush, tattered with the grime and soot of the streets. The jacket was gone, as was the hat, recycled into some unknown usage.

An illusion, this snowman. Something created through the enthusiasms of the young with no real substance, and bound to disintegrate slowly, dripping its way back to where it truly belonged, and what it truly was.

— ♦ —

Donal sipped his scotch, finished the glass, and poured another. He went back to his chair to wait for Annie, to block out this tired day, and to count the drops falling against his own puzzled and tattered heart.

He could not articulate it. Although he saw himself as a man of words, Donal found none to define the acidic discontent that ate away his days. And Annie sat in its crosshairs.

As time went on, they argued more and more. The little things eroded their intimacy and passion. Annie increasingly found Donal lazy and careless. She would have liked him to take better care of himself, to dress better, to wash more frequently, to floss his teeth and to clean up his frequent spills in both the kitchen and the bathroom. He had told her that he would write a novel, that that was his true passion and that his job was just a means to buy him the time and space to do so. Not a word had been penned.

Donal did not react well to her suggestions, which, as they were largely ignored, grew to demands. But beyond that, Donal began to find Annie dull. She no longer bounded into their time together. Their weekends hovered around the responsibilities of home and budget, their weekdays consumed by jobs that carved the time away and left them both numb. The passion of their nights, always limited by Donal's standards, grew to little more than duty.

And all of it had too soon grown tedious.

Donal Mannion had pursued Annie Maxwell, a woman just slightly beyond his grasp. But who was this woman, really? And, when it came right down to it, who was Donal Mannion?

On those nights when Annie worked late, or when she met

her colleagues for drinks, or when she just decided on her own to stay downtown longer than might be necessary, Donal felt the claustrophobia of walls bounding nothing but an empty silence. Those nights became more frequent, sometimes toppling one upon another, and Donal's confusion festered all the wrong things—bitterness, resentment, and the clinging doubt of his own worth.

"You know I'd rather be here with you, don't you, man? But it's Jenny's last day, and we need to celebrate her. She's been there since I started, and she's always been so nice. She and her husband are moving to Baltimore for his job."

"Any chance I could join you? I've met most of these people. I could be your date."

"Oh Donal, you'd be so bored. They'll talk about work, and make fun of the clients, and gossip about everyone who's not there. Besides, you're so different from them. They're all so buttoned-down."

"And I'd be a bit of an embarrassment, is that what you're saying?"

"No, babe," and she kissed him on the cheek. "Of course not. But you're definitely not an attorney."

"Neither are you, Annie."

"Ah, but I know how to talk to them. I won't be late," and with a final antiseptic goodbye peck, Annie swished out the door.

Donal would not spend this night eating cold food in front of a numbing television screen. This night, he would find a bit of his own way. The Black Hand, in the old neighborhood, and maybe one or two familiar faces. If nothing else, a meal he didn't have to cook or reheat, and a pint or two.

But the walls of the old place echoed as hollow as those of his own apartment. No one there but a handful of sullen drinkers plodding through their beers, sitting at the bar and blinking up at a television screen flickering some sports talk show. Donal ordered a hot roast beef sandwich and a Guinness, then took one of the booths that lined the side wall. His sandwich came out of the kitchen cold and chewy, its gravy little more than globules of fat. The Guinness went down smoothly, though, and so he ordered another. Then another.

And still a depressing quietude hung over the bar as the old drinkers left and were replaced by others equally grim. *No life here. No life at all.* Donal ordered a shot for the road, then took a cab back to the apartment.

When Donal walked through the door, Annie was already there. "Hi. I didn't expect you home so soon."

"So soon? It's after ten. Where the hell were you?"

"You went out, so I went out. I grabbed a bite to eat and a drink at a bar. Felt better than sitting here alone."

"More than a drink, Donal," an unpleasant edge to her voice. "Jesus, you're half in the bag."

"I'm fine, Annie. Really. I just wanted to get out for a bit. Didn't want to sit home pining for my bride." With a silly smile he tried to wrap an arm around Annie's waist, but she wanted none of it. She pushed him away and turned toward the bedroom.

"I have to sleep. I've got work tomorrow. And so do you. I suggest you sleep this off."

By the time Donal washed up and undressed, Annie had shut herself off, her eyes closed in feigned sleep and facing the far wall. "Annie?" he whispered to no response.

And then Donal Mannion once again climbed into a bed as cold as the night he left behind. He struggled to find his own sleep, but the dripping kitchen faucet disturbed his already restless memories.

Donal sat at his cubicle. He looked across the way to the window that faced K Street, through the rain streaks and through the perpetual grime that no cleaning could clear. Rain poured down, had poured all day. He had gotten soaked on the walk to the Metro, the rain falling almost sideways and defying his cheap umbrella.

Now, distracted by the rain, by the mindless thrum of his work, but mostly by the confusing realities of being Donal Mannion, he stared at nothing, and thought of everything. This morning's chill had never left him.

Donal swiveled his chair back to the clutter on his desk. He sighed from deep within, a fatigue that no amount of rest would conquer. He had done this. He had set his sights on the very things that he now held in hand.

Illusions. The wispy summonings of an imagination yearning for something different, something purer, something untarnished by the grime of the streets that nurtured him. And in the securing of these things, in the building of the early stages of this new life, he wondered if in fact he had been unfaithful to the Donal Mannion whose soul beat and thought and lusted and loved and raged beneath these illusions.

Donal eyed the baseball game projected on the big screen television across the bar. He eyed his beer as he drank it down notch by notch. But mostly he eyed the single blond sitting by herself three seats to his left at a local bar two blocks from his apartment.

There were nights he came here in his exile. No need to flit back to his old neighborhood haunts, universally grim and depressing. This place was more convenient, brighter and more comfortable than The Black Hand. A beer or two, five or six innings, and then back home to climb into a cold bed with a cold wife and reset himself for the next day.

During those nights he had seen this woman a time or two. She drank alone, smiled politely to the bartender, paid her tab promptly after a single drink, then left her seat to walk back out to the street. She was in her early thirties, as was Donal, or so he surmised. Nothing about her was extreme or flashy, but she carried an aura, an intrigue that piqued Donal's curiosity. Attractive enough, with hair tied back from a softly rounded, calm face. And at this point, what was there to lose?

She had finished more than half her drink and the home team trailed badly. What, indeed, was there to lose?

Donal slid off his seat and walked two seats down to sit next to her. "Excuse me for being bold, but I just wanted to introduce myself. I've seen you here before, and always alone. I thought maybe you could use a friend. I'm Donal."

The woman turned her head to face him. With no expression she said, "You're the first person to speak to me here. Where have all the real men gone?" She sipped her drink, a vodka tonic. "Laura."

"Any chance I can tempt you with a second drink?"

And so it began that night, a casual dalliance that salved a festering void with anticipation, romanticism and a hint of risk. All of it proved more exciting than rational as Donal and Laura met nightly to sit no longer at the bar, but at a small table near the corner where they exchanged stories, frustrations, abandonment, and despair.

Laura no longer stopped at one drink, or even two, soon placing her hand on Donal's knee, leaning into him, licking his ear, and so the assignations began. From the bar they would head back to Laura's apartment nearby, where she lived alone and had a wide bed that they put to good use, testing the limits of their own athleticism with lust that had been sublimated far too long.

Donal came home later and later. Annie, ever loyal, ever the faithful wife, came to dread the sound of Donal's key in the lock. An interruption, it was, and a return to a normality that had begun to wear her down. She had no issue with Donal's absences, which cleared her time of any complications or deflections. She was fine by herself. Better off.

At one point a few weeks past their first coupling, Laura rolled to her side, propped herself on an elbow and with a rare smile asked, "Why do you do this?"

"What do you mean? Why do I do what?"

"Why do you risk everything? A wife. Maybe even a job. And don't tell me I'm irresistible. I know I'm not. To you, sweet baby, I'm probably no more than meat. So don't tell me that. Just tell me why you're doing this. Why every few nights I can bring you to my bed."

Donal rose and pulled a sheet around his nakedness, then walked to look out the bedroom window onto the small courtyard between the buildings. He thought, then spoke slowly. "Did you ever look closely at a geode?"

"What the hell is a *geode*?"

"A geode is a rock, I guess. Just a rock. But it's hollow inside and lined with crystals. Quite beautiful, actually, when you break it apart and look inside. It's all sparkly and pure, like something that doesn't quite belong in your hands. Something almost magical. You never know what colors will sparkle back at you when you crack it open.

"So," he continued slowly, "I feel like that geode. Hollow inside, with all this empty space. Big parts of the center missing. And it took me years to get that way, with all this pressure pushing everything out of the middle.

"But there's still some beauty there. There's still something that sparkles when you look at it closely. Something that changes in the way the light plays with those crystals and makes new colors. Something that coats the edges of all that emptiness. All you have to do is crack it open and look.

"That's why I do this, Laura." He turned back to her, threw the sheet to the floor, and climbed back into the bed. It wasn't yet time to go home.

After the first indiscretion, the others came more easily. Laura had no aspirations beyond the moment. When Donal told her that they shouldn't continue, she understood. Donal's pronouncement did not stem from guilt, or loyalty, or remorse. Instead, he felt that carrying on liaisons too close to his own home raised to an uncomfortable level the potential for discovery.

In the opposite direction, several blocks over and up, there was new territory. The Old Ebbitt Grill stood across from the Treasury Department, an institution gilded and woodened and dripping with atmosphere. A longer walk for him, and sometimes even worthy of a cab, and far pricier than the places he usually drank, but the Ebbitt fascinated Donal from the first moment he entered. To the right was a bar, long and glittery and amazingly well stocked. Beyond it in three directions were dining rooms tended by well-dressed servers who hustled their way through the meals and the guests. The place was almost always crowded.

A part of the city gathered here, that part that worked on Capitol Hill or at government agencies. In the safe harbor of the bar, they would digest the day's events, argue about politics, disparage colleagues who weren't with them, and, if luck combined sufficiently with a cavalier attitude born of too much alcohol, cheat on their partners. That last act became less uncommon to Donal's eye. The Ebbitt had its share of young women who might be interested in a man like him. So he began to make the Ebbitt a part of his routine. He took advantage of logistics.

The Ebbitt stood on 15th Street below H, and Donal's office sat on 16th and K, a short enough walk. He could stop there on his way home, have a pint, make small conversation, and scout his possibilities. If nothing presented itself, he could then take the Metro to Annie and his apartment. But if there the sparks he emitted were well received, he would call her to say he might be late, that he had to close an account, or something of the sort.

In the process, Donal Mannion became opaque. He increasingly hid himself from Annie, saying little during their times together, finding excuses to go to bed early on those nights when he was home, or to leave for the office nearly at the break of dawn. Their weekends came and went in relative silence, and with no adventures. Donal assumed this opacity would protect him, would prevent his wife from seeing below the surface to where he really lay, while he tried to make sense of this marriage and the woman who now shared his name.

And despite Donal's best efforts, the subterfuge and the deceptions, the flimsy excuses and the feigned slights, despite it all, Annie knew.

A lover lives by sense and intuition as much as reason, and Annie's instincts had been well defined by her past wounds. She had had lovers before, and each had left her, or she them, because she fell out of the initial rhythm that had attracted each to the other. Sometimes it was his fault, and sometimes hers. But she could always tell. A change in tone of voice, a body no longer responsive to the usual touches, a new boldness that presumed an intimacy that did not exist, or simply a growing disinterest, the passing of a thrill.

Donal faded from her line by line, a delicate portrait left too long in the sunlight. But she knew that each subtraction need be balanced by an addition elsewhere. That's who he was. And so when she found the telltale signs that Donal's hubris could not hide—a bar receipt on a night that he had told her he was working late, or a scrap of paper with a phone number tucked into the pocket of slacks she was about to wash, or a faint strange scent on his best shirt—she was not shocked. Disappointed, to be sure. But shock would indicate that she had no notion that this could happen. In truth, Annie Mannion knew all along the type of partner Donal Mannion would be. He had no choice. This was who he was.

— ◆ —

Annie sat back in her chair, fury subsided. What matter was any of it? She took a sip of her whiskey and regarded the hollow man sitting across from her on the sofa.

"One night you'll leave this apartment, Donal, and when you come back in the wee hours you'll find the locks have been changed." Annie sighed, and spoke softly, the energy drained by the hour of shouting and the projectiles they had hurled at one another, both verbal and physical. Her mother's old lamp had been a casualty of the evening, flung toward Donal's back as he stormed out of the room.

The lamp had missed the back but found a wall. It lay in scattered pieces on the tatty rug.

"Christ, woman, you've told me that time and again, and always I'm here, and you're here, and the rent's paid on time."

"And you think it an idle threat, do you, Donal? How much can a wife stand? I swear, my best days are when I'm numb to it all."

"Then numb yourself again, Annie. Numb yourself into a coma, for all I care."

She sank back in her chair, and again sipped at the whiskey. "So out you go again, Donal, and there's nothing I can say about it."

"Not a damn thing. A man needs his time, and I'll claim mine whenever I can. Just to McInerney's, where I go. Where I can walk in the door to pleasant conversation and no one demanding I change who I am."

"That'll never happen, Donal Mannion. You most definitely are who you are."

"Damn you, woman. When was the last time you offered a kind word or a soft touch?"

"The last time you deserved one. The last time I thought I truly had a husband."

As Donal turned to the kitchen for the one last shot of the whiskey that always seemed to draw him in on these nights, his phone rang its annoying Disney song, "It's a Small World." Why in God's name did Donal select that despicable earworm for his ringtone? Just another bite out of a sour evening.

A text it was, and Donal read it blankly. "Gotta run," he mumbled as he changed course from the kitchen to the front door. "Don't know when I'll be back," then opened the door and, like a shot, hustled through it into the dim hallway toward the elevator.

No surprise. Annie had seen him rush out like this before, a response to a contrived emergency, or a drunken friend, or a lonely woman who told him that the clock was ticking and he had better show before too much more time passed.

This was her man. This was her life. Hollow, all of it. Annie Mannion sat back in her chair, sipped again at the whiskey and smiled at the absurdity of just another flawed stitch in a very frayed tapestry, all the panels of which had faded in both color and form.

— ◆ —

Newton's Law dictates that to every action there is always opposed an equal reaction. Donal concluded that, although this law applied to the physical universe, the emotional world reacted in the same form. All his efforts, all his pursuits, rebounded with a force equal to the energy he had invested in them.

And with the despair that comes to a man who realizes that he has overreached, that he does not have the character or temperament or discipline or honor to hold onto what passed for his dreams, Donal slipped into spirits he could not control, underwritten by a simmering resentment that he could climb the mountain that so many others scaled with seeming ease. In his darkest moods, he viewed all his efforts, all his aspirations, as an affront to the natural order of things. He was Donal Mannion, and would always be so, no matter the work he pursued, where he sought to live or whom he chose to love. He could not change the stripe of his soul or expect the unseen Fates to rewrite a script written well before his birth.

Change was afoot, and Donal had neither the strength nor the will to challenge it. This he knew. And although others might see this change as a chance for redefinition, an opportunity to correct the errors that led to a dissolution, Donal calculated only the coming losses and what they would mean going forward. He was not an introspective man.

Annie would be gone, of that there could be little doubt. It would likely be contentious, although Annie earned more than he did so he would probably avoid any burden of support or maintenance. He expected that she would want a clean break, leaving behind little trace of her time with someone she had so badly failed to save. Perhaps this might be a chance for him to do the things swept to the background by all these responsibilities. He could write his novel. He would need a new place to live that might suit him more. He might find the time to work out and bring himself back into the shape he was beginning to lose. He could chase whatever woman appealed to him without having to look over his shoulder. Perhaps.

But in the back of his mind, Donal knew that his was a character that stumbled for direction. Nothing to guide him. Annie, at least, provided something of a course for his wanderings, as annoying as it turned out to be. Donal chafed at the reins of responsibility.

So the final days of this strange downtown life dwindled in a festering resentment and a brooding anger that in the end he would be no different than he always had been. He had sought a pathway out of the dingy and dim neighborhood that grew him, but he did not have the means to escape who he really was. Donal Mannion, Son of Man.

— ◆ —

Late evening, and only candlelight, not bright enough to distinguish clearly the paper beneath her hand, nor the letters that her tired fingers shaped in neat and trim lines. No matter. Annie did not need light to guide her words, nor did she need to see proof that they lay in reality on the paper below her. The words she wrote that night had emblazoned themselves against her will into her thoughts a while ago. She needed only to spill them out onto this paper, fold it, then leave it as she left this dimly lit flat.

> *I remember clearly the first time. That night when we finally surrendered ourselves to what we saw as the logic of love, the inevitable and irresistible compulsion to express ourselves to each other, as vulnerable as newborn babes and as strongly driven in our desires as mythic warriors. We lay together then, in mutual*

surrender and mutual vulnerability, naked, panting and filled to our emotional brims.

I could not want for anything more in those first moments, Donal. In some corner of my mind I believed I had waited my entire life for that very moment, for the culmination of all desire, for an immutable sense of belonging at last to someone so perfect.

But there is no perfection, Donal, is there? The years since have proven that, as if we needed proof of our failings and our flaws. They live within us and we cannot escape, no matter how hard we gloss them over or decorate them with glitter and streamers. In the end I believe our flaws define us more than our virtues. Shakespeare's greatest plays, the tragedies, revolved around their heroes' flaws rather than their glories. Our failures cannot help but taint whatever purities we hold.

But still we try, don't we? And it was that effort to regain the purity that kept me here these years. Kept me through the affairs, the first of which I found so stunning and humiliating, Later I came to accept these indiscretions as the price to be paid for the veneer of stability. Go to your women on the side, if you must. I'll still be here tending the hearth, I told myself, and be better and stronger for it. I still saw the little boy behind the brash and increasingly selfish man, and there were moments when that innocent, endearing, wondrous child stroked my heart. That was enough to balance the heartache, at least for a while.

When numbness becomes normal, we reassess. Despite our best and noblest intentions, we finally admit the damage. My heart is stone now, Donal, and has been so for a while. I expect yours is, too, and that the women and the drinking and the nights away are perhaps a desperate effort to make a heart beat again, even in an irregular and tawdry rhythm.

I don't condemn you for it. But I do need to find my own heart's rhythm again. I need a resuscitation, a revival of a pulse that only dully throbs. We've both known this, and so I expect that this note comes as no true surprise, nor does the empty closet and the bed that is not turned down and occupied with my loyal, gentle, sleeping form.

Again, Donal, I don't condemn you. We are what we are, and it's an extraordinary life that holds no heartbreak. This is the course of things. Even so, I'll no longer play either the martyr or the victim. It's time to go.

Annie Mannion folded the letter and placed it into the envelope that Donal would find on the table near the front door. She would place it there, grab her tightly packed bag, then step away into a dark autumn, into uncertainty and loss, into a season of mists that obscure the path ahead and cloud the heart within.

— ◆ —

Donal Mannion pushed around his papers and reviewed the sorry words written on them. A clerk he was, and nothing more. Davis had been very clear about all that.

It was a Thursday afternoon when the divorce papers reached him, delivered by a messenger from the court who showed up at his office. When the receptionist told him there was someone calling for him in the lobby; Donal suspected what it was. He did not flinch when the messenger handed him the envelope. He took it, said nothing, then turned back to his cubicle.

He did not read them but placed them on the far corner of his clutter. On the wall of his cubicle he had clipped a photo of Annie taken that day in the Shenandoah Valley. She looked tan and tall, her well-shaped legs noticeable as they stretched below her hiking shorts, her hair hanging wild and loose, and her smile seemed as bright as the day's pure Virginia sky. Donal leaned back in his chair and regarded that photo, regarded the fool who took it, and drew slow, deep breaths. In the midst of that sad revelry, his manager stuck his head into the cubicle.

"Mannion," he barked. Donal turned slowly to face him, said nothing.

Davis flipped two pages of ad copy onto Donal's desk. "Damn it, Mannion, this copy is five days late and tells me nothing. We need crisp writing, not speculation, and certainly not fantasy. This may as well have been written in crayon. What the hell am I supposed to do with this?"

Donal remained silent, staring at the older man. Davis awaited some response, and when none came, he raised his voice. "Did you hear me? What can I do with this garbage?

At last Donal spoke slowly, and in a low voice said, "You can jam it up your ass, Davis. Or boil it into a stew and serve it to your dogs."

"I'm done with it all, Mannion. Done with your laziness, and your lip. Last warning."

And then the fury broke.

"Save it, Champ. I'm done with it all, too." The clutter on Donal's desk went flying as he swept it with his forearm. Papers and books flew to the floor, after which one wall of the cubicle crumbled under a thrust from Donal's fist. "Done with it all," shouted one last time, as he stormed out of his last office, out of his last life.

CHAPTER 7

Donal Mannion walked the afternoon streets of Washington in a dead humor. A leaden heart pumped his thick and dull blood through limbs that did not want to move against the freakish late October heat and the humidity that pressed his skin like a wet, warm cloth. He walked in small steps. No rush to it because there was really no place to go.

The Old Ebbitt Grill pulled him like a magnet. In this deadened afternoon comfort could best come from the familiar places. Donal stepped through Lafayette Park, a block and a half to the classic pillared doorway, where he wrapped a tired hand around the great golden handle and pulled it open, Cold air slapped his face, he breathed in the scent of leathers and wood, then claimed a seat at the long bar.

"Scotch, neat. Johnny Walker Red," he said as the barman came his way. With a silent nod, the older man grabbed the relevant bottle. When the drink arrived, Donal raised it first to his nose and breathed in the rich, smoky aroma of days gone by. He sipped fire into his throat and felt its burn match the fury of his troubled soul.

Donal sipped his drink quietly. It was early, and the hordes had not yet entered. Only two other patrons sat at the other end of the bar. Mid-afternoon was a quiet time, but of late the rhythms of the day had no meaning. A drink was a drink no matter when he might have it. He relished the calm this one imparted to his unsettled thoughts, drank it down, then gestured for another.

As he received it from the still-silent barman, Donal turned to his left to look into a face he had not seen before. A young man about his age occupied the seat next to him. Donal had not seen him enter, had not heard him sit, had not felt the jostle of another body so close to where he sat.

The young man had his own drink, scotch, or so it appeared. He raised his glass and smiled over the rim of it. "I hope I'm not disruptin' ya here," he said with a most definite brogue. "This seemed to be the place for me to sit."

Donal regarded this stranger with a silent eye. The newcomer had a glint of mischief about him, a twinkle in his soft smile. About his height, sharing the same slight build, the same shock of dark hair, and nothing remarkable in any of it. Donal turned back to his own drink without a word.

"I don't mean to be presumptuous, lad, but it seems as if you might be in need of a friendly voice."

Donal sighed. "Don't really know what I need. Maybe some space. Maybe just another drink."

"I've seen you here before, I believe. Not recently, mind you, but a few times a while back. Seemed you were never alone then. And it seemed you were having a grand bit more fun than you are now."

Donal turned to study the other. "You look familiar." He nodded. "But I can't really place you. Didn't notice you here. But it's a big place, and lots of people come and go." He sipped again at a drink now a bit more necessary than it had been a few minutes prior. "Maybe I've seen you."

"You have a name?"

"Donal. Donal Mannion." There was reluctance in his reply. A conversation it would be, then, and apparently no getting away from it.

"A fine name. And how did you come here to be drinking by yourself on a summer's afternoon? That's not your habit, I'll wager."

"It becomes a habit when there's nothing else to fill the time. I come here. It's as close to comfort as I find these days."

"Not how it used to be," said the other. "I recall you drinking and laughing and making a grab at the lasses. Good fun in those days, no?"

"Good fun. But nothing lasts forever." Donal finished his drink quickly, and another appeared before him, seemingly of its own accord. He looked at the scotch, then back to his new companion.

"I took the liberty," he said.

Donal sighed once more. "Nothing lasts forever. Not even good scotch."

"So you're drinking alone now. I'll dare to ask what happened."

"Thought I was the hottest ticket ever to come out of the Northeast, and no one could possibly know more about what I should be doing than I did myself. Not even the company I worked for. I knew the issues better, I knew the heart of the clients, I knew everything we needed to do. I was smarter than my boss, too, or so I thought." Donal set into his new drink, his head lighter and his heart grown darker.

"One day I told him all that. Not in so many words, but he got the idea. Worthless, all of it, and I stormed out." Donal sipped again. "He didn't like it much. Let's just say I'm 'between jobs.'"

"Ah, but there's more to it than that, am I right?" replied the other.

Donal chuckled a mirthless laugh. "Yeah," he said. "A bit more. Turns out around the same time that my darling wife of three years came to the conclusion that I had been unfaithful. She even came down here one night when I wasn't on my best behavior. I didn't expect her." He sipped again. I haven't talked with her since, although I've tried. She won't answer her phone, or any texts."

"Sad, Donal. Truly sad. But it seems you've dealt your own hand."

"For every action there is an equal and opposite reaction. Someone said that once," and he drank again. "Do I detect a bit of Ireland in you?"

"More than a bit. I was born there. Came to this country when I was nineteen."

"I'm Irish myself. Two generations. My grandfather came over and married an Irish girl. Their son is my father. Dad named me after the old fella."

"That's how it happens. We seek out our own, especially when we're lost and a bit afraid. And I was certainly both of those things. As you are now."

"More than a bit lost, my new friend. And most definitely afraid."

"But I've come to tell you this. It gets better, Donal. It has to, or else we die. You could run, like I did. Find yourself a place where no one knows your sins. But no matter how fast you sprint from all the shite, you can never outrun yourself.

"You've done what you've done, and that's placed you where you are, but that's not all there is to it. You face it, and it gets better. Ask yourself where you need to go. What you need to do. You'll learn the proper answers."

"And you're telling me this."

"I see it. Give yourself enough time to grow new skin. You'll be amazed. New job, new woman, and a very precious, new humility that will keep both of them with you."

"You seem pretty confident in your predictions."

"They're not predictions, Donal. As I said, I see it. Annie will be a painful memory, and you'll be missing fiercely the things a taken man should have. You're broken now, Donal, but you'll grow stronger at the broken places. It'll all be fine in the end. And, if it's not fine, it won't be the end."

Donal turned in his seat to face his companion. He stared into a face still hinting mischief. Still hinting a secret wisdom.

"You say you were born in Ireland. Where?"

"In the small town of Schull, County Cork. The western part, not far from Mizen Head."

Donal's heart beat a quick tattoo, and small beads of perspiration forming near his temples. "You know my name, but you've not told me yours."

The companion smiled. "You know my name as well as your own, lad. And it's time that I go. But you'll see me again, to be sure." With these last words Donal's gaze clouded over, and a fine mist painted his vision with a delicate and fair whiteness. He closed his eyes against the glare.

He opened them to the rustling of the bartender's hand on his shoulder as his head lay on the bar. "I'll call you a cab," he said softly. "Time for you to go and get some rest."

Where can a man run when he looks behind him and sees that he is only pursued by himself?

—◆—

Donal took to walking in the evenings, whenever the restlessness spasmed his legs, to clear his mind, he told himself. If the weather allowed and he weren't too tired from the day's meager efforts, he would forsake the bus that took him from his northeast flat downtown to walk the several miles back home. And if not, he might grab his jacket and umbrella, inure himself against cold, wind and rain, and walk. Not the safest streets, but no one bothered him, a solitary man, head down, walking slowly, never a threat and clearly not a target of any value. Time of day didn't really matter.

On these walks he thought of nothing, and he thought of everything. Annie. A failed effort at redefinition. The ache in his shoulders, a new weakness in his legs. How empty the city seemed. How the traffic passed by as faceless, mechanical units, devoid even of the humanity driving them. How the storefronts grew more tawdry and bland each day.

As time went on, Annie became less present. His initial regret, thin to begin with, evaporated altogether as he reclaimed the familiar trappings of how he lived before. He had pursued her, he had won her, but he had never really loved her.

He had taken a job at one of the major downtown stores, a hand on its loading dock. He spent his days unloading trucks with merchandise he would never be able to afford, cleaning the small storage warehouse, and cataloging its contents. Hard work, boring for the most part, but Donal did not object to it. Although friendly enough with his mates, he mostly kept to himself. The job paid better than being a low-level copy editor, and he reasoned that its rigors might actually be healthy work. He could strain himself into shape, tighten some muscles, and burn enough calories during the day to offset the alcohol he increasingly consumed at night.

And with nothing to do most nights, and nothing to satisfy an aching loss of purpose, Donal found solace in the bottom of a glass. And once discovered could he plunge any lower?

— ◆ —

The glass was nearly empty, nothing but the crispy bits of ice chips floating in the final puddle at the bottom. Donal picked it up and licked out the last bits, then gestured to the bartender. "Another, Johnny, when you can."

"Walker Red is it, Donal?"

"Exactly. And be generous with your pour."

Mannion frequented The Black Hand, three blocks from his flat. Three or four nights each week found him at the bar, bantering with whoever might be near him, teasing the girls who ran drinks to the handful of tables near the back, and trading stories with Johnny the bartender and Leo the cook, and anyone within listening distance.

While The Black Hand was Donal's local, it was not his only resting place. There was Clover and Gold, four blocks over, with its Wednesday drink specials, and The Irish Coup, a bar with a horse racing theme that Donal found amusing and was only a fifteen-minute walk. In each place he knew the bartenders by name and the servers by reputation.

Johnny of The Black Hand returned with the scotch. "Anything new for you. Donal?"

"Not a bit, Johnny. All these days run together like red pants in a whitewash, so that everything comes out pink. Not my favorite shade."

"Ah, but change is the order of things, Donal. Nothing lasts forever. Not even the pink."

Donal chuckled. "Maybe so, my friend. But in the meantime, we make do, don't we?" He paused to take his first sip of the new drink. The cold, smoky richness of good scotch wrapped his throat, a comforter made of liquid rather than cloth.

"You know, it didn't always seem this way."

"Sorry, Donal, I've got to tend to these folks," and Johnny hastened to the far side of the bar, ostensibly to greet some newcomers, but in truth relieved to be away from the stories, which never varied, and the self-pity, which never waned.

"No," said Donal, now to himself alone, "It wasn't always this way."

He nursed his drink in relative silence, contemplating his lost job and wife, As it drew once more to the bottom of the glass, he looked through the wide front window of The Black Hand and saw a young couple looking inside, deliberating whether a drink in such a place might be worth their time. The two held hands, and at one point the girl looked up at her man and laughed, a gentle and genuine burst of glee. Her man smiled back at her, the two shook their heads and walked on. Donal sat where he was and watched them head to someplace else.

He did not do so.

"Johnny." He waved his empty glass. "Another, if you please. And be generous with your pour."

Wandering again the old streets, those ragged and broken trails that had led from boyhood to where he now stood, Donal Mannion perceived most clearly his nature as pocked with chips and dents, like the streets he perused. Something to do on a Saturday afternoon with time to kill. It would be a while before a drink might be in order, and he needed something to wear off the week. So he walked.

His flat lay a few blocks over, leaning toward downtown and the softer life he had left behind those years ago. A conscious choice to relocate in this direction, back to the familiar. Annie had kicked him to the curb, and so what better curbs to lie against than those that had seen him grow into who he was.

The neighborhood hadn't changed much. No gentrification here, no hint of growth or renovation. Timeless, it was, no doubt identical to how it might appear thirty or forty or seventy years before, the only alteration in the models of the cars cruising its streets, and the attire of those who walked them. Their expressions, that curious but constant mix of disinterest and touches of resentment and despair, never changed at all.

The stores, too, were as they were. No new business in these parts. It was all a store owner could do to make it from year to year, avoid the losses and try to hold his own against the prevailing winds of a depressed part of this vast city. Donal walked past the convenience store on the corner of his old block, the place where he and his mates would gather at the start of an afternoon to plan what came next. Curious, Donal ducked inside and walked up and down the small stores three aisles. All the same, the candies and snacks and sodas. He wondered if the stock had ever changed or if he might be looking at the same packages of HoHos and Mike-and-Ikes that he had coveted when he was ten.

Down the street Dominick Salvaterra's fruit stand still stood, buckets of produce arranged under the same red-and-white awning, faded now to a mawkish pink. And there Salvaterra stood, as he always had, handling the small register himself and entertaining the few customers who still happened by, most of them older and a bit hunched, like Salvaterra himself.

Donal walked over and picked up an apple, firm and red. *Still the best around,* he thought as he measured its weight. He grabbed another, then went to the register.

"Hello, Dominick. Remember me?" He gave over the apples to be weighed and costed.

"Should I?"

"I used to live around here. Years ago. My friends and I used to drive you crazy. We always managed to steal more than we bought."

"Ah!" Recognition flashed into the old man's eyes. "Mannion," he smiled at the recollection. "Your mother used to buy from me every week. I remember. But you and your friends. Thieves, all of you," he said with a small laugh. "Still, you come to expect that from young boys. We all tended to thievery back in the day, didn't we?"

Salvaterra bagged the apples. "I should let you have these free of charge. But you've stolen from me enough, so I won't. A dollar and twenty-five it is."

Donal smiled and handed over five quarters. As he took the bag, Salvaterra asked, "So, what are you stealing now?"

Donal paused. "Come again?

"What are you stealing now?"

"What makes you think I'm stealing anything?"

Salvaterra continued to smile. "You're born to it, young man. All of us here, all of us on these streets, are born to it. It's how we survive. And I mean no offense in the question. I meant it as a compliment. You've done what you had to do to get this far. Not everyone can do that - take what you need to survive."

Donal shook his head and turned to go back on his way. "So," asked Salvaterra once more. "What are you stealing now?"

"Only time, Dominick. Only time." Donal Mannion walked back onto a sidewalk that, although filled with comings and goings, suddenly felt as lonely as a winter's night.

— ◆ —

Emma Mannion took her last steps months before, when the war her emphysema waged against her lungs entered its final offensive. Since then wheelchairs and gurneys dictated her movements.

Now, on this final journey home, her world came back to her in sodden and hushed tones. The lost and fallow times that wound their way to this day and place, to the hollowed-out form that carried her name, burned down to the lowest strand of the wick.

Her son lowered her from the car, unfolded the wheelchair, tucked her into it, then wheeled her down the familiar walkway from the street to her front door. "Welcome home, Ma. You're finally back where you belong, and I'm so glad. Your room is just how you left it."

Down the narrow hallway then to the stark bedroom that had been kept as it was. No man to muss things, no complications of demands or space. David Mannion, sickened and embittered by the prospect of fatherhood, had never been a factor. He had walked out of her life forever before Donal drew his first breath. It had been better that way, for all concerned. Emma knew this and had known it for years as she watched son grow without his father's resentments.

Donal maneuvered her wheelchair next to her bed, then gently hoisted her back into her own space. He pulled the covers to Emma's chest, placed a glass of ice water on the bedside table, then touched her cheek softly. "You're home, Ma."

And indeed she was. Emma Mannion had come home to die. She had been dying, she knew, for months. For years. For her whole life.

Her legs were the first to become useless. Emphysema had robbed her of the air she needed for strength and balance. Emma Mannion's lungs were twice their normal size and stretched inside her behind her stomach almost to her hips. When they had capitulated to the squeeze of the disease, her blood lost its oxygenation, her muscles lost their tensility, and what little force her legs held evaporated. Walking became unsteady, exhausting, and, finally, impossible.

And as Emma Mannion settled into her own bed, she recognized with unambiguous clarity that she had taken her very last step on this earth. There would be nothing more.

"Your first medication, Ma.," whispered Donal as he placed a pill on Emma's lips and held up the glass of ice water. "This'll help you sleep a bit. You've had a big day." Emma had no idea of her medications, and even less concern. Let them give her whatever they wanted. None of it could ever do any good.

Nothing in a pill could give her the comforts she needed. What did any of it matter?

So she swallowed with a sip of the water that stabbed the back of her hot throat. The iciness dove down her core, chilled her stomach and settled there with the acids. Within a minute or two she could sense the pill dissolving into her thin bloodstream, and into her thinner conscience.

She had been a girl once. Of course she had been young, and when she was young, she could run, she could jump and climb, giving no thought to what it was that propelled her, that steadied her. She remembered her best friend when she was no older than ten. Susan her name was, and she lived two doors down. Susan was a year older, but more timid. Emma took the lead of their friendship.

They relished the summer months, those lazy, hot days when there was no school, when their parents sent them out in the morning and did not expect to see them again until dinner. As soon as she was out the door, Emma would head to Susan's, and if Susan was not yet outside, she would just sit on the lawn and wait. When the front door opened and Susan dashed down the steps, their day would begin.

Blurry images of those days wafted through Emma's sleep-softened, medicated thoughts. She saw the two of them riding their bikes down and through the streets, farther and farther each day. It was late summer when Emma dared Susan to ride clear across town, down streets that they did not know and through neighborhoods they wouldn't recognize. "Let's just go, and see how far we can get," and Susan hesitantly agreed.

Emma remembered the dog that had come bounding at them across an undeveloped lot, and how her heart fluttered fearfully as she realized that the two of them would never be able to outpace the dog, that the dog would catch them and, if it wanted, do real damage. But the dog had just wanted to play, to be part of the chase. He was a German shepherd, or maybe a mix. It was all fuzzy now, but she recalled how he leaped around their bikes, prancing after them as they pedaled down these strange streets. At last he tired, danced himself to a stop and barked after them as they rode away. He was not there when they made their way home later in the day.

Two days later they rode their bikes to an old quarry well up in the hills that overlooked their small town. Neither dared tell their mothers what they were about. Abandoned for years, the deep pit held mysteries—rocks and crevices for exploring, an occasional cave that went back no more than a few feet but seemed a gaping maw to a ten-year-old imagination. They had heard stories of boys who had lost their footing while climbing the quarry's slopes, tumbling down into the rocks for bruises, slashing cuts, broken bones. One boy they knew at school walked with a permanent limp brought on by a leg shattered from a twenty-foot drop onto a pile of rock shards.

But they were girls, and they were young, and they had to do this. So they did. Into the quarry, where they spent the morning scampering like mountain goats before eating the lunches of peanut butter and moon pies they had packed into brown bags.

Summertime with her best friend, ten years old, and nothing they couldn't do, and life, it seemed, would go on forever.

Emma lolled her head to the side. Her right hand ran down to her leg. *Susan.* She did not know where she was, nor what happened to her. They separated after high school. Emma had met David then, and off they went. Susan went off to college somewhere, and that was that. Still, there was that summer, with running and jumping and the bikes. Emma squeezed her leg and felt what was left of its form. All gone now, all of it. The time past, the friendship, the legs. Nothing left but the blur of memory.

As the emphysema tightened its grip, Emma's lungs worked harder to suck down the air she needed. They strained and tensed, bellowing against the clogged and choked pathways, until her elongated lungs stretched in quiet agony. Emma's heart strained to keep pace with its demands. The pressure took its toll, and her heart grew weaker by the day.

Irony in that, she thought. She had always considered her heart to be the strongest part of her. It had kept her alive, and over time, over the hardest parts, it had built up sufficient defenses to keep her safe. Strange, then, that now it should be easing her down to the final ending.

When she was seventeen, on the early fringe of her senior year, David Mannion had come along. Dark hair, black eyes and a swagger that hid the insecurities attendant on nearly every young man of an age. He was twenty, three years older than Emma, and in her eyes steeped in experience and wisdom. A ticket out of all this.

So was the beginning of that hard path. Her heart. Inviolable and strong, cracked, fissured in spots, but never completely broken.

Now, enslaved to lungs that drew insufficient air, legs that could no longer run or jump, and a body too weak to support itself, her heart strained to meet its responsibilities. But what had her heart already done? It had withstood a father's dissolution, a mother's bile, a husband's indifference, and a son's pretensions to come to this place now, beating against an irredeemable fate.

To what end? Emma thought bitterly. *Why this struggle? My heart is already dead. It's been dead for years.*

Emma Mannion lay now with her thoughts alone, her body having abandoned any pretext of functionality.

How had it been, then? A single mother tending a son she hoped was precocious and gifted, a son who would capture for herself the very things her mother had forfeited accomplishment and success, beauty and a love that infuses the blood and defines the soul, respect and perhaps even a bit of fear. She would raise him to be strong, to be self-aware. A man, not a slave.

The hands that had held him now lay at Emma's side, withered and spotted. The breast against which her son nestled sank without definition to her fragile, brittle ribs. The shoulders her son had held in desperate, lonely hugs pressed into sheets from which they would never lift. No voices left to resonate in her fading ears, no tastes for her tongue to savor. The eyes that saw each movement and gyration in the young boy's growth drained of color and dimension, looking now at nothing other than blank walls and a ceaseless IV drip that marked the time like a metronome.

Time, sifted and dispersed into bits, crafted the tesserae of a mosaic, no longer linear. Emma Mannion viewed her mosaic behind her eyes, viewed it in the deepest crevices of a tired conscience. Her artwork had been completed, and there was no chance now to amend it. No time left to create another tessera that might alter the final pattern. No nuance, or daubing dash of blush. It was time to go.

Later that evening Emma lapsed into a dark sleep, propelled by shallow breathing. No drips could soothe her, no balms could provide relief or strength or comfort. By morning she had sunk into nothingness. She drew her last breath as the sun broke through her window, sending a soft light onto her shrunken form for a final time.

Donal buried his mother on a gray and grim Friday, and as her simple coffin descended into rain-soaked earth, so too did any vestige of boyish innocence. He had heard that a boy does not truly become a man until he's lost his father. Donal had never had a father, and so this loss would provide the transom between youthful dependence and the obligations of self-sufficiency. No one to back him up. Not a wife, not a mother, not a soul. Thrust, then, into the lost time of manhood, the air of it stifling as he groped and gasped for space wherein his fancies could run without obstruction, secure in knowing that no matter how foolish he might be, he was never really alone.

CHAPTER 8

Matthew Cooney had noticed the woman before, the straightlaced older lady who walked the park in a regular circuit, her clothes well tailored to fit the season, her bearing composed and almost regal. Why she walked each day he couldn't fathom. It certainly wasn't to chat, for she never said a word to other passersby. And it certainly couldn't be to enjoy the serenity of the park. The woman kept her eyes ahead, walking almost as if in a march, with regular, patterned steps and no extraneous movement. But regardless of her reasoning, she appeared each day, shortly before noon, and made three circuits.

It was Matthew's instinct to notice such things, to notice the people on the periphery, those who might offer a challenge, or a diversion, or an opportunity. Life on the streets honed his instincts, especially the watchfulness. Matthew Cooney had become a forest creature, attuned to every noise and movement. But he was no timid deer or jittery rabbit. Matthew sniffed the air and sensed the vibrations around him like a tiger aware that a tempting prey might appear at any time, and he need be ready for it.

In the early spring, when the first few tendrils of warmth broke through the deadened winter days, Cooney rose from his bench a bit earlier than normal. The woman had drawn his attention, had made him curious. He had noted the day before the direction from which she had come, and so on this morning he grabbed his backpack and ambled that way. He took to the side of the walk, and smiled agreeable greetings to those he passed, knowing full well that he was leaving his world and entering foreign space, the well-kept, orderly streets of the walkers and the riders and those whose lives were fed by others. Not his space at all, and so best be unobtrusive.

And there he saw her, a stroke of amazing fortune, as she emerged from one of the rowhouses that dotted the square near the park. Closing the door behind her, she descended the four brick steps and turned down the street in Matthew's direction. To the park, then, as she did each day.

My God, is this an omen, and with the thought, Matthew smiled despite himself. A diversion, or an opportunity.

The woman passed Matthew without expression and headed her way. *Three circuits of the park*, he thought. *Takes her about an hour. And she had locked the door behind her, which tells me that no one else is there.*

He waited a few minutes, walked past the house, then turned and went back to it. A locked door had never presented much of an obstacle. Matthew stood on the sidewalk and watched the morning traffic go by, absorbed in their own mornings. No one paid him so much as a glance.

Up the four stairs, and with a quick jab of the lock with his locksmith's hook, the door came undone. The house was as he might have imagined—tidy, small, and as orderly as the woman who had just locked its door. *Nothing fancy here*, he thought. But there would be something. There always is. And no harm to anyone in the taking of it.

He had never been the man to steal silverware or televisions, or any of the bulky items that were always problematic. Matthew saw himself as an artist, able to find the smallest things of greatest value, and quickly dash them off without notice. So here he was, with time enough to find the best of it all.

He pulled open a drawer in a corner hutch and found an envelope with a few notes tucked inside. He'd count it later. Part of the art of it was to walk away with something that would not be noticed immediately, and this envelope would do well. Upstairs in her bedroom he found a jewelry case and took only one set of earrings and one pendant that looked as if it might have some value. He left the rest. Greed was the demise of many a thief, and Matthew Cooney always remained humble.

Down the stairs, then out the door once more, securing the lock behind him. A good day this would be. There would be food, and a bottle, and maybe even a place to sleep inside. He'd decide that later, after he counted the notes and regarded what he might get for the bits of jewelry.

He turned down the street to his park, in time to see the woman make what must have been her second pass. Matthew settled on his customary bench, the one that gave him his world's view. Brilliant, it was, this bench, and brilliant the man who sat on it, or so he thought. It would indeed be a very good day.

But not all days dawned so brightly. Most days carried a bite, and it was all Matthew could do to find what he needed to make it through—enough food, something to drink and a bit of peace. The ups and downs of such a life, but here he was.

Three days after his good day, Matthew awoke to the noxious fumes and the grinding chops of the crew that came into the square to clean it, to mow it, and to roust all those semi-citizens who slept in it. He grumbled his way into the city streets in need of clearer air and something to eat. By late morning he had found neither.

By the time the crews had done their work and he could reclaim his usual spot, the sun had risen high. The park carried its usual contingent of people mostly passing through on their way to offices or shops. A weekday, so there were no families out on a lark to run along the grass or feed the squabbling ducks in the broad pond near the center. Everyone in transition, it seemed, from one place to another.

Except for Matthew. The usual bench. The usual streets. The usual convenience store where he would buy a bit and steal a bit. The usual houses away from the park, where he knew every unlocked door, every entrance and exit, and every pot of gold. The usual faces of those looking for a bit of mischief, or an easy score. The usual girls who could be courted for the price of a bottle of cheap whiskey. All of it, the usual.

Matthew left the bench and spent the rest of the afternoon walking, farther afield than normal. He found streets that splayed into new directions, and saw the landscapes of new stores, old stores, restaurants with names he couldn't pronounce, and houses that ran down upon themselves.

All day he walked, looking for what he could not define, feeling the gnaw of a new hunger that defied satisfaction. He scanned the faces he passed, and those who noticed this disheveled newcomer with the ratty backpack and the bad smell shrank back as they passed him, or he passed them. He did not belong. Not on these streets, not in these new and foreign neighborhoods. Matthew Cooney did not belong.

And so at the end of the day he circled back to the park, to his bench. Desperation, as quiet as a church mouse, tiptoed into an unsettled mind and a lonely heart.

"Matty, how are ya, man?" Dinny Murphy came up behind Matthew where he sat and clapped a hand on his shoulder. "A hell of a day, no?"

"A hell of a day, Dinny, and nothing to it."

"Ah, how can you say that? A glorious day with the sun and the sky, a bit of light and a bit of heat. And now," Murphy leaned into Matthew with a whisper, "I'm thinking there might be a bottle at the end of it."

"Not here, Dinny. I've got nothing, for either of us. Be on your way."

"Matty, if you've no bottle, then let's go find one."

"Not in the mood, Dinny. Not tonight. Now leave me be."

"You know, Matty, you used to be more fun when you were younger. High spirited you were. Nothing to set you from your course of a good time, a good laugh and a good drink. A lot more fun where you were younger."

"I was never young, Dinny. Now get the hell out of here."

A glint came to Dinny Murphy's eye. "You know, despite it all, I never really liked you, Cooney. You've always been something apart. Seeing yourself as a bit better than the rest of us dregs. But you're no better, Cooney. You belong here with the likes of us."

Matthew rose, turned, and unleashed a fist into the man's cheek. Dinny Murphy fell backward onto the grass.

And with that, Matthew Cooney walked out of the park, and into a new night. He had no idea where he would go, but he would not stay here. He would not stay where he did not belong.

— ◆ —

"The bastard took it. I know it, Dinny."

"Ah, you know no such thing, Scotty. Just because the money's gone doesn't mean it was lifted. Damn, Scotty, you're as careless as a toddler. You might have left it anywhere."

"I know what I did with it, Dinny. Christ, do you think I'd lose sight of a bounty like that. Must have been fifty bucks in that packet. I had it all the time, in my back pocket. Until I didn't. Until Matthew came rambling by. He walked away with it, of that I'm sure. It's the type of thing he does."

"Well, then, you have an account to settle, I'd say. If you really believe that."

Scotty Kyle paced the sidewalk near the convenience store on the corner of the green. Dinny stood by him and counted his tense and angry steps. Nothing good would come of this, he knew. They were men of the streets, all of them, homesteading the ragged and cold streets of the woebegone northeastern part of the city. Comrades, of sorts, bound by common urges, and here they were again.

After a few minutes of pacing, and more than a few mumbled curses, Scotty turned to Dinny. "I'm off, then. Find me if you see him. I'll be in the park across the way.

Dinny said nothing, shook his head with a tinge of sadness and turned back into the store, where he had gone to find something for his breakfast. He'd not look for Cooney, nor was there a need to. Scotty would find him, and it would all be sorted out.

It took no great investigation to find the man. Matthew spent most of his nights in the park, on the same bench, or near it. This morning of the night before had been no different. Devon found him as he thought he would, sprawled onto the usual bench and covered by the usual blanket, still asleep. Some men are creatures of habit.

Scotty stomped to the bench, and Matthew did not stir. *Perfect*, he thought. Scotty reached under the blanket and grabbed Matthew's tattered shirt, pulled him upright, then sent his fist into Cooney's cold cheek. Matthew flopped back down to his bench, awake now.

"Jesus Christ on a pogo stick," he cried, but then he softened, surmised where he was, and his still smarting face broke into a smile. "A hell of a way to wake a man up, Scotty."

The other was ransacking the backpack Matthew kept under the bench. A few scraps of food, papers that had no meaning, a pencil, a lock, and, at last, a familiar packet. Scotty held it up. "My money, Cooney. This is mine, you thieving bastard."

"Ah, you're mistaken, Scotty. Found it on the street late yesterday. A happy accident is all. Outside Flaherty's it was, lying on the sidewalk as plain as your face. Someone must have dropped it. And before you go getting all high and mighty, keep in mind that we're all thieving bastards."

"It's mine, Cooney. You found it in my back pocket. And now it's mine again."

Matthew rose to argue, but before he could fully stand, Scotty Kyle unleashed a firm right fist to the jaw then followed it up with a solid left to the chin. Matthew crumpled with a moan.

"And if this happens, again, Matty, it'll be all the worse for you. Even among thieves there needs to be some honor." Scotty tucked the packet back where it belonged, then turned back to the street.

As he did so, Matthew sat up slowly and rubbed his jaw. "Scotty," he said.

The other stopped and turned.

"Help a man up, would you? I'll treat you to some breakfast. It's the least a man can do for one of his oldest friends."

— ◆ —

Matthew twisted the cap back onto the bottle. A final burst of the courage he might need to take advantage of a rare opportunity. He lived his life harshly, to be sure, but codes existed that provided some degree of predictability. Some degree of order. Something the sullied species of mankind had chased since first climbing out of the primordial muck. Order it was that was the basis for all families, for all clans and tribes, for the creation of the state and the elevation of kings.

Today Matthew Cooney would be a king. And he would chase his throne in the arena of these tawdry, clotted streets, the crucible of a life misspent but one which still might garner some satisfactions.

Matthew tucked the bottle into a side pocket and stood from his bench. A deep breath, the warmth of a late afternoon summertime sun, and then to it.

Indeed, there was honor among thieves. He had learned this, and adhered to this new lesson, underscored by the lingering burn of Scotty Kyle's fist. What one had stolen the others would not touch. Not usually. The lads on the street carried a quiet respect for the accomplishments of their mates, a warped form of professional courtesy, but there it was. Matthew had, even in his ignorance, respected it, although there were times when he might sneak off with a pint stolen from someone who had stolen it himself from the local store, or pick up something another might have unknowingly left behind. Matthew never abused the notion.

But temptation can beckon the strongest of souls, and what Matthew lacked in strength of character he made up in boldness.

On this day temptation could not be resisted. Nor would he even try. The challenge was to turn temptation into reward.

Around the benches on the warm nights, the men would talk, and it was two nights ago that James Dunphy had shared the story he had heard of a man they both knew, a street person like the two of them, who had happened upon a major score. He had found a wallet in the corner of a doorway. No ordinary wallet, it had been stuffed with one-hundred-dollar bills, perhaps as many as twenty, an incredible stroke of good fortune to be respected and regarded with awe by those whose own existences shared space on the edge.

Matthew did not know the man, had never exchanged a word, but he knew who he was and where he might find him. Older, a bit frail—one of those who were almost invisible in the doorways at night, dirty eyes peering over the newspapers and torn blankets.

It didn't take long. A crosstown bus, then a wander down the streets where he might be. As the sun set, Matthew found the man sitting outside a McDonald's. Despite his newfound wealth, the codger shook a cup filled with coins at the passersby. Habit, or an instinctive survival urge, or maybe just the usual way to pass the time.

Matthew approached him. "C'mon, man. Let me buy you a meal."

The man looked up at him, puzzled. "You have the coin for that?"

"Enough to share with someone hungrier than me, or so it appears. C'mon then." Matthew pulled the man up by the arm. He noticed how quickly his new friend grabbed his backpack, holding it close as they went into the restaurant. So easy this would be.

Matthew reached into his pocket and pulled out a bottle of handwash. "Before you eat anything you'll want to wash up. Here. Go make yourself clean," and the man and his backpack shuffled to the restroom down the narrow hallway.

Matthew waited a few seconds, heard the restroom door close, then followed down. No one else was in the small space where the man huddled over a urinal relieving himself. The backpack was at his feet.

A quick blow to the back of his head, and the man crumpled. Matthew grabbed the backpack, unzipped it and sifted through the grime and rags and flotsam that crowded it, finding at the bottom a swath of thick leather. He pulled it out and did not count the bills within it, not then. Time for that later.

The old man groaned up at him. "You feckin' bastard. Rot in hell."

"Sorry, old man. But you know that the wolf doesn't give a damn what the sheep think." He kicked the man into the corner of the restroom, away from the urinal and the foul stenches around it.

Back to the bus, then across town, where he would not be found, not by the old man, nor any of the old man's mates, nor his own conscience. Tonight there would be a fresh bottle, and perhaps he might even share a bit of it.

And there would be order. The natural order of wolves and sheep. But in an unquiet mind, the wolf's conscience ate into the night sky, and made it black.

— ◆ —

Winter swept into an April night like a vapor, crawling under doorways, wafting into the air, numbing those who touched it. April, when daffodils poked their tender heads haltingly toward a nurturing sky, and birds hopped from branch to branch, reveling in the simple pleasures of sun and seed and song. When a man's thoughts might turn to dance and music and love itself.

But on this night winter made a reappearance, a final thrust across a city at once too eager to see it go. Families huddled in their homes and turned their thermostats up. Cabbies drove with their windows rolled up tight, and the windows of buses fogged up with the moisture of artificial heat. Grocers sold hot chocolate and marshmallows.

In Farragut Square, Matthew Cooney hunched on his usual bench. The iron slats ran shanks of cold along the back of his legs, and he arched his shoulders forward under the tatty blanket that had tried to keep him warm for years. Another night at least before he could stuff it into his backpack and pretend that he might never need it again.

Next to him sat one of the other regulars. James, his name was. Never Jim. Or, God forbid, Jimmy. He would react almost violently if someone called him that. "My name's James, God damn it. James. Jimmy, that's a boy's name, or something you sprinkle on ice cream." Sometimes the teasing would continue, though, the taunts from those younger, and bolder, and stronger. James proudly wore broken teeth and battered bones of integrity. "I'm a man, Matty," he had told Cooney when they had first met. "A man with a man's name. Don't ever call me Jim."

Now James sat with his shoulder against Matthew's, and the two of them tried to breathe warmth into their hands.

"Ah, Matty. We should be sittin' someplace warm. Not stuck out in this damn park with nothing but our wits to keep the blood circulating. And pass me a bit of that bottle, would you?"

Matthew obliged, and James took a deep draught of the cheap brandy Matthew had snuck out of a package store around the block. Nasty, it was, but its fire lit the belly.

"Nah, James. Nothing warm for the likes of us. We're living the pure life."

"Christ Almighty!" James took one final swig before passing the bottle back to Matthew. "Think of all the worthless bastards that are sleeping in warm beds tonight and wrapping themselves around their women. And none of 'em any different than us. Flesh and blood and dreams, just like us."

"Ah, that's where you're wrong, Jamesy. We've the flesh and the blood, but the dreams are gone. Don't really know what happened to them either. But gone they are, and we're left with what we're left with. And tonight that amounts to this bench, and this brandy, and blankets with as many holes in them as our souls."

"I'd like to get my hands on one of those rich bastards," James said. "I'd show him what life is really like. Maybe toss him into a trash can and light it on fire, just to keep us warm for a bit."

"And what would that do, James? You'd show him what life is really like, you said, but what would he learn? We build our own boats, my friend, and it's those boats we must sail. He sails his, complete with the dreams we've lost, and we sail ours."

James looked hard at Matthew, who continued softly. "I don't resent those who've made it, James. They're part of the game, don't you see? Every day we play the game, seeing what we can get away with, seeing what we can take. Seeing how we can kick ourselves up a notch, or maybe knock someone else down. If there were no rich bastards, there'd be no game."

"Not sure I understand you, Matty."

He smiled and sipped from the bottle. "Not sure I understand myself, James. There's some newspapers under that bench over there. Go grab 'em up and we'll see if we can burn up this trash can. A bit of heat and a bit of light. That's all we need. That's all anybody needs."

— ◆ —

"You've been keeping yourself scarce lately, Matty." The woman spoke slowly slightly slurring her words. She slipped off her jacket, then her top, placing them over the ragged chair that held the corner of the room. A single window beside it shone down on an empty street.

Matthew kicked off his shoes, then raised the flask from his rear pocket. "Busy times, Lisa. A man's got to work to survive. But you know that."

A thin smile. "Work. What type of work?"

Matthew took a long pull of the flask. "The same as you, girl. Taking what people offer, whether they know that they're offering it or not."

Wordlessly, Lisa reached for Matthew's hand that held the flask.

He gave it to her, and she drank long and loudly, slurping away the last swallow. Matthew regarded her as she did so. She was slender, bordering on emaciated, with hipbones that arced in sharp points and ribs that could be counted. Her thin face tapered to a pointed chin, holding dark eyes, empty and black, a doll's eyes, or a shark's. Black hair hung in strands on her shoulders. It had been some time since it had seen a comb, managed only from an unsteady hand passing through it and pulling it back from her forehead. Matthew noticed her skin looked more mottled than before.

Lisa finished undressing then climbed into the narrow bed. She patted the small space beside her. "Time to get it on, man."

"Is there a rush tonight, Lisa? Not even a bit of conversation?"

"And what is there to talk about? Besides, that's never been part of the deal. You're renting my body, and a bit of my time. That's all. You can keep your thoughts to yourself, or you can mumble them out, but I don't give a damn."

"A man needs a woman for more than her body, girl. We've had some pleasant times, some pleasant talks. You're more than meat."

"Never have been, and I'm not now. Let's do this."

Matthew finished undressing then joined her under tattered covers. She welcomed him with a brief hug, then dropped her hand below his waist and began her work. Matthew lay back and let her stroke him into readiness. She worked quickly toward the desired effect.

When he mounted her, Matthew did not look at her face. Instead he focused on the wall next to the window. A bug of some sort was making its way northward, heading in slow pace for the ceiling. Matthew watched it crawl while he arched his back and propped himself on his elbows as he drove into her. Mechanical, nothing more than the exertions of the proper muscles in the proper places.

Upon release he leaned back, then rolled to his side. Lisa said nothing. She rose silently, then made her way in a few steps to the bathroom to clean up.

Matthew exhaled deeply, staring at the ceiling. When Lisa finally emerged, he threw aside the covers and went to the bathroom himself. There was barely enough space for a big man to stand. He took the towel Lisa had used to wipe himself, dabbing it under the tap that spilled out cold, tainted water.

The woman had already dressed again by the time Matthew came out of the bathroom. She dug into her purse for something, pulled out a pill and gulped it down with the benefit of water. "Hurry up," she growled.

"Someplace to be, dear heart?"

"Anyplace that's not here."

"Didn't we rent it for an hour? Still half of that for you to enjoy, girl. Warmer here than on the streets."

Lisa said nothing. Matthew pulled up his jeans, then reached into the back pocket to pull out a handful of bills. He placed them on the bed.

"It's all there?"

"As always, baby girl." He turned toward the door while Lisa counted out the money, then stashed it into her purse. "A pleasure doing business with you. Miss Lisa. I'll see you again."

He shut the door behind him, but before he had made it down a single level of stairs, he heard it open again as Lisa let herself out, then locked it behind her. Matthew thought to wait for her, but what was the point? He finished his descent, then went through what passed as a lobby to get to the street where he breathed cold air that was free and scented with the subtle aroma of a winter's night.

It would not snow tonight. Good enough. Matthew walked the few blocks to the square where he gathered his backpack from the bushes behind his usual bench where James lay prone under a thick coat. Matthew would find a doorway tonight.

As he gathered his pack, James spoke from underneath the coat. "Kept an eye on things for you, Matty."

"Thanks, James. You're a friend."

"Things go well for you? Was she worth it?"

"Always worth it, James. She's as regular as a finely tuned clock."

"Just what a man needs from time to time, right, Matty?"

"Right you are." He turned to find his own place for the night, a bit calmer than before. "Stay safe and warm tonight. No doubt I'll see you tomorrow." Matthew walked off by himself into the city's night.

CHAPTER 9

It had all begun with a mistake, born of innocence and naivete, then steeped in ignorance. Years later, she would ask herself how she had come to the place where she now sat, drinking a cup of tea against a rainy window, lonely and alone, missing the forever past gifts of beauty, and youth, and time.

"Gina"

"Hey, Jack."

Jack Stroud played football and ran track. Tall and well put together, handsome enough to draw second looks, he occupied the fancies and fantasies of most girls who saw him. He was a senior, a year older than Gina Moretti, whose unsullied dark hair and dark eyes had not been entirely unnoticed. Gina was growing up, and growing out.

"Listen, I'm just gonna come right out and ask. I'd really like to get to know you better. Do you think we could go to a movie, or grab a bite, or . . . I don't know, *something* this weekend."

"Oh my God, Jack, are you asking me out? I've never even really spoken to you before."

"Yeah, well, that's the point. Maybe we can find some time to do that, to talk and learn about each other. I think I'd like that. Besides, you're the prettiest girl in the whole damn school. I figure if I want any chance with you, I better strike quick."

Gina, her head suitably turned, stammered a response." Jack, that's so sweet. Yes, let's do something."

Her first date. She ran home after school to tell her mom and waited by the door for her dad to come home from work. Their little girl was growing up. When the phone rang the next night, it was Jack Stroud confirming that he'd pick up Gina at seven on Friday. Gina's dad asked about the young man, and Gina assured him of his pedigree.

"As long as he's a very polite young man," her father admonished, "and is good to my little girl."

Jack picked up Gina Moretti at her simple home on a Friday night in early spring. They saw a movie, then went for a drive. When Jack parked the car at the far end of a nature reserve south of town, he invited her to walk with him. "Just to look at the night sky." Under that sky, the half-moon a silent witness, he pulled her down to the cool, wet grass and gave her the first kiss she had ever experienced. He did not stop with a single kiss, and Gina, naïve and overwhelmed, could not stop his hands from finding her breasts, from unzipping and removing her jeans, from tearing through the fabric of her panties, and from the rest of what ensued.

"You won't tell anyone about this," he panted when he had spent himself. "I know you won't. No one would believe you anyway." Jack removed his T-shirt and offered it to Gina to clean herself.

On the mostly silent drive back to her home, Jack told her, "I did you a favor, Gina. You can't be a virgin forever. You've got to know that practically everyone our age has done it. There's nothing special about any of it. But it was fun, right?"

When they reached her house, Jack asked, "Can I see you again next week?"

Now, too many years on, Gina Moretti saw it all as the beginning of decisions brought about by trauma, by loss and abandonment, and by the nagging, gnawing doubt that she could evoke only the worst in those around her. *What's the point to it all, if in the end we die alone, used and corrupted, more a product than a person?* Her mind chattered. *An idiot, I am. All my life an idiot.*

Men at the heart of it. First one, then another, then another after that, and on it went. Seeking something elusive, just beyond her fingertips if it existed at all. To be valued for who she was, and what she might become. Did she have that worth? And why so hard the struggle to find it? Who was she, really, in the eyes of those who saw her?

Gina sipped her tea and regarded the rain, which showed no signs of lightning. A dead afternoon, as lost as all the others, the tail end of idiocy.

— ◆ —

Joey DiMarco was to blame. Joey DiMarco, with muscular forearms whose veins ran like thick ropes and a hairy chest that peaked over the top of his work shirt. Chain smoking Joey DiMarco who could suck down two cigarettes during a fifteen-minute break and half a dozen during a lunch hour, then returned to the dock wafting a perpetual odor of black tar for the rest of the afternoon. Joey DiMarco, with an easy smile, a bawdy joke at the ready, and a well-populated Italian family that spread throughout the region.

Joey had cousins, lots of them, and he had friends where he worked, all those drawn both to his constant good humor and his willingness to lift whatever was heaviest.

If Donal Mannion had a best friend at the loading dock, it was Joey, but even Donal would have backed away from that description. Joey was really the only one he spoke with, the only one who spoke to him. Joey's irrepressible humor drew no boundaries, and he treated Donal from the first day as someone he might have known for years.

"Mannion, help me with this pallet. That is, if an Irish guy has strength enough to lift anything heavier than a pint of Guinness." He slapped the newcomer on the shoulder and drew him to the task. From the first day it was like that, all the time. Joey with his jokes, his jibes, his encouragement, and a steady rudder that kept things on course.

"What are you up to this weekend, Mannion? Let me guess. Drowning yourself in liquor and self-pity, chasing any woman who happens by, and then waking up Sunday morning with a head full of dry rocks."

"You pretty much nailed it, Joey. The Donal Mannion formula for weekend joy. I'd recommend it if you weren't already such a stable family man,"

"Ah, how can a man live like that? You're killing yourself, Mannion, do you know that? Killing yourself. But I can offer a brief respite. I have a cousin I think you should meet. I'd be happy to make an introduction if you promise not to behave like a caveman.

"You're playing matchmaker, Joey?"

"Not a habit of mine, Mannion, but I see something here. You're a desperate, lonely loser, and Gina is coming off a rocky relationship. A couple of them, actually. She's delicate right now, and she could use the company of someone who might treat her right. I thought of you."

"Kind of you, big guy, but what makes you think I'm willing. I've never been one to have someone else set me up."

"She's into the finer things. She reads a lot, just like you, and she wanders around the museums. She's sensitive, Mannion, and despite your primitive lifestyle, I think you are, too. Call it a hunch. If nothing else, it might be time well spent. You might learn something about how to treat a real woman."

"Does she have your family traits, Joey? The five o'clock shadow, the linebacker's build, that sort of thing?"

"She's cute as hell. A slip of a thing. All her cousins want to take care of her, especially after all her heartbreaks. She's adorable."

"And you'd trust her with the likes of me?"

"I think you're different than the rest of these mooks. And besides, if you ever mistreat her, I'd beat you into gutter slop. She's as lonely as you are, Donal. Divorced twice over by rogues that'd make you look like Sir Lancelot. Give her a call."

So it began. Donal called the number Joey gave him, halting and uncertain, with none of the easy, alcohol-infused charm that worked with random women in bars. Gina, lobbied as well by her cousin, expected the call. "He's a decent guy, Gina. Lonely as hell, but he doesn't know it." No one could resist her cousin's good-natured pressures.

They met first at Rock Creek Park, leafy and broad this time of year, and with plenty of people around. Gina had suggested it, a bit of self-protection digressed. She would be at the park's entrance at Connecticut Avenue, near Calvert Street. They could walk through the greenery for a bit, and then if agreeable find a spot on the avenue for coffee or a drink.

Donal's breath caught in his throat when he first saw the slight dark-haired figure that might be Gina Moretti. An instinct, some inarticulate internal calling, which told him that this woman was not to be taken casually. That this woman could mean something. Years later he would not be able to explain it, although he knew for certain at first glance that Gina Moretti would be different from all the others, that she, of them all, might change him. *Redemption, redefinition.* Somewhere an angel whispered.

She was fair, to be sure. Dark hair with a bit of curl, thickly framing a heart-shaped face with rich lips, the soft curbing of her high cheeks and eyes that hinted both insight and sorrow. She was not tall, no more than a couple of inches beyond five feet, yet she stood almost willowy, perched on well-formed legs that tapered upward to a slender waist. She presented a quiet confidence, an assurance that, come what may, Gina Moretti was who she was, and would remain so.

"Gina?"

"Hi. Donal?"

Question marks at the start, and all of the questions behind the first one. They walked that day and found that their steps were not unbalanced. The resumes presented at first meetings, the gentle probings to find out who this new person really might be, where they had been. Both would save what they thought, what they felt, for later times. To find some comfort this day, that was all. To spend a few hours unthreatened, and quietly valued for the new guise they presented the other. There was a subtle excitement in this day without expectation or demand. Enough it was just to be Gina and Donal for a time, to show to the other bits of what they were, and in so doing, perhaps to discover themselves a touch more of who they might have the potential to be.

A challenge it is to find the one person who resonates, unspoken and intuitively, the one who might finally see through all pretense and illusion. A challenge to trust in instinct rather than logic, and to know that that course, as perilous as it might be, is the only one to follow.

— ◆ —

When Donal took the number that Joey DiMarco offered, he did so expecting little more than a casual diversion, perhaps a bit of physical gratification, a laugh or two, and then the usual parting. But it had not played out that way. Not at all.

For one of the few times in his life, Donal Mannion leaned on impulse instead of survival. *There must be something more,* he told himself. *Something more than the usual pushing and pulling and tearing. I've passed four decades and done nothing. Learned nothing except the sorry lessons of loss and boredom. Maybe this is different. Maybe I can make it different. What's to lose?*

Several weeks passed, with weekend meals, almost daily calls—"Just wanted to hear your voice"—and long walks, which to their mutual surprise they came to cherish on days warm and dry enough to allow them. It was on these walks that they made themselves most vulnerable. Something in the surrounding wrap of nature, the trees and the ponds and the goofy, squawking ducks that pestered them for breadcrusts. If nothing could disturb this untamed wild that has endured so long, then what could harm Donal and Gina suffer under its awning? It was in the remotest places that they spoke most freely.

They saw each other honestly, as they were instead of how

they marketed themselves. Gina accepted Donal—flawed, tattered, irresponsible, often indolent and fatuous. But she saw, too, his vulnerability, and the constant, pointed fears that he would not admit even to himself. Fears of aging and irrelevance, the nagging sense that he might pass from this earth and leave not so much as a footprint. She knew the way he lived, the dalliances and the drinking and the drift, masked these fears, for which he had no ready answer other than to try to obliterate them through indulgences.

And because of this, she knew that Donal would never take advantage of her, that this unspoken knowledge of the man's sorry and anxious heart would protect her from his worst impulses while allowing her to savor the best of him.

She saw his charm, his self-deprecating humor, his eagerness to please her. A little boy at times clinging for acceptance. He fascinated her. He had depth that he rarely showed, and a love of art and good food and fine wines that belied his origins. Those hungers could only come from a soul seeking challenge, seeking to reach beyond itself to something higher, even if he could not define it.

It helped, too, that Donal stood more handsomely than most men of his years. He remained lean. His work had kept him strong, and despite a tendency to spend too many nights in dark places drinking cheap alcohol, his features neither sagged nor paled. Donal had a full head of hair, now tinting attractively gray, a strong chin and sharp, clear eyes.

Gina, for her part, disclosed herself in small sips. All her life men had harmed her. They had hunted her, and captured her, and toyed with both her body and her emotions. Given all this, how should she regard herself? Her first marriage came about because this man, Thomas, had shown her a love she had not thought herself worthy of possessing. He had broached her defenses deeply enough to convince her that she was desirable for more than a night's pleasures, and so had promised her a lifetime. That lifetime lasted three years, blunted by the man's boredom with a wife who retreated from him as she realized that she had married not for a shared future, but solely validation of her soiled past.

Her second marriage stemmed from the despair of loneliness. She had met Evan on the sales floor of a downtown department store where she wafted perfume samples to passing shoppers. He had stopped, he had flirted, and she did not find him objectionable. They courted briefly and married quickly. When Gina took her promotion to the store's front office as an assistant buyer, Evan grew resentful. He hadn't wanted to marry a career woman, and so the arguments, almost in cliches, grew more heated. He left her within two years of their wedding day. She had not heard from him since they signed the divorce papers in her attorney's office. He had told her he was moving back to New Jersey where he would take over his father's trucking business.

All this made Gina cautious, and she remained so with Donal, even as his latent boyishness, the unformed and unfulfilled contours of his aspirations, intrigued her. More than any man she had ever known, Donal Mannion charmed her, showing his genuine self without realizing that he was doing so. This man was worth her time, worth her interest, and, perhaps, worth her heart.

As his time with Gina grew more frequent and richer, Donal spent less time at the bars. After returning home from work, he would spend his nights quietly, either watching television or reading. Once or twice a week he might pour himself a measure of scotch, which he would sip in the relative peace of music or a good book.

On one such night, he cradled his drink at the window that looked onto nothing. *These streets,* he thought as he looked down on them. *All I knew as a boy was these streets. Where do dreams come from? No one ever showed me.*

But I might be something more than what I've been. He sipped and stared at the empty spaces on the sidewalks. *She sees the wounds, and the wounds don't scare her.*

Is she the perfect woman? No. But she's the one who might offer me something no other woman ever has. She might be the one to validate what it means to be Donal Mannion.

— ◆ —

Gina Moretti poured a measure of red wine into Donal glass, then emptied the bottle into her own. Red wine went well with the sun, as did the lunch of cheeses and fruits, the remnants of which were strewn around the edges of the blanket. Donal leaned onto one arm, lifted the refilled glass and clinked it against Gina's own.

It had been a glorious morning. The drive to the hills had begun under the bluest of skies, sharp and crystalline, carrying the whispers of a soft cool breeze that promised to keep the sun in balance. They had found their trail and walked two miles or so into the Blue Ridge, Gina skirting occasionally off track to step into the surrounding brush or to wander a few yards beyond into the deeper parts of the woods. The Shenandoah was trees and sky, streams and flying things, and always the possibility of something unforeseen and unexpected. A chevron of geese flying low enough to touch. A deer or a bear. A kiss from a nervous lover stolen under a canopy of chirping birds.

In a clearing several yards off the trail they had spread their lunch. Now, food consumed, wine in hand and the warmth of the sun lulling conversation and the thoughts that fired it, Donal regarded the lady who lay across from him.

A wondrous journey it had been, the two of them. Almost seven months along now, through confusion and discovery, the adjustment of spirits, the unspoken absorption of one another's rhythms. Rocky, broken and bumbling, but a journey nonetheless. In the end he knew that Gina took him for who and what he was—a man understated and adrift, flawed, and chipped, but one who remained a boy at heart. Now the little boy looked at his Gina, and his heart soared.

"You're a very beautiful woman, Gina Moretti. Have I told you that lately?"

"I may have heard it a time or two," she smiled in response. "But that doesn't mean I believe it. We're both of us too old to be beautiful, Donal. Besides, isn't this just an opening line in the Donal Mannion book of seduction?"

"A book I've no need for today, Gina." He rolled onto his back, and a drop of wine bounced out of his glass onto his shirt. He paid it no mind. "Today is all sunlight and warmth and wine and Gina. Nothing else."

"The words you spin. Is there no end to it?"

"No end at all. You're stuck with me, I'm afraid, and more to it. I look at you now, after all this time, and I see you as I first saw you. As bright as the sun, and as dark as the Italian night. I could picture you in a work of great art, walking in front of Monet's Rouen Cathedral or lolling in Van Gogh's sunflowers. I think I'll see you that way forever, no matter what."

Gina turned away from her man to look across the clearing to the tops of the mountains that stretched westward. While the wine had sent Donal's thoughts and heart soaring, it had tempered her own. She felt a chill. *Words, and nothing more. Donal is a great one for the words.*

With a sigh she turned back to the figure lying now across their lunch blanket. "Van Gogh had better subject matter," she sighed. "I've grown tired, Donal. Let's head back," and she moved to gather her things into the pack she carried for the both of them.

"But it's only midday. We've got all the time in the world."

"Perhaps so, Donal. But there are no sunflowers here, and no cathedrals. I'm just Gina, nothing more. And you're just Donal."

Donal rose through a sigh and picked up the pack. Back down the trail then, and once more into what was, what was always there, with no great art around it.

Their intimacy proceeded in cautious steps, but for the first time in Donal's life, the first time since that wondrous night decades ago when it all began in the park with Janie Donovan, that sex was not an obsession. Sex had become an afterthought. He did not pressure her, made no innuendos or leading entendres, never touched her suggestively except at her bidding. In the early days of his courtship with Annie he had assumed a similar posture, but even then he knew it to be an act, a device to make him appear less threatening, and so more appealing. Sex had always been the goal—the closure of the deal, the flag to be placed on the mountaintop.

But this was different. This was Gina, and Donal sensed her delicacy. He noted the bruises in the tone of her voice, her reluctance to accept his compliments. Even as she drew near to him, she kept a distance borne of the echoes of past sufferings. Men had deceived her, they had manipulated her, they had rejected her. One had raped her. Donal knew all this, and still he found her as attractive, as refined and as fascinating as any woman he could ever hope to know. She needed care.

When at last they shared a bed, the night came softly. They had walked that afternoon in the park, taken a dinner at a bistro in Adams Morgan, then went back to Gina's apartment nearby. She offered him a drink and when she brought it to him, she placed it on the table next to his chair then curled into his lap. She said nothing other than, "It's time," and with that she took his hand and led him to the bedroom.

Donal learned from their lovemaking. He learned that passion best spent itself when it focused not exclusively on the body but embraced the soul as well. He learned that Gina Moretti, shorn of her wariness and at last willing to become vulnerable once more, could be a tender, gentle, giving lover. He learned that the best sex must transcend the physical, that the power of his release would be in direct proportion to the power of his emotions. He learned that Donal Mannion might indeed be someone a fine woman could love honestly and purely, that his own rutty pathway, his indistinct wanderings, might not be a wolf's bane, and that redemption might be something more than the stuff of fantasies.

The next morning they woke within minutes of each other, Gina first, so that when Donal opened his eyes he saw her there, propped on her shoulder, smiling through a wisp of sunlight coming through undrawn curtains.

"Hi," she said, then giggled.

"Hi back at ya," then he leaned over for the first of their morning kisses.

"You don't look any different," said Gina, again with a giggle. A girl again, in the early throes of something new and exciting.

"Ah, but I am, lady. I'm quite different. I'm Gina Moretti's lover now, which I was not the day before. And that means more than I can say."

It was weeks after that, when the weather promised a gentle warmth, that he took her to New York for the weekend. Donal had offered the trip as a brief escape. The city's vibrancy attracted him, and he sought to share it with Gina. On the train north, he told her the story of his grandfather's restive flight, taking the train in the opposite direction to plant a broken family in unfertile soil.

Gina listened spellbound. "A restless man, your grandfather. Always chasing something new. Something better. What, then, in God's name have I found in his grandson?"

"I see no need to run, Gina. My grandfather never found his peace. But that's on him. We create our own Heaven and Hell right where we are."

She cuddled against him and whispered, "So what are we creating, Donal? Will this be Heaven, or will we end up in a fiery pit of anguish and loss?" Then she stopped. "I'm teasing. Don't take me seriously."

"We'll not know until it's over, Gina. But at the moment I'm hearing more angels than demons. And I suspect it would be a great, great sin not to take you seriously."

— ◆ —

From their hotel window the avenues of the city spun away in disparate lines, each one illuminated by headlights, the doorways of restaurants and cafes, and the odd shimmer from offices well past their closing. Donal leaned against the window and watched the lights, watched the lines tremoring in their unhurried movements, and regarded the intoxication of his dreams.

Behind him Gina flitted in and out of the narrow bathroom.

The Four Seasons this wasn't, but the room was large enough to acccommodate the two of them, and clean enough to dispel any discomforts. Gina grabbed the occasional stick or roll or gloss from her travel bag, then darted back into the bathroom to complete her preparations. Rare enough that they had this time together, and rarer still when Donal felt secure enough to spend precious funds on an evening out. Dinner at the least, in a fine Spanish restaurant on Lexington, then perhaps a drink or two.

He turned to Gina as she emerged, ready now. A beige dress that complemented her dark hair and darker eyes, a soft scent of lilacs. Donal considered Gina to be beautiful, but not in in the shallow terms that most men employ. As he looked at her now, a gentle smile of anticipation and muted excitement, a form real enough to be held, and a countenance that forever whispered strength, and patience, and resolve, he saw her as the entirely beautiful, a consummate survivor who drew him now, drew his soul, embedded into the core of his tattered and tatty life. This night would be special.

"Ready, love?" A quiet nod, and then into the streets.

Later, after the tapas plates were cleared, after their meal and the last of the wine bottle had been emptied, Donal reached across the table to Gina's hand.

"You know we've tried this before, Gina. At least I have. Could never find the right words, or, more to it, the right nerve. Maybe now, then. What do you think?"

Gina needed nothing more in the way of clues. A radiant evening, and no call to spoil it with a false show of gallantry, or commitments that would look tawdry come the morning.

"I think we let the night speak for itself, Donal. There's no need for anything more. No need for words, or gestures, or promises that neither of us might honor." She raised her glass of port with the hand that Donal was not holding, then tilted her glass to the man across the table, his eyes wet with adoration.

"To us, Donal Mannion, in whatever form we take."

"Gina, there's more I want to tell you. To ask you."

"And there's more I want to hear. But not tonight, Donal. This is enough."

"Ah, Gina, the dreams I have. Be gentle with them, please. Those dreams are all I own now."

Gina said nothing in reply. She sipped her port, held the hand of the man near her, and smiled into his deep and moist eyes. When they finished, she rose first and pulled him after her. Hand in hand still, they made the walk back to their hotel room, the warmth of a summer's night cushioning the lovely, and irresistible, flow of chance, desire, and the things that were not there.

— ◆ —

Gina spun out of her bedroom and piroutted for her man, proud of the fine soft fabric that carried a bright summer print. "So, d'ya think this dress will do?"

It would be dinner tonight, then perhaps a stop at a pool hall downtown to shoot a few racks. If the mood were right, the two might even cap the evening at a jazz club that Gina knew, someplace smoky and dark, a basement where the blues wafted in the air like a thick mist and deep voices sang of hope, and lust, and loss.

"Lovely, Gina. As always." Donal sat back in the worn chair across from the bedroom and smiled. He liked the view. "But then," he continued, "you could be wearing a burlap sack and you'd look as lovely as an Easter sunrise."

"Enough of your lies," Gina replied in false protest. Pleased, she was, that her man saw her as such. She had reached a point in her life where she cherished illusions. Her earlier realities paled against all fantasy for the pain they had brought—the disappointments, the loneliness and abandonment, the tawdry and tattered ends of the best intentions frayed into nothing. Donal's illusions gave some level of comfort, even as she knew them to be wispy and spectral. Let him think her beautiful.

In a final check, Gina turned to the mirror in her small living room. The dress was perfect. What lay under it was not, though, and she saw every flaw, every line, every chunk of extra flesh. *Not always so*, she thought. *Once young men elbowed one another aside to dance with me, and to sneak a kiss. To grab my hand and not let go lest a competitor took his place. And Thomas, who cried the first time we made love, that night after our wedding, that night when the world spun around me at its center and every light, every prayer, found its way into my deepest soul. Once it was, and now I'm left with this.*

Gina's smile left her, the mirror extinguishing the playfulness of the moment. She turned again to Donal. "Am I really all that, Donal? At this stage of our lives, am I really what you want?"

Donal shifted in his chair and leaned forward. "What brought this on, Gina? Of course you are or I'd not be here with you."

"But I'm no runway model, man. And you know my moods."

"And you know mine. Christ Gina, you've put up with me longer than any woman should bear, and still you're here, looking radiant and young and alive. Why would I not want to be here?"

"Because I don't truly know what's real and what's false, Donal. At this point in my life, after the years and the loss, I fool myself sometimes. Perhaps your being here is just part of that foolery."

"Perhaps it is, Gina, but then if so we're both fools. We have each other, for whatever that may be worth."

"Will we always have that, Donal?"

"Who can speak for tomorrow, girl? We have tonight, of that I'm sure. And we'll not waste it on worry and anguish and dark wonders. There's time enough for that, Lord knows. But not tonight."

Gina Moretti turned back to the mirror and smoothed her dress. She tested a smile, and found it to be sincere. With a gentle step, she reached her man's chair, bent low, and kissed his cheek.

"I think I may be falling in love with you, Donal Mannion," she whispered softly.

For a second, Donal held her eyes and looked deep. He saw there what he had not seen for too long, a treasure too long lost.

"To it, then." Donal rose from his chair, gently took Gina's elbow and led her out the door into the night.

— ◆ —

Joey DiMarco's strong hand fell onto Donal's shoulder as he finished the paperwork for a shipment of women's shoes. The job was becoming boring, and more than a little taxing as his body tired from the incessant loading and unloading. Not the work for an aging and inherently lazy man.

But still there was Joey, who kept things moving and usually brought a smile with him. Donal marveled at the man's incipient joy, his acceptance of the obligations and demands that even the simplest life brought with it. Joey had softened the days.

"Almost done, Joey." Donal finished the review and initialed the form in front of him. "What are we doing next?"

"Nothing, Donal. At least not until we take a break. We work too hard, do you know that?"

"You do, Joey. I'm just along for the paycheck."

Joey laughed, and they sat down together on a wooden crate. "So you should take me out to dinner sometime, you know? A steak dinner, I think, with a couple of drinks before we eat. What do you think?"

"And why should I empty my pockets to do something like that? Don't we get enough of each other on the dock?"

"Ah, Donnie, you know why. Didn't I tell you that Gina was something special? She's happy as I've ever seen her. And I think you are, too. I'm of the mind that I might deserve some thanks for making this happen."

"A steak dinner might be extreme, Joey, but the next time we do a Friday night the drinks are on me. That's a promise."

"I'll count on it." He slapped Donal's shoulder one more. Then he turned serious. "Just don't hurt her, Donal. Please. I know you well enough to know that you can be an incredible fuck-up. Sometimes you just don't care enough about things. About your work, or even about yourself. Sometimes you're just a dick. But care about Gina. Please be good to her."

Donal faced his friend. "I've never met a woman quite like her, Joey. I'll be as good to her as I can be. That's a promise, too. I don't know how this will go, but I'll make it a gentle journey. As best I can."

"That's all we can do, Donal. All I can ask." The two of them stood silently, waiting for anything more. Nothing, then, no more words, then back to work.

— ◆ —

He was who he was. Donal could not deny that simple reality. His days with Gina soared, and on those days his heart felt light and breezy, unconcerned with the matters of a bruised conscience.

But there were days, too, when Donal lapsed back into a melancholy as much as part of him as the color of his eyes or the curve of his spine. Days when Gina was not available, when they did not talk, and when those days stringed together the melancholy deepened. On such days, anxiety welled up within him and he paced his small flat. When the walls grew too close, he would head into the streets, find a comfortable bar stool, and try to drink away the burning bits.

It was one such night that he sat alone in a new place, one that had opened near his local that begged a try. There were ferns, and window coverings that looked as if they came from France or Belgium. *Out of my league,* he thought, but the scotch would be same.

He sat at the bar and drank quietly, his thoughts roiling then, unavoidably, churning down corridors he would have chosen to ignore. He could not drink them away, and by the third glass he no longer tried.

"The acid in a man's soul is regret."

"What's that again?"

Donal turned to the body on the adjacent seat. "Talking to myself, I suppose. I said, 'The acid in a man's soul is regret.'"

The other man grunted. "How do you mean?"

"We live with all the things we did wrong or didn't do at all. They never leave us, and they burrow into our hearts, then dig their way out again. Regrets. They burn us away, don't you see, and leave a sorry, empty hollow where there should be flesh and laughter and joy."

"Sounds as if you have more regrets than the next man."

"I'll not bore you with them," and Donal turned back to the bar and hunched his shoulders protectively over his scotch. "But I'll wager that we each have our share. Acid, all of it."

The other shuffled in his seat, palpably uncomfortable with the older man next to him, the one with the stubble of beard and sad eyes that had seen God knows what. He rose with his glass and nodded at Donal. "Good luck with it all," then wandered to another part of the long bar.

"Ah, luck has nothing to do with it," mumbled Donal, then took a long sip of his drink. This night called for thought. Dreary and gray, the sidewalks wetted and slippery, people bustling along them heads down under umbrellas, and the already small slivers of connection obscured further by the anonymity of dark days. It was a night to sit inside and think about things.

If only . . . the two Goddamnedest words in the English language. If only. Donal drank again, finished the glass and gestured for another.

If only I had been a better husband. Annie's friends had taken to *calling her 'St. Annie' even after the first few weeks of our marriage. I didn't know how to be good. I saw it as a game, all of it. Marriage, family, a job. The game of respectability. A veneer, that's all it was. Nothing changed who I really was. Too much fun to be had to bother with a wife, even one as fine as Annie. She married down, and it cost her dearly.*

If only I had had a father to push me along when I was younger. Someone to show me another side of things, and to let me know what was right and what was just folly. If only I had had better friends growing up, and my mom had a better job and more money. If only I had lived someplace else. If only I ever had a job that I really wanted, one that I might have turned into a career rather than a simple paycheck. And if only I had spent what I earned on building myself for tomorrow instead of pleasing myself today.

If only I had met Gina earlier.

If only . . .

The next glass appeared, and Donal went right to it. Nothing to do this day but try to drink it away and hope that something better comes along the next day, or the day after that.

Ah, the acid of regret, he thought. He sipped again and looked over the bar at the television, tuned now to some football match. Wolverhampton vs. Leeds. He smiled to himself as he watched the play. *If only I had been an athlete.*

One last sip, the empty glass on the bar, and then the card to pay for it all. Donal rose. *Ah, but what matter? If only these things had not unraveled as they had. But no matter at all. I'd still be Donal Mannion. And nothing could ever change that. I'd still be at this bar tonight, chipping away the last of this wasted day.*

Once more then into the rain, and the slick and lonely sidewalks.

CHAPTER 10

A hard way to make a living, it was. Never knowing precisely where the next reward might be, never knowing who he could trust. Never even knowing what he'd be putting in his stomach at the close of the day, his hunger for food to be no less ignored than his other burning hungers. All of it a game, a gigantic challenge to define some sort of finish line and then to cross it. A hard way to live.

But it had its benefits, of that Matthew Cooney was convinced. He was no man's slave, answerable only to his own whims and fancies. Strong enough, at least for the moment, to be able to take what he wanted, if only in small bites, and clever enough to devise ways to get by off the efforts and labors of others. He slept where he wanted, took what he needed, and if a day came when he could no longer do so, he would fade into whatever oblivion waited at the end of the chase. His own terms, all of it, without compromise.

Matthew had grown a reputation. His time in jail had set him apart, although even now that time so long ago still brought him embarrassment. Not for the fact that he was convicted and jailed—no, not for that. Matthew's embarrassment lay in the foolishness of having been caught. He had been young when he thought to rob the small convenience store, and filled with hubris, the invincibility of youth. He had been snared before he could even leave the store. A five-star idiot move, and he had paid for it.

But he had also learned from it. Measure your steps and know where you're going before you begin. Plan the act, plan the escape, and leave no traces. Matthew Cooney had become a master at taking the things that fed him—money where he could find it, things to sell or pawn, food and drink—and vanish as quickly and silently as the morning mist. No traces, except the satisfaction behind his ready smile. He had become a legend of the mean streets.

Young men, new to it all, sought him out, and occasionally he would train them, taking them along for one escapade or another, a dead-of-the-night incursion into an empty house, rifling the pockets of someone who couldn't hold his liquor, the sleight-of-hand required to lighten a store, even under the watchful eyes of its owner. Matthew was a master, and apprentices flocked to him.

On a night in June young Andrew Gentry tagged along in Matthew's shadow. Said he was eighteen but might be only sixteen. Andrew did not share many of the details of his youth, which were best forgotten.

And on this night the master called his apprentice to the task. They stood outside a rowhouse three blocks from the green where they slept, the nesting place of those without a nest. A rowhouse Matthew had been observing for several days.

"So, here's the deal, Andy. Use this rod and slip the lock at the back door. I'll keep watch, but no one's going to come along. I believe there'll be an armoire near the hallway leading from the back entrance. Find it and take what's there. Simple enough, no?"

"But what if I wake them, Matty? What if someone hears?"

"There's no one to wake, boy. I've told you that. They're away, and no one's watching the place. It's as empty as your head. Now go do it."

"I don't think I can." His voice trembled as wildly as his hands. Even in the dark, Matthew saw the young man's eyes grow wide.

"Clear your mind of *can't*. There's money in that armoire, I'll wager, and probably quite a lot of it. Don't tell me you can't. Grow a pair, you stupid bastard, and get to it."

Andrew nodded once and took a step to the rear of the dark house. He turned to Matthew as he did so. "You'll be here all along, right, Matty?"

"I'll be here. Now step lightly and do the work."

Andrew disappeared around the corner of the house. *His first time,* thought Matthew. *He'll be fine.* And the master turned back to the street to await his apprentice, to await the envelope of bills he expected would be lifted from the armoire. All these people kept sums of money in their homes. Spending cash for them; lifeblood for the rest of us. It was time young Gentry learned the facts of the streets, and how to make his way through them.

Matthew of course would pocket most of whatever Andrew found. He'd pass the boy a few bills and praise him for his effort. Boost the boy's confidence and give him a leg up, that cost nothing.

In minutes Andrew rushed back to the street from the rear of the house, breathless and gleaming. "I got it, Matty. Just where you said it might be." He extended an envelope. "I didn't count it, but it looks to be a lot."

Matthew took the envelope and cuffed the lad's ear. "Well done, Andy boy, well done. Let's go divide this and enjoy the fruits of your labor. There's a bottle under my bench. We'll toast the beginning of a fine and long career, the apprenticeship of Andrew Gentry."

It had actually been quite easy, this first mark. So easy. With Matthew standing watch, he had slipped to the back door of the rowhouse, slipped the lock with the tool Matthew had provided, then slid down the back hallway to the sitting room, where, as Matthew had anticipated, a large armoire stood in one corner. Unlocked, of course, and filled with surprises. Had his nerves not been so tight, he might have rummaged a bit to see what he could find. But there was an envelope in the top drawer, again as Matthew had promised, and it was thick with bills. He grabbed and fled out the back.

Now, in the green parkland where he would spend this night, and several to follow, Andrew drank a heavy draught from the bottle that Matthew had handed him. The warm liquor— whatever it was, something brown and thick—burned its way down his throat and sought to calm his emotional kaleidoscope of nerves and adrenaline and euphoria.

"Well done," said Matthew, alternately sipping from his bottle and sorting the bills. "A grand haul, and enough to keep us well for quite a while."

"Beginner's luck," Andrew said with a smile. "And a proper teacher."

"Ah, enough of that. No need for false modesty, boy. My guess is that you're a natural. You'll do well."

Andrew drank again from the offered bottle. A burgeoning calm lifted up from his warming belly, and from the quiet night around him. Stars pocked a black sky, and the city lights painted a glow around its edges. No traffic this time of night, no people rushing by. Just the green of the park, the hint of a breeze, and the whisper of conscience.

"Ah, I'll do well, you say. Not a career I'd ever have anticipated. But I can see its advantages."

"So where did you expect you'd be, Andrew Gentry?" said Matthew, his grin sarcastic and his tone carrying hidden bitterness. "A fine young one like yourself."

"I wasn't going to tell you any of that."

"And I shouldn't be asking," said Matthew. "None of my concern."

But young Gentry, loosened now by the liquor and a strange satisfaction of accomplishment, kept on. "I come from a comfortable place," he said. "You wouldn't know that, of course. But my family was fairly well off. Dad was an attorney, and a good one, or so I heard. Alexandria, where I grew up. Good schools. Good food. Good friends."

"Like a Norman Rockwell painting."

"Something like that. Except behind the painting there was my father, with his bottle, and his women on the side, and his clenched fists that spared no one. Mom stayed and took it all. My brothers, too. I did for a time, but after a particularly bad knock one Saturday night I headed out. We had a piano in the sitting room. That night my father thought I'd be served by shoving my head into one of its corners. I figured I could live by my wits better than I could survive in that hellhole. A warm bed just wasn't worth the pain. That was two months ago."

"And here you are."

"Here I am," Andrew drank again. "And learning from the best."

"More to learn, always," grunted Matthew. "We're an unlikely duo. I'm twice your age, and never knew a warm day when I was young. Never counted on a meal, or a friend, or a happy word. And you come from what you call *comfort*. But where does that comfort really lie? It's out here, Andrew, without any complications from family, or the law, or that fanciful idea of what's right and what's wrong."

Matthew paused and took a long drink of his bottle. He emptied it, then stood to fling it as far as he could into the darkness. From under the bench he pulled another bottle and uncapped it.

"And now here's a toast to a new friendship. You'll have to tell me more about this family of yours," he said in a low voice. "Their habits. Their comings and goings. Where they keep things. And how to find them. We may well have more work to do together, young Andrew. So we drink now to a glorious future. All ahead of us, boy, and nothing of regret behind."

With time and practice, and with the confidence of fools, Andrew Gentry grew bolder in his exploits. His introduction to life on the streets had been exhilarating. Each day was his own, no teachers to bore him with drudgery, no father to flog him with belts or fists. The air itself seemed purer, cleaner, and drew into his lungs effortlessly. Freedom, and if the price for it was a dodgy pursuit of food and a place to sleep, then so be it. A man, even a young man with thin wings, needed to be himself, whatever that self might be.

It had been nothing less than miraculous that he had struck a friendship with Matthew Cooney, who was older, wiser, stronger and more clever. Cooney knew the cafes that might toss him some bread or a few pieces of fruit, and the stores that let him buy on the credit of an earnest smile. He knew the unlocked doors, the untended cars, and the loose women. Cooney was a master of this life, and he lived it well. He had taken Gentry under his wing, so to speak. An amazing stroke of luck it was that he found himself in the orbit of Matthew Cooney.

He taught him things, and Andrew was an eager student. Simple jobs at first—breaking into a home whose owners were away, taking small things that wouldn't at first be noticed, stealing the occasional untended purse or wallet. Matthew showed him how it was done, and Andrew did it. Sometimes, when the job was trickier and needed a lookout or a distraction, they might work together, apprentice and master.

On a night in early autumn Matthew stepped to the bench where Andrew regarded the setting sun of a glorious afternoon. With a smile he sat beside the younger man, then dangled a key.

Andrew glanced at Matthew, glanced at the key. "Unlocking something, are we, Matty? A key to your dreams perhaps."

"To both our dreams, young Andrew. Or at least our immediate pleasures. D'ya know what this is?"

"I'm sure you'll tell me."

"This key unlocks the back entrance to Doherty's Pub, the place over on Wyndham that caters to the high-minded set. The ones that spend three times as much as a drink is worth. A friend of mine lifted it from the afternoon manager. Clever move, that. He gave it to me. 'You'll know what to do with it, he said.' And I do."

"And what's that, Matty."

"Tonight, after the place is closed, in we go. I've been told that things inside are rather loose, and there's not much security. No alarm on the back door. Money left in tills, bottles left on shelves. We can take whatever we can find."

And so, in the wee hours of morning, well before sunrise, Matthew and Andrew snuck to Doherty's back entrance. Matthew inserted the key. Nothing happened.

"Damn, this thing is stuck."

"Try jiggling it."

"What the hell do you think I'm doing?" This went on for several minutes. At length Matthew told Andrew to watch the alleyway behind him.

"What are you going to do?"

"Sneeze," said Matthew.

"What?"

"Just sneeze. Fake a sneeze, a couple of sneezes, and do it loud."

As Andrew complied, Matthew's elbow shot up to the window above the door. It shattered in tandem with Andrew's phony explosions. Sloppy, and no alarm, just as he had been told.

Matthew reached around and unlocked the door. "In we go, boy. Now we're cooking with gas."

"What d'ya mean, Matty? We gonna cook something in the kitchen?"

"No, you idiot. Just something my mother used to say when things finally got set right. Usually when she got a new bottle of scotch. Let's see what we can find."

"What would we have done if there had been an alarm?"

"We would've run like hell. But there wasn't, so in we go."

So simple it could be, this life. Back to the park for a few hours of sleep, backpacks filled, consciences at rest, and a new day ahead. Andrew Gentry, free man, apprentice to the master, and lord of all he surveyed.

— ◆ —

Matthew Cooney stretched his full length on the bench and let the younger man's enthusiasms roll over him. He had rarely seen Andrew

Gentry so animated, so full of the false claim of hope that this life offered. But here he was, holding forth in a far corner of the square, away from all other eyes and ears, only Andrew and Matthew sharing this chance.

"I'm tellin' ya, Matty, he's the one we've been waiting for. The president of a bank, for God's sake. I've studied him all this while. Leaves the office every day at the same time, stops at The Lion's Tap for a pint, then heads back out right after darkness. I know his route home, and there's a narrow alley off H Street. You know H Street, with all those rich rowhouses? And everyone tucked inside them and no one paying attention. We wait in the alley and snag him as he walks by. He'll never know what hit him, and we'll have a bank president's wallet."

Matthew nodded slowly. He'd heard Andrew's ramblings before. The young man had nerve, he had to admit. "We're not thugs, Andrew. We take the things that opportunity offers, that people leave untended. We don't go about knocking heads like common thieves."

"But this is opportunity, Matty, don't you see? A rich man, careless in his manners, the top of the pyramid where we lay at the bottom. We owe it to ourselves. We can do this."

Matthew sighed. Andrew indeed had nerve, but he lacked direction. "I have a sense, boy, that you'd do this even without me. And I can't have that. I'll help you along with it," and Andrew's face broke into an even wider smile. "But," Matthew cautioned emphatically, "we do it gently."

They prepared that night with a shared pint of cheap whiskey, just for the nerves. Matthew needed it less than Andrew.

"Jesus, Andrew, calm down. You're like a cat in a room full of rocking chairs." Andrew just smiled, and the two made their way to the H Street alley.

At the right time, Andrew peered around the corner. "It's him," he whispered. "Coming down the street. Get ready," and when the lone figure passed the thin opening, four hands pulled him into the dank and dark lane. A quick knock from Matthew's club—hard enough to leave him senseless but carefully placed to do no lasting damage—and the victim lay sprawled at their feet. Andrew dove to his form and began rifling the man's pockets. Matthew stood watch.

"Get on with it, Andrew. What've you got?"

Andrew continued to search, pulling open the pockets of both trousers and topcoat. He had a wallet, but nothing was in it. Andrew sifted through it, then looked up at Matthew. "This isn't the guy."

Matthew turned sharply to the younger man. "What the hell do you mean this isn't the guy? You've been watching him for days, you said. How could you finger the wrong guy?"

"He's not the one. This guy's a bus driver, it looks like. At least he's got a license for it. And no cash or cards. Sorry, Matty."

Matthew reared back and gave Andrew a hard kick that knocked him over, then kicked him again. "You fuckin' idiot," he hissed. "Do you know what we risk when we do things like this? Do you know the chances we take?"

Andrew moaned, then rose to his haunches. "I know, Matty. I screwed up."

Matthew knelt down to try to put their victim back together again. He readjusted his trousers and coat, then took the wallet from Andrew and placed it back into his pocket. From his backpack he took a pencil and a scrap of paper to write, "Sorry, friend. A case of mistaken identity. Hope you're well with no damage."

When he was done, Matthew extended a hand to Andrew, then pulled him to his feet.

"Come on, you ignorant git. Let's go find something to eat."

As they moved furtively back into the early night, Andrew touched his sore ribs, the mark of an imperfect apprenticeship.

— ◆ —

Heat smothered the city, smothered those who lived in it, smothered the urge to move, and to think. An effort it was to rise and face the day, wrapped in the humidity and stench of an urban summer. Tempers ran short and were easily triggered. A brush of shoulders on the sidewalk might lead to an argument. Women fingered the edges of kitchen knives and fantasized about life without their husbands, and young men swaggered through the sweat and the tension, strutting as wannabe alpha males, their hormones fueled by the incessant press of time. Summer in the city.

Matthew Cooney, his life bound to these heat-forged streets, found it a fertile season. During the worst of the hot days, there was always someplace for him to go—a shelter or a hostel. Most would give a meal along with their cool space. The city was generous in that way. People stepped away. Those who could fled to the beaches, or the mountains out west, or even flew out of the country altogether. When they did so, windows were left open and doors remained unlocked. A fertile season indeed for Matthew, who welcomed the heat.

On one of the August nights, so heavy that traffic did not move and dogs did not bark, Matthew sat on his usual bench in Farragut Square. He wore ripped jeans, too stifling, and an old sleeveless shirt. Others in the square had discarded their tops altogether, including Old Jenny, an institution who had been living this life for God knows how long. In her sixties, or maybe just well-worn forties. Harmless, and more than a little crazy, and now on this summer night she took off her own top and rolled in the dry grass. No one paid any mind. Her anatomy differed little from most of the others who likewise were shirtless.

Andrew Gentry and sat next to him on the bench. Matthew took some pride in the boy, though he could be a pest. There were times when Matthew shooed him off. A man needs space, especially a man like Matthew Cooney, who often converted that space into reward.

"How was your day, Matty? Get anything done?"

"Not a damn thing, Andy. A few hours at the shelter. You know, they'll let you take a quick shower there, the one over on 18th Street? Felt fine to wash off, if only for a minute. A sad day when that's the highlight of it."

"Ah, but now it's nighttime, Matty. What can we make of it?"

Matthew chuckled, then turned to look off toward the street. No one was out tonight, and the sidewalks were empty. Too hot to move. "We make of it what we will, friend. Like every other night."

"I saw a place a few streets over, Matty. People heading out with suitcases, and a rear door in the shade and shadows of trees. What do you think?"

Matthew sat back on his bench and sighed. "What do I think?" All the years of this had turned him into an older man, one who's traded youth and strength for the flimsy notion of freedom. A spirit unlicensed, unbound by convention, and answerable only to what passed for his own conscience.

"What do I think?"

Every night the same, differing only with the nuances of the passing seasons and the changing faces around him, different in the particulars, but bound by the same deadening routines of desperation, and loss, and fanciful schemes that had no chance of succeeding.

"What do I think?" I think a man might shine brightly like a passing comet, then burn himself out as he disintegrates into an atmosphere that destroys him.

"Come on! What do I think?" At last Matthew turned back to Andrew.

"Andy, I think I don't want to do this tonight. Maybe not for a few nights."

He rose from the bench, then turned back to the younger man. "Come on. Let's see if we can find some new faces to share the time with. Maybe some girls if we're lucky."

Andrew looked up at him, puzzled. "New faces?"

"Yeah. We all look alike out here, don't you know? We'll all look alike forever."

Matthew turned toward the empty streets that he would walk that night, breathing the heat.

Heat gave wave to the chill of autumn, then the frosts of winter. Andrew Gentry did not consider the change of the seasons. The city remained the same through all weathers. For Andrew, it was a city of opportunity, a city filled with targets. There were those so careless that they almost begged to be taken. The unlocked doors, and the open purses, and the windows left ajar. Too easy, and not to be ignored, challenges his young ego could not resist.

These were the ones who wore their good fortune. They drove the best cars, lived in the finest houses, wore clothes that glittered. These were the ones that drew Andrew's imagination. He had no refined sense of social order, no notion of economic inequality or unfair income distribution except as it pertained to his own circumstances. He wanted what he did not have, and those that had these things became prey.

Younger and stronger than most, even if less clever, Andrew made his way through these new targets. He found ways to break into houses, entering through basement windows that were usually fragile enough to jimmy and never had an alarm attached to them. He became quick enough with his hands to snatch a purse then disappear into an alleyway or down a flight of steps before the owner had a chance to react. Usually he saved his work for the early evening, that time of day when there is light to see his work, but not so much that it isn't obscured.

Once or twice he mistimed his tasks and was interrupted by a homeowner or a woman whose purse he could not grab quickly enough to prevent her from fighting back. Unfortunate for Andrew, who had to improvise, and more so for those who did not play along. The young man would not hesitate to thrash anyone who came across his work, men and women alike. A homeowner coming down the stairs to investigate strange noises in his basement might end up bloody and unconscious in a far corner, and a woman protecting her purse could find herself thrown roughly to the ground and kicked into silence.

In the back of his thoughts, Andrew knew that there were risks to all this. But he had no power to resist the lure of what lay just beyond his grasp. He did his work as carefully as he could, thought of all angles and variables, then pounced.

Matthew had taught him the craftsmanship of survival, for which Andrew would be forever grateful, but now it was his turn to refine it, to launch it to new heights, and new rewards. Besides, Matthew was too passive, too ready to let things come his way and appear rather than chasing them down. For Matthew the hunt had little thrill. For Andrew Gentry, the hunt became everything.

Andrew pampered himself after his successes. He bought the best liquor, ate regularly, and on occasion would take a hotel room for a few nights to get away from the worst heat or the worst cold, or just to feel something different. Andrew had found his place, and with it something at which he excelled. He grew in his own mind, and he perceived that the others had begun to look at him with respect and even admiration.

With a new swagger, Andrew Gentry felt himself at last.

Matthew Cooney pulled his coat closer and drew deeply from the bottle he kept even closer than his coat on these cold mornings. Stark winter wind shot in from the ocean, bringing with it the bitterness of newly frozen streets, darkness and another chapter in a book nearing its end.

On such a morning Matthew huddled close on the bench. Tonight he might find a shelter. There he would present himself as a meek, stricken homeless soul, just to gain entry. He found it humbling, this effort to absorb the comforts offered by the collective guilty conscience of a community that would not so much as look at him on the normal days. There would be a hot meal and a warm cot, but it would not be Matthew Cooney who consumed them. Rather, it would be a shortened version of the man, his energy and aggression abridged by the need to increase his chances for survival. He hated these nights, even if they were necessary to keep him whole.

Matthew would have to contend again with the problems that came with the cold. People nesting inside warm homes, leaving them too rarely to create easy targets for his quick and silent thievery. Overcoats that covered wallets and purses in new, thick layers. Benches that froze at night and left their marks striped across his back as he rose from them. A darkness that lasted too long, even for one who sought the night as coverage for the core of his living. And, worst of all, the tired, dreary strain of waiting for the warmth, days and weeks and months away, when he might again feel blood in his veins and purpose in his heart.

The square this morning showed little life. A few of the respectable people rushed to their jobs and buses, largely empty, belched their way down the numbered streets. Andrew Gentry appeared from God knows where and stood before Matthew's bench, flapping his arms like a penguin to warm himself.

Matthew looked up at him without expression. Andrew had continued to attach himself to Matthew like a remora to a shark. At first exhilarated by the adoration, Matthew had grown to find it annoying.

"A sip of that bottle, Matty? It would do me good."

Matthew sighed and handed it up to the younger man. "A sip, just one, and then off with you. I've no mind for company this morning, Andrew."

Andrew took a long swallow and passed the bottle back to Matthew. "Ah, Matt, I thought we might scout around for something we might tackle together. Not many people around. Should be some easy marks."

Matthew stood and faced him, almost nose to nose. "Like the

bank president we cuffed? The one who turned out to be a bus driver, as poor and as pitiful as we are? Or like the bakery where one of us dropped the payroll packet as we left the premises and came away with nothing more than a couple of cinnamon rolls? Those types of easy marks?"

Andrew stepped back. "Jesus, Matty, anyone can make a mistake. We've done some good things, too."

"And most of those good things I did on my own, with you lapping behind me like a lost puppy. Step away, boy. I want no part of your incompetence today, or maybe ever."

Andrew turned to walk away, and mumbled, "Jesus, Matty. What's gotten into you?"

Matthew sat, paused, then sighed. He shook his head, then gestured to the younger man to come back. "Sorry, Andrew. Winter. It makes me mean." He reached into his pocket again for the bottle, and held it up, the best penance he could offer. "Here. Warm yourself."

And the day's light, dim to begin, grew dimmer as the wind blew new clouds. A soft rain began to fall, and the two men huddled against one another on a city bench, orphans lost in winter.

— ◆ —

He had grown older, this he knew. Matthew Cooney felt new aches and heard his bones and sinews make new sounds. Inevitable, even though he had never considered the possibility. He had never looked too far into his future. For too long it had been enough merely to make it through the current day and find a new one on the other side of the night. Those days had strung together to bring him into his forties. He had never really expected to make it this far.

But the privileges of age accrued even in his hardened life. The younger Cooney was more brutal, more ready to use his fists at any provocation. He realized now that he did so more out of fear than aggression. He had come to the streets from two years in jail, a time that buried his soul behind bars and thick concrete. While there he fought often, throwing himself against the aggressions and advances of others, young and strong enough to fight them off enough to claim his own space. He kept to himself once it became clear that he was no easy mark.

Those fears never left him. And there was much to fear, both within those walls and out on the streets that became his home. He feared the approach of those he did not know. He feared that the little he had was viewed by others as an open market. He feared touch, and talk. He feared that each day might end in pain, and that each night might be his last. And so in the beginning he established himself as he had in jail—distant, relatively silent, and not to be trifled with.

Through the unmeasured time he learned regret. Something in Matthew allowed him to climb over the walls he had built around himself to see others more clearly. Perhaps it had started with Johnny Duncan's Christmas Eve kindness those years ago. Perhaps something instinctively translated a young boy's trauma into the eyes of those he had victimized. And now, years on, he regretted every blow he had ever delivered that was not made in defense. He regretted everything he took from anyone who might have needed it just as badly. He regretted the liberties he took with the truth when he told himself why he did it all—the thefts and the beatings and the deceit. *To survive*, he told himself. *I don't have the luxury of caring about anything beyond that.*

A young man sees the world differently than an old man. Matthew was not old in societal terms, but on the streets he had lived a dozen lifetimes. He felt pains more sharply, and regret more deeply. Survival it was, but in a new way, something a young man could not understand, and would not understand unless he took the time and thought to regard himself without obfuscation or illusion. Better to take what comes, to be a gatherer rather than a hunter. The other way, the way he had lived for too long, drained the soul of what little humanity it still had.

In the strange hierarchy that governed these ungovernable spaces, Matthew was recognized as someone to be respected. He had strength, but more, he had wisdom. Andrew Gentry was not the only younger man who gravitated to Matthew, who sought his approval and, in the best of times, sought to join him on his escapades. There was much to learn from the street sage.

Andrew continued to occupy most of Matthew's attention, the closest someone could be to an understudy. Despite his swagger, and Matthew's many admonishments, the young man acted impulsively, and Matthew knew that impulse on the streets led to the unpredictable. And Matthew knew that unpredictability led to mistakes, to exposure, and perhaps worse. Matthew had indulged him, and they had been lucky, so far. Matthew had no faith in luck, and he knew good fortune to be merely the product of anticipation and preparation.

Andrew lacked wisdom, was rash, arrogant and unpredictable, and had never really taken things to heart. He remained essentially as Matthew had found him, perhaps even more callow than before. A sad conclusion; Andrew Gentry was most likely irredeemable.

— ◆ —

In the dark part of the city that Matthew Cooney made his own, the winter sun made a grudging appearance. The dead days of January, so bleak that the sky itself came to life reluctantly. Better to lay low in covered warmth and leave the fallow time alone.

Matthew's warmth came from a thick coat lent unknowingly by one of the neighborhood's better positioned citizens, lifted quickly from an entryway closet inside a door too poorly locked. With the coat came a pair of boots that turned out to be so small as to be uncomfortable, and which Matthew eventually left in the square for some other soul to claim. It was the way things worked. Between the coat and his backpack, which doubled as a rather lumpy pillow, Matthew could navigate a decent night's sleep on even the coldest nights.

Andrew had found Matthew on a bleak mid-morning. "How are ya, Matty?" the younger man perked. "How was the night?"

"Not sure where you were, Andrew, but my night was cold as hell."

"Yeah, of course. Mine was cold, too. I found a heat grate, though. Had to fight off a couple of others for the space, but that's where I spent the night."

"And these others you fought off, where did they go?"

"Don't know, Matty, and don't care. They're able to fend for themselves."

"You know, Andrew, I've yet to see a grate that couldn't accommodate a few at a time. That heat radiates. I presume you kept it all to yourself, warming up that ass of yours while others shuffled off to God knows where. Tell me, how did you fight them off? A few strategic whacks, fist to fist, or did you pull a knife?"

Andrew shifted uncomfortably. "I did what I had to do, Matty. To claim what was mine. You'd have done the same, I'll bet."

"And you'd lose the wager. Jesus, Andrew, this isn't a game of King of the Hill out here. We share what we can, when we can, unless there's no other alternative. You had an alternative last night. Another lesson for you, Andrew. And once again, you failed it."

"Ah, Matty, don't tell me that. I'm just trying to get along, like all of us. Like you."

"No, not like me. How many more chances are you going to take, Andrew? How many more screw-ups until something goes really wrong and you end up in prison, or dead? How many careless things will you do that cause other people who are already suffering more grief than they merit? Jesus, Gentry, you don't know how little you know, and that makes you dangerous. Stay away from me. If you see me on the street or in the square, walk away. It's hard enough to make a go of it out here without having to watch the follies of Andrew Gentry, the boy beyond all learning."

Andrew rose, looked down at his shoes, then turned away. After a few steps he turned back to Matthew with a sneer, and for the first time, showed his anger. "You do this to me, Matty, and you may yet regret what comes of it. Old man, you are. And old men fade away for younger men to do the things the old men can't do any more. Think about that, old man." He trudged off to the far side of the square.

Matthew leaned back on the bench. "Better done with it. It's the foolish young men who squander that youth, and never learn enough to grow older." The morning wind picked up in sharp needles. Matthew pulled his coat tightly around him then wandered off to find something to eat. And as he walked onto the cold morning streets, Matthew thought back across the years, back to when he was Andrew Gentry.

— ◆ —

When he was new to it, Matthew Cooney had learned as he went along. He learned that in summer the streets are kind, or kind enough to make a day of it without too much discomfort. There was grass upon which to sit, and most days too much sunshine, the beating down of heat that leathers the skin and turns a man's energy into tiny puddles of sweat. People tended to be easier, in better moods and not so ready to walk on by. Summer days were fine enough for this type of life.

But it was the nights that imbued their true worth. There were shelters throughout the city, but on clear and warm summer nights, why accept surrounding walls when one could sleep on the fresh grass and breathe air as free as ever intended. Matthew relished his summer nights in the square, the banter with friend or stranger, and sleeping away the day's frustrations.

Winter, though, ah, the winter days of river-fed winds and breath so hard that it might seem to freeze mid-air. Winter, when the city burrowed inside itself, heads nestled in cloaks and scarves, hands shoved deep into pockets, and every door locked and closed. Shelters filled and heads turned away. Survive the winter and find spring on the other side, that was all one could do.

On a January evening years ago Matthew unwrapped himself from the tatty blanket he carried with him and stretched himself along the bench where he spent his afternoon. He had found a rare space the night before. The drug store on M Street had a recessed doorway and a small heat vent above it. An old man he did not know occupied it when Matthew came to it in early evening. The old fella sat on a fold of soiled cardboard and had a smell about him. Matthew rarely noticed the odors of transients like himself. After a time, one became immune to the fetid blend of alcohol, stale food, bad breath, and human waste.

The old man looked up at Matthew and shuffled back on his cardboard. Matthew bent to him. "This is my space, Dad. Find another."

"I don't see no name on it. You're the one to move along."

"That's where you're wrong, Dad." Matthew pointed to the drug store name on the entry door. "Reade's Drugs," Cooney said. "And I'm Reade."

The old man scoffed and spat a green wad on the sidewalk near Matthew's feet. "Like hell. This place is mine, ya smug bastard."

Matthew smiled then drew back to his full height. He knew what would come next. It was not a fair fight, not at all. The old man went flying into the sidewalk. Matthew picked up the cardboard and the small bindle that the old man had placed next to it and tossed them to the form now sprawled on the cold cement. "You'll be needing these," he said.

The man looked back at Matthew. His eyes blurred, caught between anger and tears of frustration, loss, and despair. Matthew noted the small bead at one eye's corner. He went to the man and offered his hand. "Get up, Dad. There's probably room at the shelter over on DeSales. And even if there's not, they'll take you in. Deference to age, and all that. The shelter's where you belong anyway. Not out here in this cold, snuffling through the snow like an Arctic fox." He pulled the man to his feet.

The other said nothing, gathering the cardboard and bindle that constituted the end of his world, the last definition of his humanity, then, without a glance, shuffled down the cold street in the direction of the DeSales shelter. It was all an old man could do.

Matthew settled into his newly won space. *Is that me, thirty years on? Where the hell am I now?*

But the space was warm enough, and the blanket did the job against the cold. Here he would spend the night to no one's notice. And no one ever noticed Matthew Cooney, unless he wanted them to.

Now, twenty years on from that cold night, Matthew nurtured the lesson of the memory. Regret and shame still burned after all this time. He saw them all. The old man on the grate, Scotty Kyle reclaiming with a fist what Matthew had stolen, the old man he had beaten up in a McDonald's restroom to steal the small fortune that the other himself had found. He had become that old man, the one to be bullied if a younger man could, the one who had to fight now to retain his perch.

From across the square, Andrew Gentry stood and stared at him as he walked to the streets. Matthew did not know it and would not care if he had. But Andrew burned with the passion of a young man blinded by the glow of ambition unsoftened by the weight of wisdom.

— ◆ —

The fog of early morning lifted more quickly than the fog of the preceding night. That fog, the one that came through a needle and flushed the veins with liquid heat, the night fog that would take longer to dissipate. Andrew Gentry regarded the wonder of a gray and misty morning within the context of his own gray and misty body. His bones had turned to gelatin, and for the first time since his last fix, the edge had left him.

He relaxed into the corner of the small tent he had set up in the far reaches of Farragut Square, beyond the places where anyone would take notice. The night before a man he knew only as Truck had set him up a nickel bag. Truck had no more substance than the morning fog. He wisped into and out of the streets with a sly transparency, visible only to those who needed him. He seemed to have a hidden sense of when to appear and what to offer, a unique talent that Andrew found most welcome. Last night, Truck had appeared, agitated at the mouth of an alleyway near the square, almost miraculously. Andrew had the money, and he had the need.

Andrew had tried the softer drugs, found some peace in weed and the occasional pill. Here was a chance to do something different. He was not afraid of it.

Now, several months on, he sought out Truck on those nights when his body quivered and trembled, when his mind raced to the plateaus of panic, and when it seemed that all that could ever matter was ending the pain for a bit, finding a place to float, so that when he came down he could make it a while longer.

That corner of the square, the place where Andrew pitched his small tent, was where they all came, those who needed Truck. On this foggy morning Andrew stretched out and watched the wafting, shapeless forms of the misted sky. As he lay there, an older man, one Andrew knew on sight and who often shared this space, stumbled down next to him.

"Hell of a morning, isn't it, man?"

Andrew grunted in reply, unable to think of a cogent response.

"All the mornings are like this after the right hit. Don't you think?"

Andrew looked up at him. His eyes blinked in the morning light, and he noticed a thin coating of dew lining his forehead. "Just another day," he mumbled.

The older man cackled a broken laugh. "Right, boy. Quite right. Just another day in Paradise. Here, in the Junkies' Grotto." He cackled again, then got up to wander to another part of the square.

Andrew rose at last, then folded his tent as his head cleared into a dull throb. *This is why I do what I do,* he reasoned. This was why he stole and thieved and bullied. For these days. For the paradise of this forlorn and lonely grotto.

— ◆ —

Matthew Cooney blew into his hands, then wrapped them around the mug of coffee that sat before him. James Barry occupied the seat across the table and sipped his tea. Cold enough to call for the warmth of hot liquid and the rush of caffeine.

Other than the two of them, the shop was empty. Apparently, few felt the need to venture out on a bitter December morning. Matthew and James had little choice, though. They had spent the preceding night in one of the city shelters, scratching some sleep under tatty, worn blankets and flipping about to find some position of comfort on too-hard cots. But it was warm enough there, and the others who had stumbled in for the night remained quiet. Morning came, and it was back to the streets.

Matthew and James sought shelter in the small coffee shop that sat near the corner of their square. The servers passed no judgment on their clientele. This was a safe space, and on this cold morning, it was a safe space that served what they needed.

"D'ya think we might head over to Georgetown today, Matty? I think I'd like to. Change of scenery, and all that, and maybe a bit of luck there."

Matthew smiled across the table. James came as close as Matthew might claim to being a friend. Of similar years, of similar experiences, and James placed on him neither demands nor threats. Two old fools stumbling to a vague finish line that neither could define, but that neither feared.

"I think I'll stay around here, James. I seem to be losing my hunger for new faces."

"Ah, the same, Matty, the same. It's just that a man has to do something to break up his days, you know? Otherwise he can fall into a rut." James gave a low and throaty chuckle. If there was anything that defined their hardscrabble existence, it was the sameness of their days. Some ruts ran too deeply, and they both knew it.

They sat in silence and sipped their drinks. People on the sidewalks outside bundled by with heads down and their hands in pockets. Wispy clouds floated upward as they exhaled into the cold.

Matthew was about to go back to the counter to beg a day-old bagel when the shop's door flew open and a man Matthew knew by sight but not by name dashed in, breathless and flushed. He ran to Matthew, grabbed his elbow and panted to catch his breath.

"Cooney. You got to come with me. Come on. Now, you gotta come."

James Barry rose to where they stood. "What is it now, Frankie?" He knew this man. Another one from the streets.

"Can't say, can't say. But you have to see this. Follow me."

Matthew nodded to James. With that, the three went into the cold. Down the block and around a corner to a narrow alleyway, and then to the dumpster in back of the restaurant that catered to the weekday downtown business clientele.

Frankie pointed, then turned his head away. Matthew went to the edge of the dumpster and leaned over the rim.

There, amid the discarded food and the squalling of the rats that sought it, the lifeless eyes of another young man of the streets stared up at him. Blood congealed around a wound in his stomach, soaking his shirt and exciting the gnashing rodents.

Matthew recoiled, then caught his composure and turned to the others. "What is it, Matty?" whispered James Barry.

"One of us, James. One of us for whom it ended badly."

James stepped back. Frankie stayed to the side, his hand over his eyes. "What do we do?"

"We leave him here, James. We're not the ones to deal with it. He'll be found soon enough, and then the right people will take over. He'll find a pauper's grave."

"Did you recognize him, Matty?"

"I didn't look too closely, James. Nor did I ask for identification. But I recognize him. I've seen him. Here, on these streets. With us. And I reckon I'll see him again." He turned back to them.

"Come along, both of you. There's nothing for us here. I'll at least buy you both another coffee."

CHAPTER 11

"We're just floating along, you know. Like two butterflies flitting together from flower to flower." Gina Moretti turned in the chair that sat next to the window overlooking the garden across the way. She sipped her wine.

"What's that, Gina?"

"It's true, Donal. We dance along and fly about looking for the good times. We're ornaments to each other. Nothing more."

"Ah, Christ, Gina," but really what more was there to say? Donal rose from his own chair across the room and walked to the window. He regarded the view of the garden. A lowering sun darkened the gentle hues of the flowers that grew there—hydrangeas and fuchsia and bold, exploding peonies. It was a gentle season, this time of year when the wild things grew and blossomed.

"And, you know, one of the things about butterflies is that they tend to dance around the edge of things. They may dive into a flower's belly from time to time, but mostly they just float and flit and fly, rarely landing and never leaving a mark."

"I believe you've left a mark on me, Gina. Some would see it as a very deep one."

"Ah, but have I, Donal? Here we are again, and nothing different than on the first days. We talk, and we eat, and drink our wine, then go to bed. We'll find a pub, or a concert. We look for the good times, but do we ever really look at each other?"

"You're sounding bored, Gina." Donal paused to take a deep sip of his wine. The silky warmth of his swallow cut through him and eased his thoughts. *No need to flail at this. Heard it before.*

"Not bored, Donal. Jesus, there's nothing boring about you. I never know when you'll call me to ask for a favor, or to propose a wild trip that we'd never take, or, as I might remind you, once to ask me for rent money."

"That was all a mistake, Gina. Christ, we've been over all this."

"Yes, Donal, and never boring. But when are the butterflies going to land somewhere? That I'd like to know. We can't keep just flitting about, with no end to it."

"And why does there have to be an end? Why do we need a goal? Isn't it enough just to *be,* just to know that we have a safe space with one another? "

"Donal, you've lived your whole life in a drift, at least as long as I've known you. You get by, nurse a pint or a glass, have a good meal and a toss with your lady, and you think that you've all you'll ever want. But what does all that amount to, Donal? It's running a soft pace, to be sure, but you're running in one place.

"So no, Donal," she continued. "Not boring at all. But stagnant. Very stagnant, and soon to grow altogether stale."

Donal walked to the back of Gina's chair and placed his hands on her shoulders. He leaned over to kiss her neck. "What you say is no doubt true, Miss Gina. And I'll work on it, that I promise. I'll work on bringing Donal Mannion back to life, and with it offer a bit of new spark to the lovely Gina. But tonight I don't want to think about any of that." He kissed her again.

Gina felt the kiss, savored the pressure of his hands on her always tired shoulders, and sighed in a usual resignation. If she herself had the courage, was not herself a butterfly, she would have risen from her chair and left, walked back to her own place or called a girlfriend to meet her across town.

Instead, she leaned back into the chair, into Donal Mannion's strong hands, and counted in her mind how the rest of the evening would play out. It would not be unpleasant, nor would it necessarily be boring, merely the flight of two butterflies, weightless, to the nearest, cleanest flower.

— ◆ —

Gina shut the clasp on her carry-on bag, a scarf no longer needed in the warmth of the bar tucked next to a gathering of cosmetics and the book she'd read on the flight south. She fluffed her collar, now free of the scarf or any covering, and smiled back across the table. On the other side, Donal Mannion sipped his scotch.

"You're bent on going, then?" he asked. "No way I can talk you out of it?"

"No choice, my love. We've been over it too much already."

"Your ma's eighty-seven, Gina. What are you really hoping to accomplish?"

"Yes, and I want her to see eighty-eight. Company and care, and all those things that become more precious as we grow older."

"But she's been on her own forever, Gina. Ever since the old fella passed, what, twenty-five years ago. She's got her jigsaw puzzles, and her television, and her cats. She can walk and drink and cook. Christ, Gina, she won't starve, and she won't be spending her days any differently than how she's been."

"Except I'll be there. In case something happens."

"Except you'll be there," Donal sighed again. "And I'll be here. And no telling for how long."

"It's got to be done, Donal. We'll talk, and send each other silly messages, and maybe even text each other naughty pictures. Time will pass. It all will pass." Gina turned to gaze out the wide windows of the bar. In an hour or so a plane would bear her in presumed sterility fifteen hundred miles away in a gesture of daughterly obligation that she could not allow herself to doubt.

Gina sipped the last of her wine, gathered her things, and pushed back the chair from the wooden table. Donal already had the check. One last sip of the scotch, and a quick suck of the dwindling ice cube that floated on it. *Courage, Donal. Courage, lad.*

"Gina, I need to ask you something before you go."

Standing now, Gina looked to the door, then distractedly back to Donal. "My cab is waiting, Donal. What is it?"

Donal hesitated then stammered, "You know, I've never met anyone like you. What we've had . . . what we have."

"Jesus, he's honking for me. I've got to go Donal." She leaned forward to grant a quick peck on his cheek, placed her mask back in place. "I'll text you tonight," she said over a shoulder disappearing out the door, into the cab, and then away.

Donal Mannion sat. No rush now. No need for courage. He summoned the server.

"Another scotch. A double if you can."

Donal reached into his wallet and took out the picture he carried of Gina and him taken last winter in front of a Christmas tree, taken before the smothering cloud of viruses and masks and restrictions wafted down onto them all. He placed the picture on the table. *The before time,* he thought. *Will there ever be an after?*

He drank the scotch slowly then ordered another. By the time he left the bar, Gina's plane would have landed. He searched his phone for a text, but no message had been sent. Donal Mannion walked back to his flat, staggered, through the detritus that grew deeper each day.

Three weeks later Gina returned, and both discovered that the rhythm they had played to before her departure remained intact. They spent their time well in the usual ways, and through it Donal perceived to rift in the subtle symbiosis he had grown into with his lover.

— ◆ —

A mountain morning, so crisp and bright that the air itself seemed to crackle with every breath and the blue of the sky burrowed behind the eyes to settle into one's thoughts and calm them. Such a morning it was, after days of rain. Donal Mannion opened the door to his cabin, stepped to the narrow porch, filled his lungs and looked through the trees to the mountain ahead.

"Gina," he called over his shoulder. "Come see this. It's a morning that God himself has been holding in reserve."

Behind him, still in bed, Gina stretched one last time and tossed the covers to the side. Over a cold floor that sent a chill through her feet and up her legs, she came up behind Donal and wrapped an arm around his waist.

"Gorgeous. Purely gorgeous. And what does such a morning say about the day ahead, Mr. Mannion? What shall we do with all this beauty?"

Donal turned to her and cupped her face. "We need do nothing with it except to live it, girl. We're here, and we're breathing this air. The rest will take care of itself."

They had come here, these two, to save it all. Two months before, Gina had headed home to her mother, claiming that her mother's heart condition had suddenly worsened and that her time might be limited. But it was not her mother's health that had worsened. Gina and Donal had fallen into a torpor that paralyzed their hearts, a disease all its own and one without a ready cure. Gina felt that, if anyone's time was drawing short, it was theirs.

Donal for his part sensed it, too. His response was both desperate and drastic. On the day Gina took her plane south to her mother, he had thought to ask her if she'd ever consider marriage. Not a proposal, to be sure, but a testing of the notion. *What could be the loss?* he had reasoned. He wanted her to think about it, to think about putting the pieces back in order, rearranging the dysfunction into the regularity of shared expenses, shared responsibilities, shared challenges, and an energy that had somehow been lost. Stitch the disparate parts together with a piece of paper and a judge's words, then see what happens. Think about it, that was all.

But Gina hurried off to a waiting cab before Donal could summon the spirit to make the ask. Just as well, he considered in retrospect. She would probably have said no. Or worse, she might have just laughed him off.

No, better this way. Wait for her to come back and feel the vacuum when she was gone, then hope she felt it, too. They had been together off and on long enough to grow into each other, at least in part. Passion might fade and lust grow cold, but their love itself was mutable, an energy that flowed and ebbed and changed itself as necessary to meet the needs of its hosts.

When she returned, Donal looked at her as he once did, the girl new and fresh, the one to be courted. When he suggested a getaway to the west, a week away in the Blue Ridge, Gina had not turned him down. A marriage proposal it wasn't, to be sure. *Small steps,* thought Donal. *See what the days bring.*

Donal kissed her softly in that morning's soft and bright air. Gina leaned into him and returned the kiss. "Feed me," she said. "And let's find something to do. I don't want to waste a day of this."

Donal Mannion looked once again to the mountain ahead, brilliant in the morning sunlight. "To the day ahead," he whispered, then walked back inside in small and measured steps.

She steadied him, this he knew. His rough edges smoothed into softer curves, although they did not lose their flaws. He drank, but drank less. He eyed the curves and lines of other women, but he did not act upon the urges they sparked. He did not commit to finding new work, something better for himself, but he no longer let the nothingness of his work eat away his pleasures. At the end of these days, there would be Gina, and so the days were worth spending.

What did not return immediately was his courage, and the question he had nearly asked before Gina's departure remained unsaid, until at last circumstances compelled Donal finally to take his chance.

"I've something to tell you, Gina."

Donal took a sip of his scotch, the pathway to his courage and the herald of his greatest mistakes. It was wine that soothed his soul, and scotch that fired it. This had always been so, from the days of his first taste of each, a thirteen-year-old boy running the streets with his equally wild friends. He had formed a quick and lasting relationship with both, wine his confidant and scotch the instigator of mischief, of boldness, and, in the end, of honesty. Tonight was a night for the scotch.

Gina sat back in her chair and held her own glass. The banter of the evening had been tense from the start, none of the easygoing banter between lovers accustomed to the other's moods and rhythms. Gina had prepared a simple dinner of salmon and rice, most of which Donal had uncharacteristically left on his plate.

"Something to tell me? I can only imagine."

"Ah, Gina." Donal took one last sip, then leaned forward. "It's hard enough to put it out there without your darts. Please just listen."

Gina said nothing through a thin smile, then sat back in her chair, cradling the wine glass.

"Okay then, here it is. You know we've made something of a path together these past months. I've tried to tell you how I feel, tried to crawl inside that locked vault that passes for your heart. I still don't know what's in there, to be sure. But I'll tell you what's in mine."

He continued through another small sip. "You know me for who I am. All the flaws, all the tempers. All the losses. You're perhaps the first woman I've ever known who's seen me away from any romanticism or idealization. Not that there's ever been much to idealize. So I know to you I'm no ideal, and God knows I'm no Adonis."

Gina held up a hand. "Wait, Donal. Just wait. I don't want this to go any further," but Donal plunged on.

"You recall that afternoon when I took you to the airport when you flew home for your mother's illness. I was trying to bark out these things then, but the time ran out and I lost the nerve. Same things on my mind today, and in my heart."

"And I don't want to hear them, Donal. Damn it, man. I've told you from the start that commitment leads to tragedy. We have no need to punish ourselves beyond what we've already suffered. So stop it, and let's carry on as we are. There's enough in that for both of us, I think."

"Ah, Gina. I know all that. But this is you and me. And next month the lease on my flat runs out and I was hoping maybe I could join you here, a place for the two of us."

Gina sipped the last of her wine, then flung the glass into a far wall. The tinkling of shattered glass reverberated for several seconds. If this were not her own apartment, she would have headed for the door. Instead, she turned to her man.

"So what's in your heart is rental space, is it, Donal? Perhaps a place where you can lay your head and ride your lover after she cooks you her meals and pays for the very place you claim as your own. Damn your ass, Donal Mannion. You've just put the blessing to all my thoughts. And all my fears."

Donal sat back in his chair shyly. "It was just a thought, Gina. Just a notion. Might do us both some good."

Gina sat back, quietly brooding.

"Christ, you didn't think I was going to suggest marriage, or something foolish like that?" He gave a small laugh. "I've thought about that, I'll confess. But then I thought that, even though I'm fond of you, girl, I'm not suicidal."

"No, Donal," she sighed. "You're not suicidal. Just a user. And very cunning at it."

"Aren't we all, darlin' Gina? Here, you sit back. I'll fetch the broom and pan, and get this mess cleaned up."

"Renew your lease, Donal. For both our sakes."

— ◆ —

Gina Moretti paced the small space of her living room fearful of wearing a path into the already thin and fraying carpeting. She changed her route to include her bedroom and the few steps that constituted a hallway. The movement of repetitious footfalls created a lulling rhythm that cleared away her thought's distractions. Decisions to be made, and the needed space to make them.

A shower and clean clothes created a remade Gina. She sat herself back in the living room and waited for her man. Donal may show up at the appointed time. Or he may not. Of late, his already erratic behavior had become more so. She had no real notion what was amiss, nor did she have the energy to try to sift through the wispy clues that masked her loving enigma. Perhaps it was the drink again, or perhaps the inevitable onslaught of age and time, the twin demons that had compromised her man's vitality and promise. Or perhaps he had just sunk into a different place, a new depth different from all the others, something peculiar to the man himself and his besotted flux. She didn't know, nor did she really care to.

At half seven Donal finally appeared at her door. "Sorry, Gina. The afternoon got away from me."

"Come on in, then. Shall I get you a drink? Perhaps we can celebrate the hole in your day that allowed me some space."

"Ah, now, Gina, what do you mean by that? Are we going to start the evening with a spat?"

"No, Donal. We've done enough of that." She returned with Donal's glass, and one for herself.

"But you know that every spat has its consequences," she said as she sat back down near the window. "And I fear I've tied myself loosely to a man adrift."

"That again," muttered Donal.

"Yes. That again. We're going nowhere, Donal. And I'm not sure I believe that we have anywhere to go."

"Ah, Gina, please." Gina turned to look out her window at the graying, drab street below. Donal sipped his scotch and said nothing. Neither spoke, and silence hung above them and around them like smoke from a distant fire, as if the countryside had flared and slowly wafted the many miles into the city. Here now, at last, this smoke, and it stifled breath, and thought, and time itself.

Donal finished his drink in silence. Outside the window a car horn blared into the creeping night, and a dog barked at an invisible shadow. Nothing else.

Donal placed the glass on the table next to him. "Well, then," he said at last. "I suppose it's best I be off."

Gina said nothing in response, nor did she move her gaze from the window. Nothing to see out there. Nothing to see in here.

"I'll be seeing you, Gina. We'll try again." He moved to the door and gently pulled it open. Silently he stepped into the hallway and closed the door, his footsteps ringing down the tiling, and he was gone.

After the echoes had subsided, Gina rose and pushed open the window. Despite the night, despite the autumn chill in a bitter city, for the first time all day she breathed fresh air.

— ◆ —

A late September afternoon with nothing to fill it. The blighted mark of a sky pocked with gray clouds that carried the implicit threat of rain in Washington, which did not nourish those things which were already consigned to wither and fade. All it did was create great pockets of mud and sludge and soaked the skin of those unfortunate enough to be caught in its falling.

Donal Mannion sought to kill an hour or two before delving into what would probably be an equally uneventful evening. He would see Gina, that he knew, but even his nights with her had begun to grow stale and withered like the city's browning foliage. So predictable, all of it. As predictable as the September rains.

A walk it would be, down the street of his flat and around the square blocks that contained what passed as his neighborhood. He might stop at a coffee shop or stick his head into the dollar store. Maybe McKenzie's, a stopgap if he didn't want to go the few blocks to The Black Hand. Even more downtrodden than his local, to be sure, but scotch was still scotch, no matter where it was poured.

A block over the neighborhood turned residential, lined with modest single-family homes in various states of repair. Most of Washington lived in boxes, and most of those boxes held multiple residents. The single homes here were small, often past the point of usual maintenance, and always narrow. In front of one such home a man near Donal's age raked the brown, yellow and red leaves that had gathered in his small yard. As Donal passed near him, the man paused his work, looked up and smiled.

"A good day for this," he said. "Not too hot to get it done without melting away."

Donal grunted a nonreply and kept walking. He had no mood for idle or bright conversation. As he did so, fragments of the raked leaves caught in the light breeze and swirled around his feet.

Autumn, he thought. *How many more of these will I see in this short and contorted life? Worn down and old is what I am. A piece of leaf blown into a gutter, too stubborn to be swept entirely away.*

Donal felt again the sharp leg pain that slowed his stride and caused a slight limp. He did not know what caused it, only that it was a relatively new sensation, an unmistakable sign of what was to come. Weakness, decay . . . irrelevance. But when, really, had Donal Mannion ever been relevant?

As he rounded the block the wind picked up and the first drops of what would be a brief rain hit his face and shoulders. *Walk on*, he told himself. One foot after the other, through rain and broken leaves and a broken spirit. Still warm enough for it all but growing colder by the day. Winter was coming, that he knew, with its constant whiff of isolation. Winter, whose cold air matched the deepening cold of his own soul. How many more of these, then, until there were no more winters at all?

Donal limped his way down the street. The Black Hand was a few yards off, with its tatty entrance and cracked walls and surly bartender. But the scotch would be warm, and the afternoon would pass away under its comforts. Then into the night, into the autumn, and finally into the dying time of winter.

He pushed against the rusted door and went inside.

— ◆ —

"Johnny. Another, if you please."

"Coming on to last call, Donal. Just so ya know."

"Then I'll have to accelerate the pace of my consumption." A fresh glass appeared before him, and half of it disappeared in a single swallow, its familiar burn the length of his throat to a stomach unsettled by the foul food that passed for his dinner, and by the dark, dank cloud of depression. He raised his head long enough to note that he was the only one left at the long bar. Just the two of them, Donal Mannion and Johnny Whatever, the keeper of the lonely bar. Last call indeed.

"Tough night for ya, Donal?"

"No tougher than most. Just another day, Johnny, and well done with it."

"Well, drink up to the end of it, Donal. And hurry a bit, if you can." Johnny went to the bar's far end, where glasses waited to be rinsed and bottles sorted back into their proper places.

The end of the night, then. The end of many things. Donal sipped through to the glass's bottom, slipped on his thin jacket and headed for the door.

"Okay, then. Until next time, Johnny."

"Take care of yourself, Donal. You're becoming my best customer, ya know. I'd hate to lose you."

Then into the night. Not to the flat, although it was only a few blocks away, through quiet and dead streets that would show no life at this time of the early morning. At two, when thoughts flew through a disquieted mind like bats, flitting side to side and up and down, elusive and beyond grasp or capture. Not to the flat, then. Donal chased his thoughts in the opposite direction. Chasing the bats. He needed to walk.

With no one about, he ambled almost blindly, his gaze cast within himself. He would be easy enough prey for anyone with bad intentions—more than slightly drunk, distracted, and vulnerable. So be it. He had become accustomed to vulnerability.

I'm losing her. A single thought repeating itself, crowding out all others. *I'm losing her.*

Inevitable, most likely.

Donal considered that he had been losing Gina since the first day he met her. An attraction, to be sure, but what was it really? All surface and convenience. It takes time and patience to plumb the depth of another soul, and Donal Mannion used those commodities sparingly. He was a creature of the moment, and he couldn't change who he was, no matter the motivation. Gina had been fading incrementally, a bright light increasingly obscured by the harsh sunlight of who he really was. He was losing her, and nothing to be done about it.

All that needed sorting were the final details, the way it would be done. Would she make a final confrontation, or would it be a silent withdrawal? Perhaps she would just disappear altogether, the way most of the things he had valued during this tattered lifetime had passed from him. One day here, the next day gone. But those were merely the details. What mattered was the passing, and there was no avoiding it. He was losing her, and she would be gone, with all the rest of it.

Donal walked until the sun glimmered in the eastern sky. By then the scotch had worn off. The conclusions, though, remained.

He was losing her. He understood this. It was time to go home and try to sleep a bit.

— ◆ —

This damnable time of year, the tattered and tatty backside of the great holidays, the detritus of celebration all around, laying silent in the cold, and the snow, and the boredom. Donal Mannion shoved his hands deeply into his coat pockets and made his way through the wind and a chilling rain down sidewalks as empty and barren as the days themselves.

No place really to go, but no call to stay in his flat, other than the warmth it offered. But how long can a person remain embryonic, his life a fetal coil in space that offered safety without comfort and security without stimulation? The streets—tawdry and tight and shiftless—promised at least a contact with something outside himself.

On this January day something new and different was unlikely. The world died in January, and it stayed dead until the days lengthened enough to allow sunlight and commerce and movement. Donal clicked off the days one by one.

What drew him to Gina's street he could not say. Some seed within a guilty subconscious, perhaps, or maybe the constant unspoken impulse to recover the lost days. On this rainy afternoon, though, his aimless wandering led him to her building. He stood on the sidewalk and looked up at the same window he had looked out of countless times.

Up the steps and into the entryway where he saw her name printed above her bell. *G. Moretti.* And with the instancy of impulse that shoved all thought and consideration into a far corner, he pushed it. Once, then twice, then a third time. Donal waited in the entryway for a response and paid note of the dense silence interrupted only by the tapping of raindrops on the doorway. After a few minutes he rang again. A rainy afternoon, and Gina no doubt had somewhere she needed to be, or so he told himself.

"Ah, it was just a notion anyway," he muttered. "She'll be all right."

Mannion turned back to the street and dove his hands, wet and needing warmth, once more into the deep pockets. An afternoon as wet and empty as the day, as wet and empty as the month. Damnable January. As wet and empty as his life.

Where to go now, and what to do? Donal Mannion turned down a familiar street and walked through the familiar door of The Black Hand, where the inside was warm and dry.

"Johnny Walker Red," he nodded to the bartender whom he had known for a great long time. "And be generous with your pour."

— ◆ —

"And so, Donal. I trust you've been well enough."

Donal Mannion opened the cracked door that stood as his border against an indifferent world. On the other side of it Gina Morretti leaned against the adjoining wall to balance herself as she toted a box filled with the debris of love gone wrong, or possibly just wasted away through the boredom of familiarity.

"Jesus, you're about the last person I'd expect to come by. Here, let me take that," and Donal hoisted the box away from her. "Come on in now. How've you been?"

Gina stepped around him and into the center of the still too-small living space. "I see you've done nothing with this room since I last saw it. You live too simply, Donal Mannion." She turned to face him. "Too simply by half."

"Ah, but what's the purpose of fixing things up then?" he replied. "We're all just passing through, aren't we? No point in digging in too deeply."

Gina took off her coat and shook her head. "That doesn't preclude making the effort, man. You live like a bear, and this place is a very dark cave."

"It does me well enough. And I do get out, you know. I'm not in hibernation."

"And I know the places you get out to. Each one the same, and each one with a man standing behind a bar pouring you drinks. Not much of a life, Donal."

"So what brings you here, Gina? I'm sure it's more than just commenting on my social habits." He smiled. "Those habits you found pleasurable at one point, as I recall."

"Unlike you, I tend to declutter when things have passed their point of purpose. These things I've brought are yours. Or should be. I've no use for them, and each of them has your fingerprints on it. I thought they best belonged here."

"Sweeping me away altogether," said Donal, and he moved to the box. On top was a jade bracelet, one he had bought for Gina at a small craft shop they had found at the end of their day in the Blue Ridge. Nothing fancy, but at the time a fitting talisman for a day well spent. Underneath it was a book of Mary Oliver's poems, and a novel by Niall Williams, both of which were holiday gifts from two years ago. Donal lifted the bracelet.

"You disapprove of my taste in jewelry?"

Gina sighed. "Just no sense in keeping it. Or the rest of it."

"The books might do you good. Some fine writing there, and an insight or two."

"I've read them. And the insights faded like morning dew. They're yours again now."

Silence. Nothing more to say. "I'd offer you a drink, but my guess is that you'd decline. Too early in the day, and all that."

Gina smiled. "I've put the bottles behind me, Donal. You should, too, but I know you never will."

"It's who I am, lady friend. It's who I'll always be." He shook his head slowly behind a thin and saddened smile. "And so it ends again. Like this. Probably as it should be, don't you think?"

"You're taking all this rather well, Donal. I'd have expected a bit more confrontation. Perhaps a beg to reconsider, or a pledge of undying love, or at least the admission that the heartbreak I'm imposing will ruin your life. This is a significant blow to my ego."

"No begging, Gina. I'll miss you, to be sure. I've missed others, and if I'm fortunate, I'll have others to miss as I go along. Nothing to do about it. We do what we need to carry forth. That's all."

Gina picked up her coat and walked to the door. "So. Take care of yourself, Donal Mannion. I expect I may see you from time to time, and I hope that when I do, I'll see you well."

"You'll see Donal Mannion, Gina. Nothing more nor less. Donal Mannion as he's meant to be."

She nodded, opened the door, turned, and was gone.

And as her steps rang down the narrow hallway, Donal Mannion, as he was meant to be, said to no one, "Done, then. All of it done, and to another day."

— ◆ —

The afternoon rain did not abate, and watery streaks ran down the windowpane to blur what was already a dim view. Gina's window looked out to the street, onto asphalt and tacky storefronts, and the detritus of the gutters. On the best days she might catch a glint of sunlight, and the swatch of a blue sky above the apartment complex across the way. But this was not one of the best days, and all there was to see out her window was rain, and cars coughing along a bumpy street.

Gina finished her tea and took the cup to the sink. A Saturday this was, and no calls upon her time. Once she would have relished the peace of these weekend days, the absence of demand, the rare leisure of time. But those simple pleasures had grown tawdry. Weekends had come to carry their own demands—to fill the empty spaces with something, anything, that might touch a deadened spirit. And now, on these hollow days, she would often find herself looking forward to Monday morning when she would once again drag herself to a sterile office to pursue meaningless work among people she did not know and who did not know her. There would be at least a predictable rhythm.

It had been this way for a while. Gina had always been attractive to others, had always been able to find a partner to share the time and to stimulate what passed for her feminine senses. Two disastrous marriages had not deterred her from the ideals of companionship, from the wispy illusion that romance might in fact be possible. Missteps. Every woman was entitled to a few. You learned from them, that was all. Her basic instincts remained intact.

But now, years on from those mistakes, her wisdom had not brought her comfort. It had, instead, brought her Donal Mannion, and now he was gone. Or rather, she had sent him away. At what point did his vulnerability turn to indolence, his sadness to resignation. When Gina failed to respond to him in the usual ways, he had done nothing, sagging into idleness, or maybe just accepting that all good things were destined to end.

Now, on this hollow Saturday afternoon, with nothing to keep her company other than the raindrops, she steeped a new cup of tea and brought it to her small desk in the corner of her bedroom. She took out paper, and she wrote:

Donal,

No doubt this note will come as a surprise, as I've even surprised myself in the writing of it. No point to it really, other than to tell you that I hope you're well. I regret not being with you, that you should know. You know the reasons why. But that doesn't change the simple fact that I consider you to be a fine man, despite your own doubts and despite your capacity to massage and knead your good qualities into something of a lasting shape. I hope you do, though. I hope you find a place, and a person, and a purpose. I miss you.

Gina

Gina Moretti slipped the note into an envelope, addressed it, then set it aside. *Jesus,* she thought, *I've become a cliché. Something out of a Jane Austen novel. God help me.*

She brought her tea back to the chair beside her window. Still the rain fell. Still the tea ran down her throat in warmth and bitterness. Still the clock hanging near the kitchen ticked away, a relentless beating of the relentless and empty time.

CHAPTER 12

A clear day it was with moderate heat under a sky broken with the occasional cloud and a breeze that came and went just long enough to cool skin. Days like this were rare enough, a departure from the oppressive heat and humidity that beat down Washington's streets and made those who walked them cross and sore. Late summer in the city.

But this day dawned differently, and Donal Mannion rose with a mind to take advantage of it. Begin at the corner bistro with the treat of a fine breakfast and then see where his feet might take him. The city was built for walking, everything accessible within the rectangles and diagonals of its well-ordered streets, ample parks, and greens along the way to rest, sit under some shade, and talk with the birds. This day, this bright anomaly within this withering season, would be his alone.

Within this city of museums and monuments, someplace glittering and alluring could be found. The Museum of Natural History, or perhaps the magnificence of the National Art Gallery, those strong and proud buildings along the Mall that drew tourists like gnats. One of those places that sparked something deep within him and stirred life into hopes and ideals dormant or afraid to show themselves. *A day to savor the grandest achievements of man,* he thought.

Donal bused from his neighborhood to the northwest part of the city. Once there he began to walk southward, down Connecticut Avenue toward DuPont Circle with its bookstores and cafes, the shops and boutiques that lined the northwest streets, then to the Mall beyond. A grand day, and Donal felt it in every vessel, every artery, every spark of idea or thought. Great it was to be alive on such a day, and in such a place.

At K Streets and 14th Street a crowd had gathered, milling about, with faces drawn, or some leaning forward to see through it all to what lay beyond. Something to see here, and Donal crossed 15th Street to see what it was. He pressed himself into the mass of bodies.

"Ah God," he muttered when he saw the trickle of red behind the police line. Donal nudged the man next to him. "D'ya know what went down here?"

"No idea. A drive-by shooting. Or a random one. Who can tell? Another one."

"We've got quite the body count this year, no?

"Every year, friend. We just keep shooting ourselves, and there's no end to it."

A young man lay on the other end of the trickle, a white covering that could hide neither his form nor the blood that ran from it. Another one, and more to come.

Police kept the line tight, and the crowd began to disperse. "Move along, folks. Nothin' any of us can do." The officers moved in well-practiced procedures, expressionless and automatic. "Nothing any of us can do."

The National Art Gallery, where the grandest achievements of humankind hung on walls while the brutality of the day played itself out in regular rhythms. Donal shrugged, then frowned, then turned back. The Old Ebbitt Grill was around the corner, and this day, bright, beautiful and more typical than he had thought, called for a drink.

A fine day, yet nothing good to it. Damn it all. Damn the sunshine, and damn the wind when it comes, and damn the rain that visits too often. And damn this bitter sense of nothingness behind it all.

Donal lifted himself from his thoughts. Despite its fine start, this day beckoned clouds, which lurked on the horizon, heading his way.

Autumn loomed ahead with its promise of bursts of wet, bursts of boredom.

Through the scent of blood and a mist of red behind his eyes, he felt a need to fight through these streets, through the people crowding them, against the flow of traffic and the flow of life itself. On such a morning he should have remained inside the dinginess of his flat and let the world tend to itself.

— ◆ —

Capital Taxi, a local firm, a speck in the shadow of the larger companies, but still one that commissioned its drivers and let them keep the fares they earned. Mannion turned onto DeSales to find the dark door with the tinted window next to it displaying a bad drawing of a cartoon taxicab.

A job this would be, another in the series of low energy, low risk, low reward pursuits that helped him pay his bills. Donal knew how to drive, and he knew this city well. He had walked almost all of its streets through the years, knew its curbs and its alleyways, knew its rhythms and dysfunctions. If he belonged in this city, if this city was truly a part of who he was, then he may as well turn that knowledge into income.

Twenty minutes later, he re-emerged from Capital Taxi. "Welcome aboard. You can claim your cab as soon as the background check comes clean. Give it a day or so. I'll give you a call when you're set." No need for congratulations, and none forthcoming from the squat, gruff cabmaster who would fill in the long line of bosses that commanded Donal Mannion's days. Perhaps a bit gruffer, a bit less refined, than many of the others, but there was a blessing in that. No need to read him or play the political games that could turn a workplace into a house of mirrors.

Back to the streets, and the rain. He debated a stop at the Old Ebbitt on the way home. A drop or two might fight the chill, and, at heart, Donal was feeling quite spry. He had a new job, one with flexibility that would allow him to work at his own pace and provide ample space for the daydreams that still flitted through his consciousness, a place of fantasies. He had a place to live that, however dingy, was warm and dry. And he was still strong enough to make his way through these streets. So, to the Old Ebbitt then, to raise a glass against the chill, and to the security of his cobbled, jerry-rigged life.

At M and 16th, a young woman dashed her way across the rain-splattering streets. As she reached the corner, her foot caught the curb, and she launched headlong onto the wet sidewalk. Small waves splashed up against her as dropped there, as those on the street kept their strides. Some gave a glance but kept on their way.

Donal, who had been pausing under the canopy of a bistro that occupied that corner, saw her go down and stepped out to where she struggled to gather herself. "A nasty spill, ma'am. Here, let me give you a hand."

"Goddammit it all," the young woman hissed. "I don't need this. Not today, of all days."

"There are no good days for a wet spill, I'd think."

"I can't do this," she said as she rose. "I need to go home and change. It's all ruined, this day. But thank you. Seems no one else cared to notice," she said as she stood and smoothed her outfit. "I was on my way to a job interview, of all things."

Donal raised his arm and hailed a taxi. Capital Taxi, it was. When the cab stopped, he leaned into the driver's window. "Take this lady anywhere she needs to go," he said, and handed the driver a twenty. "She's had a rough morning."

"You don't have to do that," said the woman.

"It's a celebration to do so, ma'am," and with that Donal turned back to the street. No need for the Old Ebbitt. Not this morning. There were better ways to fill the time, despite the rain.

— ◆ —

Donal settled into the seat he had come to call his own, the driver's side of a beaten-down Ford Taurus that passed for a taxicab. A few days of this, now, and each one more fascinating than the last. He had not expected such diversion.

It was near the end of his second shift, the second day of navigating his city's narrow, gridded streets while listening to the banter of his fares. He quickly surmised that a cabdriver was not unlike a bartender. A presence, he was, to the strangers who climbed into his orbit, an anonymous ear to the travails and challenges and heartbreaks that seemed to permeate the lives of those who sought his cab.

He had known the giving of it, the nights spent talking idly with those who poured his drinks, getting to know them by name, recognizing which bartenders gave the best pours, and, with it, the best harbor for his thoughts and regrets and longings. He prized those who listened best, and, in the listening, sometimes offered nuggets of obscure wisdom, the things he might never find for himself.

And so it was in his cab. All that was missing were the drinks.

There was the man yesterday, one of his first fares, who gave the address of a lawyer's office, then unraveled for Donal the story of his divorce, his cheating wife and the financial shenanigans that might lead him to bankruptcy. He was followed by two young women, friends, off to an exclusive set of shops in Georgetown, spending, they claimed, outrageous sums of money on clothes that would, they told him, make their claim as fashionistas.

The older woman who climbed into his back seat, gave an apartment address, then spent the ride in muffled sobs. The couple, married or not but obviously drawn close to each other, heading to the theater, their first night out in two years. The young men later that night, already in their cups, who asked him where they might find the best hookers. And all of it as confidential and as safe as the tales told in a priest's confessional. Father Donal Mannion, Confessor to the Lost.

Now, as this day neared its end, Cabby Mannion was flagged by a man outside one of the downtown office buildings. Late in the day, it was already dark, the time when most offices have gone quiet, and their inhabitants scattered to their real lives.

Mannion turned his shoulder to face his fare as the man climbed into the back seat. "So where are we heading tonight?"

"Find me a bar."

"You don't need a cab for that, my friend. Walk in any direction in this town and you'll find one around the corner."

"Just drive a bit and take me to someplace along Connecticut. I want some distance. Any good place will do. I take it you might know one."

Donal chuckled. "A few. There's a place near the zoo that serves 'em straight and strong. The bartender is a friend. He'll do you well."

There was silence until the fare leaned forward. "Do you have a woman in your life?"

"Not really. Not anymore. Seems I can't hold on to anyone worth keeping."

"You're fortunate, then." Another pause. "She left me last night. Married for three years, and none of them easy. Left me with regret, she said, for the wasted years. 'How could I have ever found you attractive?' I expect that line alone will stay with me for the rest of my life. Left me for another man. Or other men. I have no idea, beyond her boast that there were better men she could have any time she wanted."

"That's tough. I feel for you."

"Have you ever gone through something like that?"

"Can't say that I have. I'm usually the one doing the leaving. Or forcing them to leave me."

"Rips your soul in two," the man said. "And never the same afterwards."

They drove in silence down Connecticut. At the bar, The Kingsman, Donal pulled to the curb. "Here it is."

The man said nothing and reached for his wallet to pay the fare. Donal took his card and processed it, then handed the man his receipt.

"A tough day for you, and it deserves a proper end. The

bartender's name is Frank, and he'll be there tonight, I expect. Tell him Donal Mannion said to set you to a drink or two. He'll recognize the name. Tell him to put it on my account. It's the darkest days that can ultimately give you a hint of the light."

"Thanks," muttered in dour tones. The door opened, shut again, and Donal the Confessor drove once more into a darkening night.

On the slow days, those days when the city grew strangely quiet and its pace dropped from mad dash to slow trot, Donal's cab might sit quietly on a side street, waiting for a fare that was unlikely to appear. He valued the soft times. He had no desire to rush, to hustle, or to fret about the lost minutes that might be turned to income. When it seemed as if no one in the city needed a ride, he'd pull his cab to the side, or find an alley where he could sit idly, read a newspaper, or, sometimes, turn off his light altogether and take a short nap.

A slow morning in late August, with the city on holiday, and Donal adrift in a cab that was going nowhere. Washington became a small town, one given over to tourists who often rode tour buses instead of cabs. The government went quiet, the ambassadors flew home, and the natives left for beaches, mountains, or family retreats.

Donal sat in his cab at the side of Connecticut Avenue, closed his eyes, and did not nap. Lately he had been given to reflection, the province and privilege of a man whose yesterdays outnumbered his tomorrows by a too-wide margin. And, for reasons he could not, could never, fathom, on this morning the reflective man once again looked back on a loss he had not considered.

A rap on his window, and Donal opened his eyes. "Hey, buddy, are you working?"

Donal sat up quickly and flicked on the cab's light indicating availability. "Yeah. What do you need?"

The other man opened the rear door and climbed in. "Russell Office Building. No need to rush."

Donal drove down Connecticut toward the Capitol. The city flitted around him, around the contours of his thoughts, and his memories. As the street tunneled just north of DuPont Circle and the day's light grew darker, he thought of covered bridges, the ones where no light penetrated, and all remained quiet.

The cab gave him time to think, a perfect job for this time of his life. In between fares he had space and peace. And the driving itself took him to different places, both in the city and within himself.

In the end, it's the intersection between what we have and what we wish that defines our happiness, it occurred to him. In his cab, a rainy Monday afternoon, and fares that day were scarce. *It's the wishing that does us in,* he thought. *Perhaps I should become a Buddhist.*

A young woman tapped on his window, and he beckoned her inside. "Come in from the rain, girl. Where are we heading today?"

"Thirty-three thirteen Connecticut," she said in something of a growl as she slid into the back seat and disengaged her umbrella. Water splashed onto the floor of the cab, onto the back of the front seat, and onto Donal's neck. "Damn rain," she mumbled. "And me a mess now. Damn."

Donal said nothing. *Career woman,* he surmised. *Off to a meeting, or an interview. Running her own race and looking for her own special prize. The wanting of it. The wishing.*

He no longer gave himself the enchantment of wishes, the luxury of hope. He was where he was, and there'd be no changing it. At the end of each day Donal would park his cab at the depot, then ride the Metro northeast. Nothing more to do.

It was in the fog of deadened nights that Donal delved most deeply below the twisted flotsam that marked the surface of his life. What type of debris was this, floating around him and polluting what should be clear waters, and how had it come about? Whatever it was, he would have to navigate through it with a broken rudder, that much he knew. Self-awareness had never been his strength, but this much was obvious.

He had spent too many nights drink in hand, a superficial hail-fellow-well-met persona at any bar he might fancy, and a trained eye for which women might be immediately available. His work merely bridged his days until the freedom of its final hour, and then into the night. It was only then that Donal felt the lure of the possible, the attraction of adventure or the expansion of his tired soul. The days got him through, and gave him the wherewithal to live, that was all. What mattered came after he left his workplace.

And so the parade of cheap drink and cheaper acquaintances, the kind that barely knew his name but felt enough to listen to his stories in the hope of a free round. The women drifting in and out of his space, as dissolute as he was and similarly searching for some measure of comfort against the fallow nights. The grime of late-night streets littered with spotty trash, cigarette butts, empty coffee cups and discarded newspaper, the landscape of despair.

He had moved back near his old neighborhood into a cheap flat just two blocks from the street where he had grown up. Nothing had changed, really, and many of the faces remained the same as he knew from years past. His old friends came and went as before. All of it was what he had expected when he signed the papers for his flat and took the key from a landlord accustomed to the dissipated souls that occupied his lowly properties.

Most nights Donal would find a bar for his drinking, but there were times when he preferred solitude, and the veneer of quiet. His living space looked onto the back of the stores that lines the street behind him. Beyond them, though, was a patch of greenery, a small square of grass and flowers set off by an iron railing that kept the city away. He could see it from his window if he lifted his head and peered over the stores. It gave him comfort, something alive and growing amidst the grime and soot.

On such nights he would drink his drink, and let his mind wander to the past times, romanticizing them into new shapes and stripping away their tawdry trappings. In his mind he was no longer a poor boy trying to find a place with a broken family in a broken neighborhood. Instead he was an adventurer coming to life, discovering the soft thrills that experience could offer—the rush of friendships who shared his dares, the fall of light on summer evenings, the amazing sensations of a girl's touch, the exhilarations and exaltations of youth, and power, and all that would be possible. He thought of those times, and the ones with whom he shared them, and he missed them.

The elongation and eventual negation of an entire life, he thought, gazing across to the square. *What I might have been. And what am I now? But I belong here, I think. I belong to this place. Nothing more to wish for. I had my chance.*

— ◆ —

He began his night at The Black Hand, nestling into the familiarity of the place that was his local. Here he could be anonymous, or, if in a social frame of mind, banter with the bartenders, all of whom were becoming increasingly familiar.

There would be women there, too, but Donal generally avoided them. His forays at the Old Ebbitt had lifted his standards, and he no longer easily abided any scent of cheapness, or the shallow incantations of women seeking the same tawdry release he sought himself. He had come to value the challenges of style and poise and intellect, qualities that forced him to stretch himself, and, if the stretching were successful, placed him in the intimate company of women whom he knew outshone him and with whom he carried no risk of any complicated involvement.

The faces these nights all held a clear familiarity, even if Donal had never seen them before. Regulars shuffled in, almost in formation, as smoky and as streaked as the glass that formed the bar's windows, the sad eyes that looked out from within onto the littered sidewalk. No beckoning to those who walked by. Nothing to entice or lure newcomers. Those who came to The Black Hand did so knowing the place it was, comfortable in its inherent darkness that clouded their own murky vapors and allowed them to drink away their time.

Donal sat at a corner table with his first scotch of the night and took it all in, an observer here rather than a participant. He noted the dust specks that floated through the muffled lights that shone above and behind the bar, bits of earth-powder stirred into the stultifying air. At the bar sat the slouched forms, mostly silent except for a scattered, muffled comment to one who might be seated adjacent. The bartenders kept the glasses filled, engaging when asked a question or in response to an opinion or a complaint. The usual sounds, the usual sights, of a usual night.

Into it came a familiar form. Eddie Moore, one of the neighborhood boys whom Donal had known for three decades. Head down, but Donal could notice that his old friend seemed different, sparer and drawn. Eddie had always been their nondescript friend, the one who went along with the others, happy enough to be part of the crowd. Tonight he looked faded altogether, a wraith too distracted to go about his hauntings.

Donal left his seat, went up to him at the bar and placed a hand on his shoulder. "Eddie." Startled at the touch, Eddie bolted upright, then broke into a smile. "Donal," he said a bit too loudly as he grabbed a hand to shake. "Jesus, it's good to see you. Didn't know you hung out at places like this."

"It's got a bar and bottles, Eddie. What more does a man need? Come on, let me get this round."

With new drinks, they went back to the corner table. "I still picture you as a downtown guy, Donal. Surprised to see you back in the neighborhood."

"I was never a downtown guy, Eddie. I was just pretending for a time. This is more where I belong. And you, my old friend. How've you been carrying on?"

Eddie took a long drink, put his half-empty glass back on the table and looked away at the basketball game on the television screen in the far corner. At length he turned back to Donal, then chuckled. "I just got back. Just tonight."

"There's a story there, I'll wager."

Again Eddie looked off to a safe space. The alcohol quieted him, quieted the river that raced through his tired thoughts. "A story," he said. "Not really, Donal," and he took another long pull. "Tell me," he said. "When was the last time you felt like all the pieces didn't fit?"

"When did the pieces ever fit, Eddie?"

"They fit for me, Donal. At least for a while." With that he rose and went back to the bar. He returned with two new drinks and placed one next to Donal's still filled glass.

"What's up, Eddie?"

"Mullin's got bought out last week. Did you hear about that? Been driving trucks in this part of the city for fifty years, but all of a sudden the apple of some major carrier's eye. Bought out the whole fleet so that they can absorb it, make everything more efficient. Apparently, I'm not worthy of absorption." He drank off half his glass.

"Christ, Eddie, I'm sorry. That's rough."

"Been driving for them since I left high school. Twenty-six years. No more, though. I'm in the past tense."

"What are you going to do? What comes next?"

"Don't know, but I'll tell you what I did. When I got the word, I went home to Colleen. She was there as she always is, watching some soap opera and drinking her fourth or fifth cup of coffee, her fat ass planted in a recliner. Needless to say, she did not take well to my news. The usual insults, including a few 'I never should haves.' Like 'I never should have trusted you.' Like 'I never should have married you,' that sort of thing. She was a trifle bitter.

"It's never been good with her, Donal," he continued. "Not since the kids came. She got lazy. Disinterested. Unhappy, I know, and frustrated. All she has to do is chat with her friends, clean the house once or twice, and cook an occasional meal. I guess that's not enough for her. And I know I'm not enough for her.

"Anyway," he went on, "I walked back out and got in my car. I sat there a while and tried to think of where I could go. Just to drive, you know? To think things through. And I thought how great it would be to wake up tomorrow morning someplace warm, someplace on the ocean. So I headed out of the city, headed south. I had no idea where I would go, but wherever it was, it would be warm.

"I didn't want to drive the interstates. Just the local roads. You know, the narrow, tired roads that are only two lanes and loaded with stop lights and strip malls. Route 1 down into Virginia, then God knows where."

"So why are you here sitting across a table from me, Eddie?"

"At Richmond I turned off to the east, toward Virginia Beach. Thought I might cross over to the Outer Banks and walk in the sand." He paused again to drink.

"But do you know how Virginia Beach looks in early afternoon on a winter's day? Do you know how gray and dirty the ocean looks, and how the traffic moves along in burps and farts, and how cracked and broken the sidewalks are? Do you know that Donal? I got to the beach and parked the car to walk out to the water. Big, ugly seagulls were swooping down looking for garbage, squawking this awful squawk. Cigarette butts in the sand and candy bar wrappers that never made it to the trash cans. I looked out to the water and there was this big ship way out there. Could have been a Navy ship, or maybe just a big freighter. I couldn't tell. Out there on the horizon, this flat gray shape, all by itself. Might have been five hundred crew on board, but it looked to me like a lost, lonely thing, heading nowhere. Made me sad. Sadder than I already was.

"It dawned on me, standing there in this gloom, that there really wasn't any place to go. No sunny shore, no warm sands, no girls in bikinis bringing me coconut daiquiris. Just me, Eddie Moore, with nowhere to run to. So I stopped running, right there. Turned around and drove back to the city."

Donal sipped his drink. Eddie continued to stare down into the table, not looking at the one across from him, peering instead into a place that required neither focus nor response.

"I came right here when I got back to town. Figured I could use a drink or two before I face Colleen again. I'm not even sure if she'll be there. She didn't call or message me all day. I thought she might at least ask me where I was, when I was coming back so she could yell at me some more. But she didn't even do that."

"You could stay at my place tonight, Eddie, if you want. Just to think things through. If you want."

"Thanks, Donal. I think I might, if that's okay.

"Not much of a place, Eddie, but there's space for you."

They finished their drinks in silence, then stood together. Donal put his hand once more on Eddie's shoulder. "No point in running, Eddie. At least not tonight. Let's get some sleep and see if things look better in the morning."

"This is who we are, isn't it, Donal? Two kids from the block, still on the block and nothing we can do about it. You're right. No point in running."

Donal put Eddie on his couch and within minutes Eddie's resonant breathing told Donal that he was already asleep. The next morning, when Donal woke, Eddie was gone, the blanket and pillow neatly stacked on the couch's armrest. No note, no trace. Donal Mannion never saw Eddie Moore again.

— ◆ —

Another day to the streets, the crawling, creeping, beeping streets, and those who drove them. It had been three weeks now, and Donal had found his place. A revelation to recognize that that place was behind the wheel of a taxicab, but his life to that point had carried its share of surprising revelations. This was no different, really, and, on the whole, a bit more reassuring than the other realities that had punctured his younger years.

The carnival of characters that crawled into and out of his cab kept him fresh. Stories floated through the air like the scattered remnants of dandelions, and his capacity for absorbing them, for finding each one peculiar in its own way, made the days pass sharply. At first, during the early days of his driving, he just listened, the ready ear that many of his fares had sought. But occasionally there would be a tale, or a lament, or a loss, that touched him inexplicably, and he might offer a response. Nothing profound, or much beyond the acknowledgment that his passenger had been heard by another human being, and that human being had a like heart. It was enough.

In the late morning a young man, tattered and more than a bit disheveled, flagged Donal down near Union Station and gave him an address in the northeast part of the city. The young man settled into the back seat with a dirty backpack and muttered a profanity.

"Rough morning, is it?'

"No rougher than most. It's the nights that you have to be wary of."

Donal drove, and the two said nothing until the cab turned up New York Avenue. It was the driver who broke the silence.

"We're heading for my old neighborhood. I grew up on these streets. Never really left them behind."

"No one ever leaves these streets," said the young man. "It's what we're born to, and there's no call in fighting it. Just make the most of it all, and grab what you can."

"Has the grabbing been good for you lately?" Donal asked.

The young man smiled and leaned forward, his arm on his backpack. "Yeah. A good week this has been. Let me ask you, did you ever have a really good teacher? Someone who taught you everything you really, truly needed to know, then showed you how to make it work for you?"

"If I did, I wouldn't be driving this cab."

"I do. Knows everything there is to know about these streets. Who walks the sidewalks and where they live. How they live. And what you need to do to find your way through them. How to take what you need and never think about the costs, then disappear like a whisper. Do you know how much freedom there is in knowing these things, then having the courage to act on that knowledge?"

"You sound to be fortunate, young man," Donal said. "It's the brave who are truly free. The rest of us cower into our little holes and mistake safety for comfort."

"You know these streets, you said. Do you still live around here?"

Donal chuckled. "And if I did, would I be telling that to you?"

"No worries," replied the other. "You don't seem the type to have riches stored up, at least to the point where it would interest me."

"Ah, the storing up of wealth is the stuff of vanity, haven't you heard? I'm a simple man, my young friend. And I'll spend the rest of my days in that simplicity."

"But you're not brave."

"No. Not brave at all. I'm as courageous as a church mouse."

"Then you'll never be free. And there's great freedom to be had on these streets."

The cab pulled to the curb. "Here we are. It's six-fifty on the fare."

The young man handed Donal a twenty. "No change needed."

"Jesus, that's generous."

The young man stepped out of the cab to the curb, then leaned over to the driver's window. "Consider it a gift from the Free State of Andrew Gentry." With a laugh he turned to the streets and lightly strode into his new day.

CHAPTER 13

"Mind if I join you, Matty?" Andrew had come into the coffee shop shortly after Matthew had taken his cup to a small corner table. Matthew said nothing, but gestured to the empty chair across from him, and Andrew sat.

"You come here quite a bit, don't you? They seem to know you here."

Matthew sipped, and then replied. "I'm not after being known, in this place or anywhere else. It's comfortable here, that's all. And they make strong coffee. If you want, I'll stand you to a cup of it."

"That would be very generous of you, Matty. And a bagel, too, if you can spare it."

Wordlessly Matthew rose and went back to the counter. He returned with coffee for Andrew and bagels for the two of them. "Here," he said as he set them down. "Happy to share."

"You're a good man, Matthew Cooney."

"Hardly good, Andrew. Just a man. Like you and all the others."

"So where are you off to today, Matty?" he said through a hungry bite of his bagel. "Scoping out new territory?"

"The usual. I'll wander a bit and see what I can find."

"I know you've been heading to Georgetown quite a lot lately. Fascinating area, there. Lots of money. Lots of fine women."

"And all of it well out of my reach, Andrew. The streets are more pleasant there, that's all. A good place to regard the day."

"Ah, Matty, I know you too well. You don't do much of anything without some purpose behind it. That's why I admire you, man. I admire your subtlety."

Matthew looked at Andrew and did not smile. "There's little about you that makes me think you admire much of anything, Andrew. You're a survivor, just like me. Maybe not as 'subtle,' as you put it. And maybe with a few more aspirations. But here we are, and neither of us deserving of any admiration."

"If you say so, Matty." Andrew had quickly finished his bagel, then rose from the table with his coffee. "Into the streets, then. To see what we can find. Thanks for the breakfast, and be careful out there. You never know where some mischief might find you."

"You as well, Andrew," and with that Matthew returned to his bagel. Unlike Andrew, he was in no hurry, this morning, or any other.

— ◆ —

Matthew no longer took things forcefully as he did when younger. He felt no need to exert himself, to shout through strength and violence that he walked this earth, drew his breath, drank his liquor, ate his food and lay with his women.

Still, there were opportunities that his wise eyes could not ignore. Rarer and more fleeting than before, but no less real. Behind unlocked doors, or those too casually secured, lay the means for Matthew to preserve himself for as long as he might need. All it required was a keen eye and a careful touch. He marked his time now in days, no longer within the luxury of projecting too far into the future. Aspirations beyond the immediate were nothing more than teases. What mattered was the next meal, where he might spend the night, and what comforts he could claim for himself on those fine days when comfort was a possibility.

He trained his eye on the anomalies—a door handle that might be loose, a slight tear in a window screen, a gate to a backyard that had no latch. Such things would draw his interest, and then he would watch for a time, gauge the comings and goings of those who lived within those spaces. If there were a security system he might not be able to crack, he would turn his attention elsewhere. There were always plenty of candidates in a city where people rushed in self-importance and made mistakes in the rushing.

Matthew never acted rashly. Instead he studied, and then strategized. He had done so for some time now, minimizing his risks by picking what were likely to be the least complicated targets. Unlike most, Matthew had patience, and with nothing else to fill his days, he had the time to make that patience work for him.

And so it was that on a warm evening in September Matthew Cooney sat opposite a rowhouse on New Hampshire Avenue. There had been no signs of life there for several days, other than a nightlight coming on at the same time each night. No one coming or going, and disinterested neighbors that paid no mind. Like many of these houses, it had a tiny basement door in the narrow triangular backyard that could readily be picked open.

All too familiar, this act of thievery, this act of survival. Done a hundred times and despite a few close calls, never caught, always able to take what he needed to bring him along. Matthew sat on the bench in the tiny green triangle near the corner, watched the house one more time, just to be sure, then sighed deeply. The taking and the hording and the scrambling. So very tired of it now. Not like before.

"A tough way to get by, isn't it, Matty? Taking what we can and begging for the rest."

James Barry had said those words to him that very morning.

"It is, James. But we do it, don't we? All so that we can face another day, and do it all again."

"Makes no sense when you think about it that way, Matt."

"We've long ago passed the point of logic, James," and Matthew smiled with the countenance of one who held no stock in logic, or order, or peace. Illusory things. All that mattered, the only real thing, was getting by.

On legs stiffened with age, Matthew Cooney walked slowly across the avenue, empty of traffic this time of night. Most men find a profession that brings them through their lives and imparts a measure of meaning. He had found his. Now it was time to get to work once more.

He ducked quickly through the back gate, shaded by the trees around it. The basement door was as he had expected, held together by nothing more than a bicycle lock, which he dispatched with a snip of his iron shears. As easy as it ever might be, all of this. As natural as breath.

Once inside, his instincts told him where to look. Always, it seemed, there would be a hutch, or a desk, or a credenza on the first level, and it was here that special things were often kept. Matthew found it, pulled open a drawer and saw an envelope filled with stock certificates. These were of no use. But around the envelope were various parcels and folders. And wrapped in one packet was a trove of bills, mostly hundreds, although a healthy mix of twenties and fifties mixed in. Matthew sifted through them and took a smattering of each. He would not take the entire parcel. He would not empty this packet and thereby bring attention to its losses. Later, when the money was needed by whomever placed it here, they would find it to be a little short, that was all, and they would rack their memories for the last time they might have touched it or whether they could recall taking anything away. What they were unlikely to miss would keep Matthew housed and fed for weeks.

Matthew snuck back out as blithely as he had entered. In the narrow patch that passed for a backyard, he paused to check the air, to see if any threat presented itself to his invisibility. A warm night, but late enough now that no one seemed to stir. Matthew took a deep breath, then slipped through the gate.

As he turned to set the gate in its latching, his head exploded in pain. A second hit followed the first, and he crumpled to the sidewalk.

Hands searched his pockets and pulled out what they sought.

Whatever it was that struck him sent stars flying into, then out of, his vision, followed by darkness beneath the blackness of the night. A club, perhaps, or maybe a metal bar. He may have lost consciousness for a moment or two, or possibly he was stunned insensate, his awareness blurred by the pain and shock of it. No matter the particulars. His senses returned quickly enough to hear the sound of feet running down New Hampshire Avenue in the direction from which he had originally come.

— ◆ —

The next morning Matthew woke to the bells of the National Cathedral. Miles away, north of where he slept, but in the still of a Sunday morning he heard them, softly at first, musical whispers that caressed his weary and wearying soul. He lay back and listened. He seldom heard these bells. The city was too cluttered, too loud, to permit their tones to permeate very far, but on this morning he heard them. Ringing, quietly exultant, calling him to a new place.

He had spent the night at the shelter, his bed a rusty cot, but warm enough to provide cover for the disquiet that he could not elude. His head ached, but there was no blood. A dark blue bruise welled just above his left ear. In the winter he might be able to hide it under a wool cap, but this was September, and wearing a cap would bring more attention than the bruise itself. He would carry the bruise, a mark of his foolishness. A mark of the lost time. All of it. The years of it that culminated in a physical beating that mirrored the thrashing of his soul. He deserved it, this he knew, so the mark of it provided no cause for concern.

It was mid-morning when he left the shelter. The city drew him in his restlessness, and Matthew walked a meandering walk without pattern. He knew these blocks, those that formed the boundaries of his current world—the shelter and the square where he often slept and where the others would gather to waste their days; the stores where he would be welcome, and those where he would not; the bus stops that would bring him to the finer parts of town.

Always, even on quiet Sunday mornings, there was the stench of the city, that peculiar mixture of grit, grime and exhaust mingled forever with the scent of despair. *Been here forever,* Matthew thought. It had wafted over the Capitol Dome and flitted through the filters that cleaned the air at the White House. It had permeated the public festivals and the state funerals. It had drawn into the lungs of Lincoln and the Roosevelts. And well before it all it had seeped into the tawdry shacks and tin-roof settlements of Swampoodle, where the Cooneys and the Mannions and the Duncans and thousands of their forebears had found their way, then lost it again. The city had changed through the decades, families and lives scattered to disparate corners. But the stench remained, and nothing could cleanse it from the lungs and psyche of those consigned to sense it.

Near Capitol Hill he passed a church, its façade dominated by a spiring stained-glass window. Simple in a classic design, solid yet gentle, the entire structure seemed to point its way to a welcoming heaven. Matthew stopped under a tree near its front steps and regarded the play of the morning light against the colored glass.

It had been years since he had been to Mass. As a boy his mother would drag him down the street to Saint Francis de Sales, a solemn place that gave him chills, but when he had walked out of his catechism class forty years ago, he never looked back. He had no regrets. He would abide a priest's prayers or a deacon's blessings, all the religion he needed on these streets. But this morning he had time, and a notion that the city's burn might somehow be lessened within these plain walls and the glorious, reflected light of its sunlit colored window. There would be a noontime Mass, a few minutes off. Matthew climbed the steps and took a seat in the rearmost pew. He hoped he remembered the pattern of the Mass, all the responses and repetitions, although he thought those things had been burrowed into him deeply enough to be retained. He would not presume to take the host. No matter, really. If nothing else, he might breathe a few peaceful moments.

When the Mass ended Matthew sat quietly until the church emptied. He moved to the side chapel and knelt before an image of the Virgin Mary. Tears formed behind closed eyes. Matthew rose, lit a votive candle, and walked slowly back out into the early afternoon sunshine. He wiped his eyes, and then resumed his day, repentant but unpurified.

He found Andrew in the square, his head back, eyes closed, absorbing the midday sun. Matthew waited for Andrew to open his eyes. When he did so, Matthew smiled and spoke to him quietly.

"I believe the first thing I ever taught you was never to run away from a scene. Draws too much attention to yourself. Always walk, Andrew, as if you're just taking the air and breathing in the world around you. No one ever notices a man out on a walk. But a man running? Ah, that draws looks and invites curiosity, no matter the place or time of day."

Andrew smirked. "You've taught me a number of lessons, Matty. I'm grateful for the wisdom." He paused while Matthew's gaze held his eyes. "You seem to have a nasty bruise there, old man. An accident? Or maybe a fight you didn't win?"

"Not an accident, Andrew. Something quite deliberate." Matthew leaned forward, grabbed Andrew's shirt and twisted it up to his throat, hissing through clenched teeth. "And now I'd appreciate you undoing your foolishness and giving me back what's mine."

Andrew leaned forward. He placed his own right hand across Matthew's fist holding his shirt. He was unhurried in his reply. "Don't really know what you're talking about, Matty. An old man's fantasy, from what I can tell. Maybe a touch of dementia, is that it? I'll thank you to let go of my shirt."

Matthew pulled the younger man to his feet. "If it's a test of strength you want, Andrew, I'll give it to you. Don't fight me, man, any more than you already have. Among the other lessons you've ignored is the one that says there's always to be honor among thieves. But I've never known you to be a man of honor, Andrew. You're just a thief, and a poor one at that." Matthew tightened his grip. "Now bring me back what you've taken. Settle your debts."

"The only thing I've taken from you, Matty, is your insults," Andrew spat back. "I have no idea what you're referring to. Now I'll ask you again to take your hand away before I'm forced to become violent. And I'd hate to have to strike down an old man."

With his hand still firmly gripping Andrew's shirt, Matthew brought his other forearm up and pressed it against his throat. Andrew squirmed then took a quick pivot away from the pressure of the forearm. As he did so, Matthew stumbled, just a step but enough for Andrew to gain some leverage. The younger man's fist crashed against Matthew's ear slightly below the bruise from the night before. Matthew reeled and Andrew was free. With a muted growl, Andrew drove forward and knocked Matthew to the ground. He was on him then and delivered two hard kicks to Matthew's ribs.

"We're done here, old man," he panted. "Go find yourself a quiet place to die." Andrew wiped his mouth, picked up his backpack, gave Matthew one last half-hearted kick, then stomped off across the square. No one paid him attention, and no one seemed to notice Matthew lying prone in the warm September grass.

He lay there a while, then gathered himself enough to stumble to the bench where Andrew had been sunning himself. Throbbing ribs echoed the pain in his head. In the distance he once again heard church bells, thinner and tinnier than those from the morning. No benedictions on this day. No blessings. Just another Sunday in the city.

As the afternoon grew late, Matthew stood again. He needed food. The coffee shop would do. Coffee would revive him, and there were always the day-old pastries that would otherwise be thrown out. He had come to welcome the simple pleasures. A couple of semi-stale bagels would do as well as steak and potatoes.

From the far end of the street Matthew saw Andrew step out of the coffee shop. Andrew pulled his backpack over his shoulder and headed back to the square. He would be coming this way. Matthew carried his pains to an alleyway that adjoined the sidewalk, then tucked himself flat against a wall. In his mind he counted the steps until Andrew would be passing. He heard the flop of worn boots growing louder.

As Andrew strode past Matthew sprang from the wall, grabbed the strap of the backpack and with it pulled Andrew into the alley. Matthew looked around him. Narrow and dark, with a dumpster at one end. He had been here before. And now he held Andrew, pulled backward, against his chest. He slipped his arm around the younger man's throat.

"We need to settle this, Andrew," he whispered. "You have what's mine." Matthew tightened his grip, and the pressure caused Andrew to cough spasmodically.

"I expect it's in this backpack, am I right? You're not one to trust the leaving of it anywhere or trying to hide it. You'll want all that money close to you. Close to your black heart." Matthew loosened his grip enough to pull the backpack quickly off Andrew's shoulders and toss it to the ground. He resumed his chokehold.

"Now, you can end this with a degree of honor, or I can squeeze that wasted, worthless life out of you. Your choice, man."

Andrew slumped back against Matthew's hold. His right hand grabbed lamely at Matthew's forearm around his neck. His gasping struggle created enough of a diversion for his left hand to slide down to his hip. Inside his shirt there was a small sheath, and inside the sheath was a knife. Nothing too big, but he had effectively used it before.

Andrew's first thrust found what it could, the space below Matthew's ribs. Matthew yelped, as surprised as he was hurt. His grasp of Andrew weakened enough for the other to lurch forward and throw off the arm that pinned him. When he did so, he spun around and faced Matthew fully. Mouth open, a line of saliva dripping from it, and panting desperately for enough air to feel whole again,

Andrew stared at Matthew and said nothing.

Within the breast of Matthew Cooney a cauldron boiled over. Rage, despair, loneliness, and loss, and perhaps more. Perhaps some things that were not so readily known, or passions that had no name at all, a unique brew, a concoction of spirits and emotions that mix in unbalanced measure and define his soul. Matthew felt the press of fifty-five years, the blending of all the hurt, the pain, the joys of survival, and he felt as no one ever had before, or ever could again. He was Matthew Cooney—distinctive and unique, but an avatar for all of us. Matthew Cooney, Son of Man.

Matthew dove at Andrew, hard and full in his fury. If he had paused to reason, he might have feinted one way then moved another, or sought to hit him in such a way as to disrupt his balance and bring him down. Matthew, though, was past the point of reason. With all the rage within him, he attacked through instinct, animal-like, behind a throaty roar.

Andrew absorbed his charge and stepped back, their arms locked around each other. Matthew sought to throw a fist, which did not land. He became a flurry of motion, fists whirling in every direction, while Andrew deflected the blows and held Matthew as close as he could to keep him from gaining leverage.

But then Matthew's fury disappeared at once, stunned in the moment. He let go of Andrew, then fell backward as he sensed the spearing pain beneath his ribs. Andrew turned on his heels, then ran out the alley before turning down the street. *Once again,* Matthew thought. *The running away. He may as well send up a signal flare.*

Matthew sat there amid the grit and the garbage, another discard waiting to be collected. He leaned back for a time he could not measure. Long enough to catch his breath, it was, and to gather the flying remnants of thought strewn to the wind by his rage. His fury spent now, and he could once more think of what to do, calmly and without the skewing of emotion. *What to do?*

He rose and stepped to the neck of the alley where it joined the sidewalk. The day had grown later, and the August sun hovered just above the line of downtown buildings. He noted then the wetness. It flowed down his hip to his leg, a warm rivulet that soaked into his jeans. He did not linger on the pain under his ribs. Just another pain, this one physical and a bit sharper than most, but nothing special to it.

A swath of cloth lay near his feet, the remnant of an old shirt. Matthew picked it up slowly, shook off the standing dirt and stuffed it into his jeans to catch the flow. He would have to abide whatever filth hid within it until he was able to fix things right. He could fix this, that he knew, but he would need some help.

Matthew walked slowly to the street, then looked in both directions. His legs felt too weak to take him very far, and even so he had little idea of where to go. He would have to flag a ride. Not much traffic on a late Sunday afternoon, and Matthew waved an arm at whoever drove by. No one stopped, and few even bothered to look his way.

Weary now, and his thoughts clouded over by the pain on his side, Matthew searched the streets. A cab, one of the few on the streets, and its light was lit. Matthew stepped one foot off the curb and raised his arm. The cab slowed, then veered to where he stood. Matthew opened the rear door, then dropped himself into the back seat. A peculiar pain shot through his side then up to his chest as he did so.

"Where're we headin', friend?"

Matthew said nothing, panting deeply, trying to catch breath that all of a sudden defied the capacity of his lungs. The driver, hearing nothing but the urgency of lost breath, turned at last to the back seat.

As he did so, Donal Mannion looked into the desperate eyes of Matthew Cooney.

"Ah, Jesus, man!" The cabby turned at once to his wheel and pointed to the closest hospital.

Matthew glanced at the driver's identification card, then drew a thin smile. "So how've you been getting on, Donal? Through all these years."

"Apparently a bit better than you. What the hell happened, Matt?"

"The right argument with the wrong man. Seems I've lost my touch for violence."

"Sit tight, Matt. I'll get you to where you're going in a few minutes."

"I've spent my whole life trying to find where I'm going, Donal. A few more minutes won't matter." Matthew slumped back into the seat. The rag against his wound soaked red, and drops of it leaked onto the taxi's seat. Neither had anything more to say while Donal drove fiercely through the northwest streets into the sunset.

Donal pulled into the circular drive at the hospital's emergency room. He bolted out of his seat, opened the rear door, leaned in and wrapped an arm around Matthew's shoulders. "Come on, Matt. I'll help you up," and with that Cooney opened his eyes. Mannion smelled the blood, smelled the rot on the other's breath, then tugged gently to bring Matthew out of the car. Matthew wobbled to his feet and leaned hard onto Donal.

"A hell of a way to reunite, eh, Donal," he panted. His voice had grown faint. "One of my first friends. And now my last."

"Hush, Matt. Save your breath for what matters." The two dragged a few steps before an attendant rushed out of the building with a wheelchair.

"Help this man," Donal called to an attendant as Matthew flopped into a chair. "He's wounded and bleeding hard."

"What happened to him?"

"The same dreck that happens to all of us, man. He wasted away. Like we all do."

— ◆ —

Matthew Cooney lay across town in perhaps one of the warmest beds he had ever felt, his own life leaking out of him. Donal had been shaken to see him, to find him in this peculiar and particular condition, but there was something to be gained from it, he reasoned.

Donal had lived too long in recognition of his own need for penance. He knew, too, that no penance would ever set right the accounts he had broken and ruined. If anything, this might be a call for reflection, an accurate adding and subtracting of those broken accounts. Not his style, to be sure, but something that called to him now in recognition that his tomorrows were to be far fewer than his yesterdays. *Perspective,* he thought, *and the chance to review my mistakes.*

He could not reverse his miscues and blunders or change what he was. Not that he would. Donal Mannion was living as he wanted. He sought his pleasures as he always had—the nights out with his friends, or alone at the local, a moody selfishness that tended to distance, and sometimes anger, the childish indulgences of time and shallow amusements. Annie, Gina, and the others were left behind.

His thoughts did not leave him as made his way back to his shoddy flat, much more a cave than a womb, for nothing fresh would ever birth there. Once inside he peeled off a wet sweatshirt and put on his robe before pouring himself another drink. Donal listened to the rainfall tatter the window and ran his finger around the rim of the glass holding his evening scotch. Johnny Walker was a constant friend, a confidant in the annoyances and disturbances that assaulted the form of his long and meaningless days, a comforter when those days came to their welcome close. And here the two of them sat again, Donal gazing out a streaked and blurry window onto empty streets, and Johnny Walker, tonight wearing red, warming his gullet and whispering that this was where he was meant to be.

Rainfall washed the streets, but it could not cleanse Donal's cluttered mind. The wasted time, the lost loves, the past chances that rolled and clattered against the wall like a pair of dice. And the fears. Always there had been the fears, the things that fluttered his heart and weakened whatever resolve he might have possessed.

It had started early. It had been just he and his mother back then, his father abandoning them for unknown places. He recalled poverty without knowing that he was poor. The thin and stingy meals—

dinners of cereal, or perhaps a piece of bread smeared with peanut butter, a breakfast of potato chips—and he recalled the intransigent, instinctive fear of mere survival.

As he grew, he explored the streets, running with a rough group—Johnny Duncan, Matthew Cooney, Devin Murray, the first person he saw commit a crime when boredom drove poor Devin to steal a woman's purse and dash off frantically down the street where they lived. He had been caught and punished, sent away by his father to some juvenile facility or other, lost to the group forever. A fear of authority.

That had never left him, and that fear had translated too often into resentment and rebellion. No job ever lasted, brought to dust by overly officious bosses, or arrogance, or unreasonable demands, or a thousand other reasons coupled with Donal's basically lazy, suspicious nature. From job to job he flittered into middle age, then past it, to be sitting tonight at this window.

Fear of commitment. Women, as lovely and as nurturing as they might be, brought his every latent fear to the surface. One wife lost, the product of a nature that caused him to wander, to avoid any conclusion of permanence. He indulged his urges, chased his fantasies, and lost his wife. It was bound to happen, he reasoned. No woman deserved a life with such a fool, especially not Annie.

Annie had tried to ignore it all, tell herself that it really didn't matter and that her man had a special devotion to his young and fragile wife. But the string of cheap and tawdry one-night stands did not abate. He recalled the one evening that Annie sat him down and told him that she was leaving, heading back to her mother in shame and regret.

"You're not cut out for this, Donal. I saw that early on. The laughter and the drinking and the good times, but no basis to any of it. I thought I might make you different. But I'm tired, man, and I can't take any more of the lying and the loss. Can you know how that makes me feel? The disrespect and grief? I'm done with it, and I'll be gone in the morning."

"Ah, Annie, can we give another go? I'm not like that, not all the time. I love you, girl. You know that."

"I know you tried your best, Donal, but it was never enough. It can never be enough, not with a man like you."

Annie had left him in bitterness, and he saw her seldomly in the years since. His first mistake. No, not the first. There had been countless mistakes before Annie, smaller in scope.

And then Gina, the freshest of his wounds. Gina, too. The one woman he might have truly been able to love. But what chance did they have, really? She was too fine, and for reasons he could never quite believe, seemingly devoted to him, protective of his happiness, protective of his heart. And if Gina were not the one to shatter his heart, then he, Donal Mannion, would have to do it himself. Another chance squandered. Another woman lost. Another fear confirmed.

She had been different from the start. When he was with her, he approached each day in wonder that a woman so intuitive and wise could find comfort with a man like him. But he knew now that that wonder masked his fears. For if an insightful woman like this, so remarkable, stayed with him long enough, and close enough, she would see right through him. She would see the heart of his very flawed soul—his lack of purpose and place, his innate weakness to define himself, his inability to focus on an endpoint of any kind, and his foolish efforts to obscure these realities. And when she did so, when she at last came to this clarity, she would leave him, as would any reasonable woman. In the face of such fears, how could he commit beyond the moment?

Ah, but those moments were sublime. So natural with her, and so easy. A loss, she was. Gina Moretti, better off finding her own way absent the albatross of Donal Mannion around her lovely and delicate neck. He had let himself fade away like a train's whistle in the night.

He saw her again, quite by accident. One last time on the downtown curb at the end of the day, arm raised to signal for a ride.

The wind whipped her scarf and sent her hair flying behind her like a dark cloud, her face furrowed in the discomfort of a spring evening made vicious by fierce blowing and the debris it carried with it. When he saw her, when he recognized the moment, Donal smiled, then drew his cab to her side.

She entered quickly and did not glance at the driver as she gave a familiar address. As she tucked her bag beside her she looked up, and in a spasm of disbelief, checked the taxi license displayed behind the driver's seat. Her jaw dropped.

"Good evenin', Gina. And please close the door now, would you, before all our warmth is gone."

"Donal," she said slightly above a whisper.

"The same," and his smile widened.

"I had no idea you were doing this."

"Picking up lovely ladies on the street? You seemed to chide me for that once or twice, as I remember."

"Driving a cab. I had no idea."

"For the past few months. And yourself, Gina. How've you been getting on?"

She paused. "I admit it's less exciting without you in my life, Donal. Is that what you wanted to hear?"

"Only that you're doing well, and as reasonably happy as those of our humor might expect. Is that so?"

"I haven't considered it. Happiness. Such a vague concept. I work, I sleep, I eat. What more is there?

"Ah, you know the answer to that as well as I do."

"We had our chance, Donal. I'm grateful for it."

"Have you found another man yet? Forgive my asking, but I want to comfort myself that you're not alone in the working and eating and sleeping. Someone with less of a drift than I had with you. Someone with more substance." He paused, then added quietly, "Someone you deserve."

Gina looked out the window. "I won't answer that. Just know that

I've never known any man quite like you, Donal." She turned back again and watched his eyes reflected in the rear-view mirror. "I don't regret what we had."

"Nor do I, Gina. I only regret that it wasn't enough for you. I suppose I never thought it would be, even when I was telling myself something different."

They drove in silence, Donal maneuvering through the familiar streets now to the one that would take them to Gina's apartment. At length he drew the cab curbside. "Here we are, Gina."

She hesitated then drew her credit card from her bag to pay for the ride. "Seems like there should be more we can say to one another."

Donal took the card and ran it through the processor. He smiled as he handed it back to her. "We've said enough to know each other quite well, Gina. And there's no sadness, at least as I see it. We made our run, and I had my chance. You made me better. I'm grateful for it. For you. For all of it."

Gina smiled awkwardly, then opened the door. "No sadness," she whispered.

Donal turned again to the back seat. "Hey, you know there's space there to add a tip," and he gestured with a grin to the receipt he had handed her with the card. "It wasn't a bad ride, was it?"

Gina took out her pen and added a number. She looked back up at him with amusement. He could always make her smile. "Still hustling, I see," then added softly, "It's good to see you, Donal."

She eased out of the cab onto the sidewalk and the wind and the swirls of dust and grime, then walked to the entryway. There she would pass the lobby and press the elevator button to the fourth floor, where an empty apartment waited.

As she did so, Donal put his taxi into gear and pulled away. *What a fine thing*, he thought. *What a fine thing indeed.*

Now, as the summer drew on and the days grew shorter, Donal felt the pang of a special mistake, one that tore at his heart the way pain now tore at his back. He eased back into his chair, and, for the first time in memory, felt a tear form in the corner of an eye closed in sadness.

And now it was just he and Johnny. On some evenings he might turn to his Hispanic friend, Jose Cuervo, but mostly it was Johnny Walker who calmed the fears. He looked back out the window and watched the rain. The only movement below came from a sad, soaked dog who slinked between buildings, looking for some kind of shelter.

He thought of Matthew Cooney, the boldest of all of them. Donal had always regarded him with a quiet awe. Matthew had walked through their shoddy youth with a smoldering anger that absolved him of all fears, and in so doing he became as close as these lost boys might have to a leader. They followed him in wonder, in amusement, and in respect.

Donal had not seen him in more than thirty years until Matthew bled into his taxi. It had only been by chance that Donal was even driving this day. Nothing to do on a Sunday, so he may as well take a turn behind the wheel. In doing so, through the grandest of accidents, he came face-to-face with who he was, and what he might have been.

What happened to Matthew in these intervening years he could not know, nor even truly imagine. They had been rough years, and Matthew's brashness had not survived them. His friend lay tonight in a hospital, close to death with all his strivings for whatever pleasures and satisfactions he treasured behind him now, never to be revisited.

Broken and bleeding, Matthew embodied the inevitable devolution of man's aspirations, his energies, and the false bravado of youth, or so it seemed to Donal Mannion on this sad night. Nothing to do about it. He might check on Matthew at the hospital tomorrow, but, really, what did it matter? Donal had seen all he needed to see.

On the table by his chair lay a report his doctor had sent him two weeks ago. He had called, they had talked, their voices thudding and heavy. The doctor said he would summarize everything in writing, and so he had. Donal picked up the report and flipped through it, not for the first time. In fact he had committed its central points to memory.

Pancreatic cancer, and it would very quickly grow worse. So he had been told. He had been told his options, too—the various forms of treatment, chemotherapy, radiation, even an experimental surgery.

But none of it was for him, and none of it would even matter. He had spent his life chasing illusions, pursuing those wispy things that would always be just beyond his reach. He would not do so again, chasing an illusory cure for a disease that held him in its crosshairs. He would approach his end on his own terms, facing it fully without the crutch of sorrow.

Donal sipped his scotch, then rose to refill the glass. As he sat back down, he thought of rainfall from another time. Years ago. A thunderstorm raging, with lightning flashing between the roars and a menacing rain so thick that shut out the light. Another fear. And his mother on this night, in the storm and the rain, sitting next to him as he whimpered lowly.

"It's alright, Donal. It's alright, boy. Here, hold my hand." He had done so, and the rain eventually passed, the thunder ended, the lightning faded. It had been alright.

Tonight, Donal Mannion watched the dog across the way, sipped his scotch, and felt the icy smoothness of the glass. He glanced down at his hand, cold, lost, and trembling with fear.

Matthew Cooney's mind faded into undefined levels bridging consciousness and the spirit. Images of the before years came to him in snippets and spasms. As the blood ran out, the memories flowed in, a neap tide of thought and feelings for things gone by and forever vanished. The lot of time was there only for the regarding, for the evaluation of gain and loss, and nothing more.

Memories in their vague, wispy forms, unsorted and random, flitted before him and around him. Matthew had no sense now of physical space. He did not know where he was, not really. A bed of some sort, and there was strangeness enough in that alone. He had known too few beds in his day. His slumped body had grown accustomed to the benches and grasses of the square, to the unforgiving cots of the shelters, and, when his resources allowed, to the bug-infested beds of cheap hotels. Here, though, he lay in some comfort. He could not recall with any precision how he had come to this place, nor did he know who the shifting forms were who gathered around him to poke, prod and study what was left of him.

Thick as flies on a summer's night the memories came to him. He saw himself once again as a boy, chattering through his days, bearing the bruises, both visible and invisible, of being Jock Cooney's only son. He saw his mother, gone these many years, sleeping on a ragged couch, and heard the fall of her bottle as it hit the floor and spilled the remainder of its contents onto the tatty rug.

He saw Johnny Duncan pull at his arm, dragging him reluctantly to school, sixth graders then and rawer than most of their mates. "Come along, Matt. Let's get on with it. We've got to go, and you know you'll end up there anyway."

And he saw again the inside of the classroom where the torments of learning left him numb. Matthew felt the urge to fight what he could not grasp, to shake it and pound on it until whatever it was gave up and left him alone. So it was with the boys on the street, and so it was in this classroom with most of the things his teachers put in front of him. He recalled a math lesson where, called to the board to add a string of numbers, he froze and looked confusedly at the figures before him. They may as well have been Egyptian hieroglyphics or Icelandic runes, and the vision of his friends' laughter came clear. In his wrist he felt again the throb where the teacher's ruler had whacked his unmoving hand.

He had learned to fight. He had learned to steal, to thieve, to hoard what he had and give out none of it, neither the material goods that comprised his store, nor the emotions of the young man who had stolen it. He saw the crumpled form of an old man of the streets, bent under fists that had taken him down then taken his treasure. He saw the limber and lithe forms of every woman whom he had bedded, and he felt again their warmth and validation they had bestowed upon how he saw himself.

Matthew Cooney learned to walk alone, to stare into a night sky and see only a single star, ignoring the rest of the firmament. One light was enough.

Now, at the end of it all, these things came back to him. He had no control of the matter. There was no order to it. The jumbled, chaotic, and severely broken mosaic that was Matthew wafted into and out of his memory in its broken, faded pieces, each piece with its own sharpened edges.

Time now to pass it by. A heart broken years ago grew weaker and wearier by the minute, and the spirit that fed it packed its things to go.

Matthew opened his eyes once more and looked around him as best he could. Strange it was. All this was very strange.

In the doorway he saw Jock Cooney standing with a scowl.

As Matthew closed his eyes, he drew a long and tired breath. Before him his father's face, behind him all that was, ahead of him the vast darkness and uncounted balances of a life at once too short, and yet far too long.

"I am thy father's spirit, doom'd for a certain term to walk the night."

EPILOGUE

Gina Moretti turned the page on her sixth decade and clung to the notion of being in the full ripeness of middle age. She remained vibrant, committed to all the right things, and very much alive. Still attractive enough to lure her share of attentions from the men she encountered, still energetic enough to hold a stable of good friends of both genders, still sharp enough to pursue the best books and go to the concerts she fancied, still strong enough to take an occasional run through Rock Creek Park or spend an afternoon at the gym working the elliptical. Not young, to be sure, but certainly not old, Gina faced the days with grace and acceptance. She had always done so.

But as the calendar moved past sixty, she reasoned that, given the unlikelihood of living to be one hundred and twenty, she was no longer middle-aged. She had buried her reflective tendencies years before, during the confusing times when Donal Mannion befuddled her intentions with his quiet charm and gentle wit. He had been an intoxicant for her, a man unlike any she had ever known.

He had wafted into her life effortlessly, seemingly making no effort to impress her or win her over other than being himself. There was no artifice to Donal Mannion. He was who he was, and would always be, and apparently Donal trusted that would be enough. He was drawn to her, clearly. The times they spent together were light, pleasing and devoid of the tension that had wrought Gina's previous relationships. They went on, it seemed, as weightless as two butterflies skittering between the flowers.

In the end, though, it was that very nature that undid them. Donal was effortless in his pursuit of Gina, and he was effortless in all the other aspects of the way he spent his days. Donal did not chase, or plan, or strategize. He drifted through life, content and discontent alternately tumbling within him, but neither causing the burn of a deep fire or the crafting of a straight line. Gina could only do so much, and it would never be enough. He would drift beside her as long as he could, even in death, a remora clinging to a shark.

It ended, more with a whimper than a bang. Eight years ago it was, and she had heard nothing of him since. Until a friend sent a death notice from a funeral home in the northeast section of the city. "Thought you'd like to know."

Now, a birthday ending in a zero just concluded, Gina took time once more to weigh the balances of what had been. *Regrets, always,* she told herself, *and they weigh us down like magnets dragged through the sand. Small enough so that we barely feel them at first, but they accumulate, bit by bit.*

She drank her wine and listened to the last movement of Mussorgsky's "Pictures At An Exhibition" and she let the stirring and bold rise of the trumpets fill her blood. The piece lifted and exalted, celebrated the strength of the human character and finished with a crescendo of brass and tympani. The wine moved within her through the music.

When I am an old woman, she thought. *I will face down these regrets with the confirmation of who I am. I was always honest, and never false. I never cheated myself. I never cheated anyone around me. It was all I could do. And I live now with the bright freight of memories, clear to me, and me alone.*

She drank more of the wine, then closed her eyes. "When I am an old woman—" she whispered aloud, with no one to hear her.

And when the piece ended, when Mussorgsky's final tympanum

had sounded and the brass and cymbals reverberated to echoes, her room filled with the quietude of time itself.

ACKNOWLEDGEMENTS

It's such a confidence trick, writing a novel. The main person you have to trick into confidence is yourself. This is hard to do alone.

Zadie Smith, English novelist

Those who know me best know that self-confidence is really not one of my strengths, especially when it comes to my own writing. It's subjective, this writing business, and one reader's masterpiece might be another reader's waste of time. Add to this the vulnerability any writer accepts whenever his or her work finds its way into print. It was Yeats himself who once said, "It takes more courage to examine the dark corners of your own soul than it does for a soldier to fight on a battlefield."

To my everlasting blessing, I have been joined on this journey by others, wiser and deeper, who recognize the power of fiction, and the beauty of a language that can be made to soar and dance while sending forth truth like sunlight through dew-covered leaves.

There's a group of writers coordinated through the Irish Writing Centre in Dublin that call themselves The Inkslingers, a name as distinctive and playful as the group itself. We meet weekly, share thoughts and jokes, write to a prompt, then read what we've written for others to react and critique. It's a quirky bunch, diverse in what we write, filled with personality, and universally committed to the craft. Much of this work originated in these sessions, and the insights and suggestions of this group have been invaluable in shaping this book. They've become honored friends, all of them. I'm a humble Yank in their presence.

I am forever indebted to the excellent writers who took an early read of the manuscript and offered their own expertise in crafting this book's focus. Dean Cycon, whose first novel, *Finding Home: Hungary 1945*, has emerged as one of the year's best and most acclaimed works, helped trim the manuscript's fat. Glenn Miller, a brilliant new novelist from Minneapolis from whom we will be hearing much more in the years ahead, provided early counsel regarding how this book could be structured. I turned to Miguel Rivera, a debut novelist who writes in a completely different genre, to see how the manuscript might play with someone unfamiliar with my style, and Miguel did not disappoint. Steve Jam, a bright and vibrant novelist with a satiric eye and incredible social insight, helped buff and polish. Heloisa Prieto, a leading novelist in Brazil, offered gentle thoughts on how these characters came to be. I'm beyond grateful to each of them, and look forward to sharing with them the challenges, satisfactions and neuroses that bind all writers.

John Koehler is a publisher of high reputation, integrity and honesty. He's become a guru, a champion of my work, and, most significantly, a good friend. He's also surrounded himself with a team of exceptional professionals, who edit, design and market books with immense talent, flair, and enthusiasm. There's no place else I'd rather be.

This book is dedicated to Harry Browne, a longstanding and highly regarded writer in Dublin who has coordinated the aforementioned Inkslingers. Harry's grace, kindness and constant good humor provided a beacon through the creation of this book. More importantly, he stands as the ideal of what a writer can be, and how a gentle, thoughtful soul can brighten the lives and spirit of all those fortunate enough to feel its touch.

My son Michael has a critical mind, and he thinks things through, as logically, as precisely, and as thoroughly as anyone I've ever known. He helped anchor this book in ways I had not considered.

And then there's Lynn. Always and forever, there's Lynn. And, really, nothing else matters.

Milton Keynes UK
Ingram Content Group UK Ltd.
UKHW042114111124
451073UK00020B/413/J